I0599996

exploit
4102

COURTNEY CLEM

This novel is a work of fiction. Names, characters, places, and incidents either are the product of the author's imagination or are used fictitiously, and any resemblance to actual persons, living or dead, business establishments, events, or locales is entirely coincidental.

Copyright © 2025 by Courtney Clem

Registered with the U.S. Copyright Office.

All rights reserved. No part of this publication may be reproduced, distributed, or transmitted in any form or by any means—including photocopying, recording, or other electronic or mechanical methods—without the prior written permission of the publisher. The only exceptions are brief quotations used in critical reviews or certain other noncommercial uses as permitted by copyright law. Any other use of material from this book, including excerpts, adaptations, or reproductions for educational, commercial, or other purposes, requires express written consent from the publisher. To request permission, please contact the publisher at goldenseventhpublishing@gmail.com. Thank you for respecting the author's rights.

The publisher is not responsible for websites (or their content) that are not owned by the publisher.

Type set by: Atticus

First edition.

ISBN: 979-8-9919897-0-1

ISBN: 979-8-9919897-1-8 (ebook)

LCCN: 2025913104

Published in Birmingham, Alabama, USA, by Golden Seventh Publishing.

Author's Note:

This book is in no way, shape or form, meant to represent the religious ideals for all Christians. Rather, it is meant to reflect the sentiment and personal experiences this author has witnessed living in the "Bible Belt" of the southeastern United States. The characters and events depicted are fictional, though inspired by real-life observations.

It is important to note that the author intends no disrespect to any individual or religious group. Christianity is a diverse faith with numerous denominations and perspectives. This book is not intended to generalize or stereotype any particular branch of Christianity.

Beyond its exploration of faith and morality, this novel delves into broader societal themes, including the potential for manipulation and division within a population. The story is intended to provoke thought on the complex interplay between individual beliefs and larger political agendas.

Trigger Warning: This book contains themes of manipulation, medical procedures, panic attacks, and sexual abuse. Reader discretion is advised.

Exploit:

To use someone or something unfairly for your own advantage.

1

DR. MALICUS

I reluctantly crack one eye open as the alarm fades and realize that my peaceful sleep is over.

"Good morning, Dr. M-Malicus. Today is M-Monday, October 23rd, 4102. The time is currently 7:15 a.m. Would you like for m-me to continue with your m-morning report?"

The day will start, with or without you. No sense in lying here any longer when there is work to be done.

I push myself to a sitting position on the edge of the bed before answering her.

"Yes Ziva, please continue."

As I stand up, the bedroom springs to life as the dark window shades roll up to reveal more of the morning light. Overnight, the trees outside have transformed to their autumn colors. A gentle breeze blows a few yellow leaves loose and the sunlight dances between them as they float down to the ground.

"Very well, sir. The President of Earth Nations is once again m-meeting with Chancellor Cordelia..."

Ziva's voice from the intercom fades into the background as I strut over to the bathroom. I feel the stiffness in my neck from poring over my research the night before. Turning my neck from side to side, I try to stretch it out then rub the stiff spot for a moment of relief.

"The two leaders are hoping to find a resolution for the current global extinction crisis..."

In the mirror, my hollow eyes stare back at me as I take in my sleep deprived appearance. A few more white hairs are popping up in my short black hair and the fresh stubble on my face. My pale white skin looks sickly from the lack of sunshine and my grey eyes are bloodshot with little red veins. The wrinkles across my forehead are slightly more defined, even when I don't move any facial muscles. I sigh, accepting the sad reality that I am getting older, and the stress of my work is compounding on my body.

Not anything you can do about that…

I splash cold water on my face and wince at its sting. Ziva knows my routine and already has a warm towel waiting on the counter for me.

"The Institute for Cloning Organics has made promising strides towards reversing the genetic mutation…"

My stomach rumbles as I change into a clean gray short sleeve shirt and black pair of pants. Both are efficient and optimal, loose enough to allow me to move freely, but tight enough to not drag or get in my way. The perfect fit.

Turning towards a small table, I pick up the watch Ziva gave me and rub the engraving on the back "*Only the strong survive.*" Memories of our 10th wedding anniversary flood my mind, how Ziva promised we would always be together. How giddy she was to gift me this watch that had been passed down for generations in her family. It didn't even work anymore, and no one had made lithium batteries in over 1,000 years. She wanted to upgrade the watch face, so it could work with our technology, but she knew I would enjoy doing it myself. I keep telling myself that one day I'll sit down and do it, but that day has yet to come. And it certainly won't be today.

I walk into the kitchen where Ziva has left a plate of scrambled eggs and avocado toast with a glass of water. Swirling at the top of the water, I see the remnants of my medication dissolving. Disappointed, I drink it swiftly. As I devour my food, I think about my day and everything I need to accomplish. This sabbatical is supposed to be relaxing. I'm not supposed to be working. But there is a global extinction crisis at hand and as a scientist, I cannot sit by and do nothing.

I look around for Ziva but don't see her. I leave my empty dishes on the countertop, so she can pick them up later. Down the hall, I enter my personal lab and carefully shut the door behind me. Before turning around, I take a deep breath and clear my mind to focus.

It's a new day full of new opportunities. You just have to reach out and take them.

I turned around to see the remnants of my work throughout the lab: scattered test tubes, DNA samples and empty cloning stations. My home lab is a collection of varied technologies, some the most sophisticated pieces of equipment that only a few in the world had. Others are scrap pieces I managed to find and still one day hoped to replace or upgrade. It wasn't as nice as my lab at the ICO, but it would suffice.

The steady hum of the cloning machine is still echoing throughout the lab as it recreates the DNA samples with the latest code I engineered. By collecting samples of DNA, the computer runs scenarios of every combination and tells me which ones should, theoretically, work. Then it makes enough copies of the DNA to test each theory. Today there will be 785,236 samples to review from subject 21ON03.

The average person would find my work boring, comparing samples of DNA and inserting them into various test tubes while waiting to see results. But I'm not your average person. I thrive for the moment when, after running multiple tests and experiments, one finally works. All it takes is one success, one win. One sample of DNA to work with our modified code.

Two years ago, a genetic mutation appeared in the newest generation of human babies. At first, the doctors didn't think anything about it. The babies were born perfectly healthy, kicking and screaming as they should be. But within a few minutes they died. Hundreds of thousands of them died and have continued to die every day since. Across all human races, biological variations, and genetic compositions.

Scientists and doctors spent weeks studying the dying phenome-
non, trying to understand what was happening. Global conferences
and meetings were held, as panic and hysteria broke out among
the common citizens. Expectant mothers worried their unborn baby
would follow the same pitiful death and cried when confronted with
the grim reality. There were no symptoms or signs to look for. The
greatest threat to our species was a silent, cold-blooded killer that
we couldn't understand.

As a renowned geneticist, I was part of the initial conferences,
pulling all-nighters and working with the most intelligent scientists
in the world to try to figure out what was going on. Days later, and
with every major working artificial intelligent robot in the world, we
found it.

The chromosomes responsible for holding our DNA together, repairing it and facilitating natural modifications could no longer perform its functions independently. Throughout a woman's pregnancy, doctors couldn't identify any birth defects or abnormalities because it didn't exist until after the fetus was born and separated from
the mother's body. Because the issue lay at the very heart of the
DNA, it impacted every single organ within the fetus's body.

The magnitude of the issue is profound. Over the last millennia,
we had manipulated our DNA through various cloning processes to
create the ultimate superior race. We were supposed to be invincible
and perfect. Better, stronger, and smarter than ever.

Instead, we set ourselves up for failure. For generations, the problem had built up until the right combination of gene clusters created
a looming global extinction. We were at a loss for where to even
begin repairing it.

The Institute for Cloning Organics, or more commonly called ICO,
kept a record of each new addition, modification, or removal we
made. Not just for everyone who currently lived on the planet, but
also everyone who had been born for the last thousand years. I knew

if we were to find a solution, we had to start by looking at the records to learn at what point the deviation first occurred. Then we would need to create a new DNA combination that is compatible with our modern DNA and does not include the traits of the mutation.

As one of the leading board members for the ICO, I secured emergency clearance and funding for my team to lead the research project. I hand selected the very best and brightest scientists of our century and together we went to work evaluating the ICO's records and testing DNA samples. Each person possesses over 70 trillion different chromosome combinations, of which barely 1% of those were, theoretically, suitable for our purposes.

While identifying the deviation was rather quick, testing the chromosomes presented its own unique challenges. Starting with the most recent records, my team worked our way back through the years to identify DNA samples we could use to create new embryos.

Beep, beep, beep, beeeeeeeeeeeeeeep.

I turn around and walk towards the finished DNA samples, pushing my inner thoughts away.

Alright, time to work. Let's see how much closer we get today.

I wave my hand at the holographic screen, analyzing the report. The large '0' on the screen glares back, taunting me. None of these 785,236 DNA combinations solved our issue. I wave my hand again, to see the next '0' on the screen. It confirms that none of the DNA samples are compatible with our modern DNA. I sigh and proceed to the next screen to see a break down of the failures. 82% weren't growing in interphase, 13% were dying during prophase and 4% weren't able to divide in anaphase.

My heart stops as I realize this report contains four lines of data. Not the normal three lines I am accustomed to seeing. The fourth and final line shows 1%: chromosomes failed to divide into two daughter cells during telophase.

I flick my fingers to pull up the DNA combination that made it to the 4th stage of the cell cycle. After two years of research, I finally had a DNA combination that almost completed the cell life cycle. My fingers are sweating, and my heart is now pounding from the rush of adrenaline that I am getting closer to a solution.

"Run theoreticals from past experiments against this DNA sample to identify possible combinations that could successfully complete the telophase cycle."

As the machine processes my request, a new number appears. It shows how many DNA combinations there are with this similar sequence that might help it complete the telophase cycle.

308 billion.

I click my approval for the machine to create the DNA matches and double-check that it is working before walking away to read more ICO records. As much as I want to hope that this time is it, the logical part of my brain knows better. I have too many years of experience in this field to stop working now and hold on to a false sense of hope. I must keep researching for the next sample I want to test because most likely I won't find the solution in the current sample that is running. It is just the most likely to get me closer to the solution I want.

It truly is ironic that out of every issue our species has faced, it is the one we have created to advance ourselves that will kill us all. No war, disease, famine, or humanitarian issue for the last 10,000 years came close to what we were facing right now.

New reports flash on the screen before me, and I dive into them to see if this time I am closer to saving our species.

2

GRACE

"What is today's date?"

"July 21, 2015."

The receptionist answers without looking up from her computer. I scribble down the date and my name before turning away to find a seat in the waiting room.

Almost half the seats are filled with women, some still expecting and others cradling their newborns. I walk towards an empty seat beneath a poster of a happy, smiling couple. The petite woman is cradling one arm around her pregnant belly and the other behind a man who must be her husband. He appears tall and strong, with one arm wrapped around her shoulder. A perfectly happy couple. At the bottom of the picture, there is a quote: 'I am proud of many things in life, but nothing compares to becoming a mother.'

I take a seat underneath the poster and glance around the cheery waiting room. The walls are covered in colorful ads promoting pregnancy, birthing classes for new mothers, and weight-loss support through a new wellness shot the doctors can provide. In the corner is a set of children's books and toys. I notice two young children playing with the toys while a mother sits nearby reading a magazine. Occasionally she glances up to check the children before turning her eyes back to whatever page she is reading.

It appears that I'm the only woman in the room who is here for my annual appointment. It's one of those things that sucks about being a woman, but it's necessary to ensure I'm healthy.

My yearly trip to the gynecologist is more of a formality than any-thing else. I'm still a virgin, so there is no way I could have an STD or be pregnant.

Yet, as I continue to wait, my nerves build up. I don't like undressing and sitting naked on the table, waiting for a strange man to touch my breasts and stick his fingers inside me. Religiously, I'm not sure how God can forgive such a sin. That doctor would never be my husband. He is 40 years old and married to another woman, with their own children.

But my father insisted I start visiting the gynecologist when I turned 15 because his mother died from breast cancer. He was worried that my sisters or I might somehow inherit the same disease. I'm sure, on some level, he was also worried one of us might get pregnant in high school.

Maybe that would happen to Hope, but not to me…

I perk up as the door opens and a nurse calls out another woman's name. I collapse back down in my seat, looking around the waiting room again. My fingers start to twitch, and I grip the cross on my necklace.

'Children, obey your parents in all things, for this is well pleasing to the Lord.' Colossians 3:20.

I am dedicated to my religious faith, praying and reading my Bible daily. If I can help it, I never miss Church on Wednesday night or Sunday morning. I obey my parents and try to be a good daughter. This summer, I even began paying for my own tithes when I started my first job. I am not without my flaws or sins, but that's what Jesus is for. His sacrifice washes away all the wrongs we have done or will ever do.

Lord, please give me strength to endure this.

My mind races ahead to the endless list of items I still have to do today. I am supposed to meet my Church group at 11:00 a.m. for a ministry outing. Mom usually cooks dinner around 5:00 p.m. and tonight I also have my Christian women's Bible study at 6:00 p.m. I glance at my phone to see that it's only 9:33 a.m.

"Grace Wilson!"

I jump in my seat at the sudden callout for my name. I pick up my purse and follow her through the door. Unlike the colorful waiting room, the hallway she leads me down is stark white. There are no happy couple pictures or posters on the walls. No colorful ads for weight-loss programs. The lights are too bright, and the sterile stench of a cleaning product fills my nose. I recognize the bleak, cold welcome from my previous visits.

"So, you are 18 now, right?" she asks solemnly.

"Yes ma'am."

"Step on the scale, and I'll record your weight," She directs, motioning toward the scale.

I do as she says and smile softly when I see the weight is half a pound less than I weighed the day before. She scribbles it down in her notes and points to the chair where she wants me to wait again. After taking my blood pressure and collecting a urine sample, she moves me to the exam room.

"Everything is on the table ready for you. Just undress and the doctor will be here in a few minutes."

She turns away and shuts the door before I can answer. I undress and shiver as the cold air in the room hits my exposed skin. Looking around, I find the empty chair that is always in the corner, put my clothes and purse on it, while leaving my flip flops on the floor next to it. I grab the two sheets of paper on the table.

I always forget how thin these things are.

One is a paper vest to cover my breasts. The other is simply a large paper blanket to sit on top of my legs. It's supposed to make me feel more comfortable and dignified, but all it really does is make me feel stupid. The paper is so thin, it would be transparent if it weren't for the little raised pattern on it. I slide the vest on and take a seat on the table. I situate the paper blanket on my legs and pull the vest close in an attempt to cover myself as much as possible. My fingers subconsciously find the cross around my neck, twisting it around.

'Children, obey your parents in all things, for this is well pleasing to the Lord.'

I wait impatiently on the table for several minutes. Finally, the doctor knocks on the door at the same time as he opens it, and I jump from his sudden entrance. He greets me with a smile and a "how are ya!" that echoes off the walls.

I smile and give him the small talk he wants while he washes his hands and grabs the stethoscope around his neck. The nurse who brought me to the room closes the door behind him and watches from the corner.

"On paper, it looks like everything is fine. Your weight is fairly consistent, and you appear healthy. Do you have any questions or concerns you want to address?" He asks as he places the stethoscope on my back to check my breathing. I respond with a shiver at how cold it is before answering his question.

"I've been having some really bad cramps in between my periods. Like it's normal to be in pain while I'm on my period, but the last few months I have been feeling the pain in between as well."

He motions with his hand for me to inhale or exhale each time he moves the stethoscope. I can hear the nurse taking notes on her clipboard in the corner. He listens for a moment before answering me.

"Ya know, it is common for a lot of women your age to struggle with endometriosis," He explains. "It's possible your pain is just that. It is very common and nothing to be alarmed about. Endometriosis is where your uterine lining grows on the outside instead of the inside. It just makes it harder for your body to break it down each month for your cycle. Common symptoms are cramps, bloating, chunky discharge, and pain between periods. I believe you have good insurance. Why don't we just set you up for an ultrasound to be sure nothing else is going on?"

"Yeah, that would be great, just to make sure it's nothing else. My grandmother died from breast cancer, and I know it worries my parents that I might inherit it from her." I barely finished answering before he motions for me to lay back on the table. His cold, wrinkled hands slide under the paper vest. My body tenses for a moment, but his voice distracts me.

"Yeah, I'm sure you have endometriosis. But we can set up the ultrasound today before you leave to confirm. Betty, can you remind me to put in the order when we leave here?" He half turns to the nurse behind him, and she shakes her head with her quick "yup" as she scribbles more notes down on her clipboard.

"Alright, now here comes the not so fun part! I need you to put your feet here and scoot down to here."

He commands me, pointing to everywhere he wants me to position my body. I do as he says while he turns to the nurse to grab whatever medical instruments he needs for the pelvic exam. I lay back and stare up at the textured ceiling, feeling the cold air hit between my legs. He is still talking, but I am too uncomfortable to provide any more feedback than a "yup" or "nope." I feel his fingers first, then the metal rod. He continues to prattle on to explain the treatment for endometriosis, occasionally deviating to give the nurse directions for items to add to her clipboard or tasks for her day. I try to focus on his words instead of what he is doing to my body.

'Children, obey your parents in all things, for this is well pleasing to the Lord.'

"Alrighty kiddo! You're all done. I'll put in that order for the ultrasound and Betty will give you a call in a few days if there is anything wrong with your test results. Silence is a good thing! Take care and see ya next year." He smiles big and leaves the room with the nurse.

As soon as the door shuts, I bolt up and use the paper blanket to wipe away the excess lube between my legs. I rip off the paper vest and toss them both in the trash. After I put on my bra, t-shirt and leggings, I slip on my flip flops and grab my purse. My fingers wrap around my cross necklace, and I take a deep breath before leaving the room.

Dear Lord, forgive me please. I don't like these exams, but I don't have a choice. My parents say I have to get them done to make sure I am healthy. Wash away my sins for this moment and please help my future husband to understand why these exams are necessary. Amen.

Back in the hallway, Betty leads me to another exam room that is very dark. There are big machines in the room, some of which I vaguely remember seeing when my mom was pregnant with Faith. She instructs that I will have to take my leggings off again, but I can keep the rest of my clothes on. She hands me a fresh paper blanket to use and leaves the room while I undress. Once I lay back on the new table, I spot a clock on the wall and am annoyed that an hour has passed since I first signed in.

I need to get out of here soon or I'll be late.

Several minutes pass before she finally returns. She preps the machine before picking up the ultrasound probe. My eyes bulge with surprise at how large the probe is and the realization where it is about to go.

"I know it looks big, but it shouldn't hurt much. If the pain is too much, just let me know and we can stop the procedure at any moment. Okay?" Betty explains.

"Okay," I say back nodding my head.

"It won't take long at all, I promise. Now lay back and just relax. Everything will be fine," She encourages.

Betty lubes the probe and gives a small warning before inserting it. I silently wince at the pain and close my eyes tight. She pushes a little deeper and then I am able to breathe easier. She positions the probe, clicks some buttons on the ultrasound machine and then moves the probe to repeat the same clicking process.

I need to leave here and go straight to the Church. I'm supposed to park in the back lot, so it is easier to get on the minibus before we leave. Oh, I'm so hungry! Sister Rebecca said they would be providing lunch, I really hope it is...

"How many c-sections have you had?" Betty asks curiously.

"None. I've never been pregnant," I answer quickly, a little taken aback by her random question.

"Have you had any surgeries?" She asks, confused.

"None, I've never had any surgeries. Well, aside from my wisdom teeth. I had those removed a few summers ago."

"That's odd, I see a tear in your uterine lining..." She trails off as she makes some more clicks on the machine.

"Oh, well, the doctor said I probably have endometriosis. It had something to do with the uterine lining I think," I explain.

"Ahhh yes, that's right," she said, recalling the doctor's diagnosis. "He did say you probably have endometriosis. I bet that is it then. Well, I'm glad we had this ultrasound to confirm it. I'll make sure to get these reports over to him. And I'll file it with your insurance provider, so you don't have to worry about paying for it."

She makes a few more clicks before finally removing the probe. I nod to acknowledge her and my stomach growls.

I have got to eat something soon.

Twenty minutes later, I'm finally back in my car and speeding off to the Church. It wasn't until I was halfway down the road that I realized I didn't say my prayers before driving off.

Jesus, please forgive me. I have been distracted and busy today. I normally don't forget to pray before I drive. Please ensure that I travel safely, and no harm comes to me or my car. Amen.

I fly into the Church parking lot, heart pounding nervously until I see the minibus.

Oh good! They haven't left yet.

I sigh with relief, park my car, and speed walk to the minibus. Pastor John and his wife, Rebecca, are standing on either side of the minibus doors. They are the ideal couple, who married in their early 20s and came from wealthy families. He is tall and handsome, with dark brown hair and green eyes. She was petite and beautiful, with brown hair and brown eyes. Both of their skins are glowing from their recent cruise to the Bahamas. Everyone knew them because of how active they were at the Church and in the local community. They even worked out at the gym together and ran marathons on the weekends.

"Grace! We are so happy you were able to make it. I was starting to get worried that something happened," Pastor John exclaims.

"I'm so sorry Pastor John, I was at a doctor appointment, and it took a little longer than normal. But I am so glad to be here! I'm excited for today," I respond back, relieved to see the familiar red and white Chick-fil-A bags in their hands.

"Here you go Grace, we have one sandwich left just for you," Rebeca says, as she hands me the sandwich. "There is a pack of waters in the cooler on the front seat. Help yourself to one of them."

"Thank you, Sister Rebecca!" I exclaim, grabbing the sandwich eagerly and climbing up the minibus stairs. I grab a water bottle from the cooler and take a seat toward the back of the bus. Head bowed, I bless my food:

Dear God, thank you for this food I am about to eat and the opportunity You have given me to share Your Gospel with others. Bless this food to the nourishment of my body, so that I might better serve Your needs. Amen.

As I open the wrapper around my sandwich, the mouthwatering scent of greasy chicken fills the air, making my stomach rumble. I vaguely hear the minibus doors close as I take the first bite. My body jolts forward as the minibus takes off, but I immediately refocus on my meal. The minibus quickly fills with chatter and laughter. I take another bite of my sandwich then look up to see who showed up for today's youth event.

Up front, I see Jessica and Ashley, huddled in a seat together, whispering and giggling already. I'm sure Jessica's mom dropped them off, since neither one can drive yet and Ashley's mom works a day job. Across the aisle sits Michael, Christopher and David, already engrossed in the latest football team debate. School would be starting back in a few weeks and all three boys were trying out for the varsity team this year.

In the back of the bus, Taylor is slouched down, headphones on and glaring outside the minibus window. His newly dyed black hair has grown longer and casts a shadow over half his face. He recently got in trouble for smoking weed and now his parents were forcing him to attend Church events on a regular basis. I believe Jessica said they even took his phone away, so I wonder what he could be listening to in his headphones. Or maybe his parents gave him his phone back for the day, I think they both still work during the day. Elizabeth is sitting by herself with her back against the window so she can talk to William and Tyler who are sitting behind her.

Hope is nowhere to be found, but that wasn't surprising. Ever since she started college, she had avoided anything and everything to do with the Church. She even signed up for summer classes, so she could stay on campus. I still can't believe Mom and Dad let her get away with it.

Where is Megan? I thought she said she was coming today...

Searching for her familiar blonde hair, I scan the minibus one more time but still don't see her. Megan has been my best friend since I failed the first grade and had to repeat it. She also happened to be my cousin, and we were both thrilled to be in the same first grade class the second time around. We quickly became inseparable, doing everything together: school, cheerleading, pageants, and Church. She was the one person I could always count on to show up. Yet, she didn't come for today's event.

I pull out my phone and text her. Several minutes pass by and she still hasn't responded. I check her location and see that she is still at her house.

She better not have stayed up late and slept in again. She knows I hate going to these things alone.

All too soon we arrive at our destination. I look outside the minibus windows to see the familiar sign where two angels are holding a ribbon that says, "Welcoming Wings." Our Church worked frequently with the nonprofit because Welcoming Wings was a Christian organization that provided shelter, food, and other supplies to poor families in need. Many of the families have children who could use our help to guide them to Jesus, so they don't turn to drugs and violence on the streets. Every Tuesday and Thursday this summer, our youth group came to read Bible stories to the children staying at the house. We usually came for a couple of hours during lunchtime, to provide relief for the workers.

Most of the children are 10 years old or younger, so sometimes they have a hard time sitting still for the two hours we are there to spend with them. It can get annoying when you are trying to read a Bible story to them, and they don't listen or try to wander off to play with the toys. When that happens, I always have to say an extra prayer that Jesus will give me patience to deal with them.

As we exit the bus, Sister Rebecca, hands each of us the Bible story we will read for the day while Pastor John splits up who would be going to each room. I take my book and glance at the cover, delighted to see that I have the creation story. Armed with the Word of

God, we march off to save the innocent souls. Pastor John placed me with the 6-8-year-old group today, and they were not happy when I walked into the room to end their playtime.

The woman who had been watching them is someone I had met several times on my previous visits. Her name is Mary, she is a short, beady woman with terrible highlights and an apple-shaped body. She looks relieved to see me walk into the room and as she comes to greet me, I am overwhelmed with the smell of her cheap perfume. Mary thanks me graciously and takes off to enjoy her lunch break. I round the kids up and once they are all sitting on the reading rug, I take my seat in the chair and start reading.

"In the beginning, there was nothing…"

I pause for a moment to show the children the picture book. A few of the kids stare at it, wide-eyed and full of curiosity. One of the boys towards the back is playing with the car in his hands, ignoring everything else going on. The boy next to him can't decide if he would rather listen to me or play with the car. Another keeps fidgeting, rocking back and forth. She's the same one who asks a million questions every time I read a story. I don't think she has ever set foot in a Church before or learned anything about God.

A text comes through on my phone and I glance at it quickly to see who it is. Faith's name pops up and I briefly see the first few words of her message: Hope is home.

She better not ruin my sleepover with Megan this Friday.

I swallow my frustrations, put my phone in my pocket and open the book.

"On the first day, light was created," I show the children the pictures on the page, depicting the light on one side and darkness on the other.

"On the second day, the sky was created," I turn the page to show the picture of the sky with white, fluffy clouds.

"On the third day, the land, sea and trees were created." The next page shows the land, lush with green trees and the ocean.

"On the fourth day, the sun, moon and stars were created," I continue. Now the page depicts all the elements created so far, with the sun on one side lighting up the Earth. The moon on the other page represents the nighttime.

My phone vibrates with what I assume is another text from Faith.

She can never just send one text message.

"On the fifth day, the birds and fish were created," I turn the page to show the birds flying in the sky and giant fish in the ocean. One boy squeals with happiness and yells, "Shark!"

"On the sixth day, the animals and people were created." I show the next page to the children, depicting a variety of animals surrounding two people in the middle.

"Then on the seventh da–"

"How many people were created?!"

I jumped at the sudden outburst that came from the fidgeting girl.

"Uh, two," I respond. "God created Adam and Eve."

"Who did he create first?" she asks.

"Adam, then Eve," I answer sweetly, with a forced smile.

"Why not Eve first?" she asks.

Here we go...

My phone vibrates again.

"Well, because He wanted men to be the head of their families," I respond matter-of-factly, hoping my confidence will stop further questions. "So, naturally men should be created first. Then, He took a rib from Adam to create Eve, so that all women would be part of the men."

"Why can't women be the head of their families?" She asks, scrunching her face up in confusion. "I don't have a daddy, so does that mean my mommy is the head of mine? Or, she can't be the head of mine, because I don't have a daddy?"

Oh crap.

"Oh, well, in that case, your mommy is the head of your family," I respond reassuringly. "Until she gets you a new daddy. Then, he can be the head of your family."

She shrugs her shoulders, responding with a chipper, "Oh okay!"

I breathe a sigh of relief.

Suddenly, the race car driving boy in the back is paying attention. His voice fills the silence. "I don't have a mommy, is God going to make one for me from my daddy?" I feel all their eyes on me, waiting eagerly for my response.

Oh, this keeps getting worse.

"Um, well," I struggle to find words. "It doesn't exactly work like that."

My phone vibrates again.

"Why?" he immediately asks.

"Well, uh," I struggle to figure out how to explain. "Because that was just in the beginning. When God created the world... um."

He doesn't even miss a beat. "Why?"

"Yeah, why?" another kid chimes in.

My phone vibrates again.

Why can't they just let this go?? And what does Faith want?!

I bite my lip and breathe deeply.

"Because that is what God decided to do when He created the world! He wanted to make Adam and then Eve and that was it!" I snap.

One or two children flinch at my sudden outburst. The girl who started all the questions remains unphased and speaks up again.

"That doesn't make sense. If he can just create people, he would have created my daddy."

Oh no.

I take a deep breath to calm myself. "Ya know, there are just some things in this world that we are not meant to understand or question," I reply, softening my tone and forcing another smile. "We will find out all the answers when we go to Heaven and see Jesus."

"My mommy tells me to always ask questions," She states matter of fact.

"And you do such a great job of it," I retort, not even trying to hide my attitude.

I'm so glad they are too young to know what sarcasm is.

My phone vibrates again.

"Okay, story time is over," I command, slamming the book closed. "Why don't you all go play now?"

Shrieks of happiness and laughter erupt from all the children as they disperse to find whatever toy or game they really want to play with. I roll my eyes and breathe deeply.

Annoying kids...now let's see what Faith wants.

I pull out my phone and see six text messages from Faith.

> Hope is home...

> OMG

> She cut off all her hair and dyed it purple.

> Mom and Dad are going to freak out when they see it.

> What is she wearing??

I tap on the picture to make it bigger. It looked like Faith peeped out the upstairs window and took it through the blinds. Hope's hair used to be halfway down her back. Now it is super short, pixie-cut-she-could-be-a-boy short. She also dyed it the brightest, most obnoxious purple color I have ever seen. Her baggy pants and V-neck shirt look like she bought them from the men's section at a local thrift store. Not a cute look at all.

I type out my response to Faith, letting her know I have one more hour left and then I'll be home. Right as I press send, I hear a loud crashing noise and crying.

UGH. What now?!

I looked up from my phone to see that one of the boys climbed up a bookshelf, and it fell over on him. The bookshelf is small, not even up to my waist, but it is heavy wood. I rush over and pull it off him, then help him get up.

"You're fine! Everything is fine, stop crying. You'll be okay," I rub his shoulder and look him over quickly for any signs of blood. "You need to be more careful next time, okay?"

He quiets, rubs his eyes, and shakes his head softly.

"Now go back to playing," I say nicely, giving him a slight pat on the back to join the other children.

The next hour drags by until Mary returns from her lunch. She thanks me again and I return to the minibus. On the way back to the Church, I realized Megan never responded to my text. I check her location again to see that it still showed her at home.

Should I double text her? Maybe she is busy with something impor-tant… but she tells me everything and I can't think of anything else she would be doing right now.

I decided to send another text to her:

> The 6-7 year olds were extra annoying today. You wouldn't believe all the questions they asked.

As we pull into the Church parking lot, my phone vibrates. My heart races with excitement and quickly deflates with disappointment as I see Faith's name, again. Only this time she is warning me that our parents just arrived home.

Great. Can't wait to walk into that mess.

I quickly say my goodbyes to Pastor John and Sister Rebecca, then rush to my car. I crank it, blasting the air to try to push the crazy 101-degree heat out and say a quick prayer.

Dear Jesus, please keep me safe as I travel home. Help me to make good decisions and avoid anything that could cause a wreck, or a ticket. Amen.

I leave the Church parking lot and head home, going as fast as I can, but never over the speed limit. As I pull up to the house, I see Hope's car parked on the street. Her army green Subaru Outback is covered in new window stickers that I hadn't seen before. The one that immediately catches my eye is the Pride flag, followed by "Coexist" that features various religions with each letter.

My face turns red, and I can feel my breathing getting heavier. A few weeks ago, Pastor John had warned us about the Coexist stickers and how they are suggesting that we should step aside to welcome all the religions in the world. To "coexist" as a human race. As a Christian, he said we should protest such things because they are temptations of the devil that are trying to pull us away from God. There is only one religion that should exist: Christianity.

Hope is a Christian, so why does she have these stickers on her car now?!

I park in my grassy spot next to the driveway, grab my purse and head inside. Right as I reach the front door, I hear a loud crashing noise and yelling.

3

DR. MALICUS

My stomach growls and I glance at the time on my holographic screen to see that hours have passed. The DNA samples are still whirling behind me, and I turn back to the holographic screen to check the progress.

180 billion remaining.

We are getting closer, but not quite there yet. I turn back to the ICO record I had been reviewing, just as Ziva announces from the intercom that lunch is ready.

Right on time.

I walk into the kitchen to see my protein shake waiting on the counter. The silent room is empty, which means Ziva is probably practicing her calligraphy or putting a puzzle together in the other room. I grab the glass and quickly drink it. My protein shake includes extra vitamins and additives to give my mind a boost. It's also convenient and easy to swallow, so I don't waste time trying to eat an actual meal.

I leave the cup on the counter for Ziva to clean up later and return to my lab, adjusting the watch on my wrist after it snags on an arm hair. Almeta should be calling any minute with her latest status report, and I am anxious to hear from her. This morning's press release was bleak and vague, so I'm hopeful she has more information on what is happening at the ICO headquarters. While I wait in the lab, I continue reviewing the ICO record.

Gender: Male
Birth: 02/17/2548
Death: 05/19/2690
Age: 142
Sample Collected: –

I sigh at the blank *sample collected* line. The Institute of Cloning Organics was established in 2505, but it wasn't until 2568 that universal sample collecting was mandated when each new baby was born. It was controversial from the start - many government leaders at the time lacked the ability to comprehend why the data collection process was necessary.

Then issues arose as some gene modification companies lied about their processes and quality. People became angry when they were promised certain genetic traits and characteristics, only for their child to be born without them. At the same time, World War V occurred and destroyed many genetic modification companies based in the countries previously known as the United States and Canada. All the progress the companies had made were lost forever.

Under the united leadership of the new Earth Nations, the ICO worked with the global president to establish rules and processes for collecting data samples to preserve in public records. As a scientist, this made it easier to access and obtain copies of historical DNA samples for research projects. The records also include which company produced the modified DNA and ensured that those companies were meeting quality checks each year.

It is a shame that those companies' data were destroyed in the war and incomprehensible it is as to how much progress was lost. Their quality genetic modification was the best in the world at that time and had solved many issues such as Cerebral Palsy, Crohn's disease, Hypothyroidism and Diabetes.

Who knows, they probably had what could have been our solution for today's global extinction crisis…

A quick beep and a hologram of Almeta appears before me. Today her dark brown hair is pulled back into a tight bun at the base of her neck, and she is wearing her lab coat. Her young, youthful face is smooth and soft, with a sprinkle of freckles across her nose and cheeks. Normally, her tan skin appears honey-brown, but over the last few months it has lightened from a lack of sunlight exposure.

"Good afternoon Dr. Malicus." Her enthusiastic voice echoes throughout the lab, matching her bright blue eyes.

I give a curt nod of greeting as I respond. "Hello Almeta, what do you have for me today?"

Her face transitions to a slight frown. "I'm afraid we haven't made any more progress from our last conversation, Doctor."

"And why not?" I calmly ask.

"These new rules and regulations are slowing our research and discovery process down," She speaks carefully. "It is taking too long to get approval for each new test. Then, once we have approval, it takes longer to get the necessary supplies and verifications for each scientist to participate. They've even installed new biometric scanners that have questionnaires updated based on the progress for the project…"

Fucking politics.

"Furthermore," Almeta pauses, avoiding eye contact briefly before continuing. "Dr. Kayitesi and Dr. García have decided to invest more of the team's research focus on Medical Engineering Modification."

"I knew this was coming," I shake my head in disappointment. "Dr. Kayitesi has always resorted to half-assed measures. It's no surprise she would push for this and that Dr. García would follow her lead."

She shakes her head in agreement. "Yes, Dr. García is fawning over her work, as per usual. They believe that it is time to focus on adapting technology to assist the fetuses for sustainability, rather than developing a genetic modification to be integrated with the existing DNA."

"When is their Phase 1 deadline?" I ask.

"Next month, sir," Almeta responds quickly, as if she anticipated my question.

A whole month? Where was that when I worked there? Cordelia has gotten too lax with the rules.

"Do you have any idea if they are progressing on time?" I ask, as I pull up a calendar view.

Almeta grins slyly. "Actually sir, I was selected to be on the research team. And our team is also invited to the upcoming ICO Global Conference on December 1st."

Hell yes.

I nod my head in approval, never taking my eyes off the calendar. "Oh really? Well, for once that is good news."

"Don't worry sir, I won't let you down," Almeta speaks confidently.

I meet her gaze and give her a soft smile. "I have no doubt about that."

She flashes a quick smile then recomposes herself. "Is there anything else you require of me, sir?"

"Actually, there is one thing…" I pull up a list of items I made and transmit it to her. "I am running low on the last DNA samples we had, and I need more supplies for cloning and testing. I just sent over the list of items that includes everything I need."

She nods her head to confirm she received the list. "Making good progress, sir?"

"Oh yes," I answer, turning my attention back at her. "Very good progress."

"Good. Just be careful sir…" She hesitates. "You really aren't supposed to be working on your sabbatical."

I nod my head and roll my eyes. I know she is just concerned for my well-being, but she does tell me this every time we talk.

When she realizes I'm not going to say anything, she continues. "I should be able to secure the supplies within the next day or so. I'll bring them to you as soon as I have them."

"Thank you, Almeta, you are turning into an excellent scientist," I deliver the praise with a solemn tone, so she knows I mean it.

She beams with pride. "Thank you, sir, I'll be in touch."

As soon as her hologram disappears, I sigh with frustration and run my fingers through my salt and pepper colored hair.

Those idiots are throwing away all my hard work. They can't seriously think that medical engineering modification will actually work… It is such an insult to our species and the genetic modification progress we have made for thousands of years.

For years, Dr. Kayitesi and I had competed against one another in the scientific field. Constantly trying to outperform the other, she had been a strong competitor that helped me to redefine what my own limits were. It was rare that we agreed on anything, and Chancellor Cordelia quickly realized she needed to keep us separated on research projects. That competitive tension only increased further when the global crisis developed.

Two years ago, Dr. Kayitesi had proposed creating devices to regulate the fetus' bodies, so they can live on their own outside of their mother's body. Dr. García had been torn between helping me find a genetic solution or Dr. Kayitesi find a medical engineering solution. It seems while I have been away that Dr. Kayitesi has been busy recruiting help to her own project instead.

It is reassuring that Almeta is on their research team though. She will keep me updated on their progress and have an easier time getting access to the supplies I need for my own research.

Beep, beep, beep, beeeeeeeeeeeeeeeep.

I turn toward the machine to see that there are still 148 billion samples left to be created. Confused, I step closer to read the red error message: *cloning incomplete.*

I read further to see that the machine ran out of the DNA parent sample.

Damn, already?!

I sigh and rub the sides of my head. I'm certain I have used all the travel serum I had, but I walk over to the cabinet to check anyway. I open the doors to see all the empty vials, perfectly stacked on the right-hand side in their rack. On the left are the empty racks, where the vials once stood when they were full of travel serum.

Almeta will need to take these empty racks when she comes back.

I grab the racks and pull them out to sit on the table. A sharp *clink* erupts at the back of the cabinet and my heart races.

Did I somehow miss one of the vials? I really hope so...

I reach back slowly, feeling for where the vial could be on the shelf. My fingers brush the glass, and I reach further in the direction where the vial is. I pull it out to see the yellow serum inside, still perfectly sealed, and intact.

HELL YES!

I check that my bag has all the supplies I need for carrying back the parent DNA samples. Everything is exactly where it should be.

"Ziva, I'm leaving for a bit, and will return soon." I call out into the empty lab.

"Be safe dear!" she answers from the intercom speaker.

I grab my transporter watch off the shelf and insert the yellow serum inside. While I clip it on to my right wrist, I can't help but compare it to the watch Ziva gave me on my left wrist. The transporter watch is dull and bulky, but functional. Whereas the one Ziva gave me is sleek and stunning, but broken.

Looks can be deceiving.

I click a few buttons to select where I want to go on the transporter watch and hit the side button to confirm. I look out at my lab, as it all fades away and the last thing I see is the error message taunting me back.

4

GRACE

As I open the front door, I hear Hope yelling.

"You never trust me to do ANYTHING! Do you really think I didn't think this through?!"

I don't see anyone in the living room or dining room except for a few overturned chairs. Our mother's voice yells back at her, confirming that they must be back in the kitchen.

"You should have consulted us before you changed your degree! We are paying for your college after all."

"It is MY degree, for MY career that will support MY life when I leave this damn place!" Hope screams back.

"You will not speak to your mother that way!" Our father's voice explodes, echoing throughout the house. "You will NOT cuss in this house and tomorrow you will go to the first hairdresser you can find and fix this mess on your head."

I cringe, feeling awkward to be privy to every word of their fight. I hear footsteps shuffling in the kitchen and panic. I flee upstairs to the safety of my room before I somehow get pulled into their fight.

Hope's voice follows me up the stairs. "It is MY HAIR! MINE! You can't tell me what to do with it!"

"Listen here young lady..." Mom's stern tone responds back. I can tell she is trying to remain calm and refocus the argument on Hope's degree change.

I softly shut my door and breathe a sigh of relief as their voices are muffled. As I drop my purse on the nightstand, Faith swings open my bedroom door, and I jump from her surprise visit. Even though we have the same light brown hair, button nose and blue eyes, we look completely different. Where I took after our mom, with my short body and wide hips, Faith took after dad. She's younger than me, but already taller by a few inches with long lanky legs and arms. Her jawline is more defined, and her face is smooth, where mine is hidden by a layer of fat and small pimples. Somehow, even her blue eyes look prettier and brighter than mine. Seeing how much more beautiful she looks in a simple T-shirt and shorts only enrages me further.

"You need to knock before you come in!" I snap at her.

She rolls her eyes, knocks on the already open door, and then shuts it behind her as she enters the room. I glare back at her.

"Oh come on! Don't you want to know what they are fighting about?" She is smug and bouncing with excitement.

"I kinda got the gist of it already, but sure, tell me." I retort with annoyance.

She makes a small hop and runs to sit on my bed. I plop down next to her, fighting the urge to smile at her silliness.

"Did you see the pictures I sent you?! Of her hair?! And her clothes?!" Faith rattles off the questions, not bothering to wait for an answer. Her blue eyes are wide with excitement over the latest drama. Subconsciously, she starts to grab her soft brown hair to pull it into a ponytail.

"Yes, I did. It looks awful."

"Oh my God it is SO awful!" She exclaims, slapping her hands on her legs and ignoring my response.

"Hey! Don't take the Lord's name in vain," I scold.

She ignores me, continuing. "I cannot believe she cut it all off and dyed it PURPLE. Of all the colors, why purple?!"

I shrug my shoulders nonchalantly and wait for Faith to continue, but I don't have to wait long.

"I mean, she always had pretty hair, but she could have used a few highlights. Not dyed the whole thing a crazy color that will make it hard for her to get hired. Ooooooh not to mention, she changed her degree and didn't tell Mom or Dad."

That piques my interest more. "What did she change it to?"

"Political science!" Faith exclaims, completely appalled. "Can you believe that? What is she going to do with that?"

I squint my face in confusion. "What even is that?"

Faith pauses for a moment and subconsciously scratches her arm. "Hmmm. I have no idea, but it doesn't sound like it would make any money."

"Or like something a good husband would be okay with and appreciate," I chime in with my support. "At least if she was a nurse or teacher, it would be respectable for her future husband."

Faith scoffs in agreement. "Oh yeah, I know!"

"How long have they been fighting?" I ask cautiously. Even though I'm pretty sure the fight is just getting started.

"Hmmmm," Faith thinks for half a second. "Like maybe five minutes before you came home. Hope was here for a while before they came home. And of course, they immediately started fighting because of her hair."

More yelling erupts from downstairs, and we pause our gossiping for a moment. I can't tell what is being said. Then the front door slams and I hear Hope's car crank. I make eye contact with Faith and then we rush to my window to see which direction she drives off towards.

She takes off flying down the street, before turning the corner, but I have no idea why she would go in that direction. Maybe she is going to her friend's house. I look at Faith for an answer and she shrugs her shoulders.

"There is no telling where she went," Faith says as she plops back down on my bed to look at her phone and knocks off a pillow in the process. When she doesn't make a move to pick it up, I grab it for her and roll my eyes.

Tossing the pillow on the bed I say, "You need to leave, I have stuff to do."

"Like what?" She doesn't even bother to look up from her phone.

"It doesn't matter! Get out!" I yell.

"UGH FINE!"

She slams her hands down on the bed as she pushes herself off. Her stomps to the door are heard downstairs because I hear Mom yell our names. Faith yells back at her as she shuts my bedroom door. Then, her footsteps fade away as she retreats to her own room.

I lay down on my bed and breathe a sigh of relief. Finally, peace and quiet. My phone vibrates as a text message comes in. I grab it and look at the name on the notification: Megan.

Took her long enough! What has she been doing all day?

I open the text to see she ignores all my previous messages and instead asks if we can hang out tomorrow.

Grace! Can you hang out tomorrow?

Sure, but I have to go to work at 2.

Want to eat at Chick-fil-a? I can be there by 12.

You know it's my fav place lol

Lol! Still wanted to ask. See you then!

Megan has gotten into trouble a few times for sneaking out with boys, so her mom will occasionally check her texts. She must have something really juicy to share if she isn't willing to text it.

I glance at the time to see that it is only 2:30 p.m. I'm not sure what I want to do with my free time before dinner. It would be nice to watch some TV, but I'm too scared to venture downstairs.

Mom should have returned to work by now, but I don't recall hearing her car leave after Hope did. I glance outside my window to see if her car is still here. I see the faded top of the maroon 1995 Blazer and the smaller navy 1998 Malibu still in the driveway.

She didn't go back to the bank? That is unusual.

It also reassures me that the safest place I can be is in my room. When enraged enough, Dad has a tendency to lecture at anyone who gets in his path. Even if they weren't the person who originally made him angry. If both of them are downstairs, then they must be having some serious conversations.

My fingers twist my cross necklace as I look around my room, trying to figure out what to do. There is a stack of clothes on a chair in the corner, waiting to be hung up in the closet. Above the chair are two of my favorite music posters: a purple one with butterflies and a red British phone booth.

On the opposite wall hangs a corkboard with dozens of papers thumbtacked on it. Most are Bible verses and quotes, with the occasional plastic flower sprinkled in. My summer reading and school supply lists are the latest editions, tacked to the bottom right corner.

I search the top of my dresser, hoping there is something fun to do that I missed. A collection of old CDs, ponytail holders and nail polish are scattered across the top. It's not a big bedroom, but at least it's mine.

I already did my Daily Devotional this morning, so there is no need to do that.

Daily Devotional is one of my favorite parts of the day and I enjoy doing it first thing when I wake up. It's my time to sit alone, read my Bible and be with the Lord.

Each week, Pastor John will give us a passage of scripture to review. The one passage is meant to last the whole week, so it does not come across as overwhelming for those who normally don't read their Bible every day. However, I read my Bible daily and usually complete his assigned passage the very next day.

I will read other passages throughout the week or revisit one of my Daily Devotional books. One of my favorites is a book with different passages of scripture for each day of the year. The scriptures focused on the role of women, how to strengthen my faith in the Lord and prepare for my future duties as a wife.

I guess I could paint my nails.

I select a music playlist from my phone and grab a nail polish that is a dainty pink color. I decided to make it a slow drawn-out process, cleaning my fingernails and then toenails, painting them, and even massaging lotion on my feet. Two hours later, I'm satisfied with the results and can smell the dinner Mom started cooking.

I should probably wait a little longer until the food is closer to being ready.

I plop down on my bed, phone in hand and scroll through Pinterest. I look at a variety of pins for hair tips, clothing styles and home decor. It's not until I hear Faith running down the stairs that I realize Mom is calling for us.

I put my phone on the charger and walked downstairs, cautiously entering the dining room. The food is laid out on the table, Dad is sitting on one end, and Faith is in her normal spot. Mom is walking in from the opposite side, bringing a glass of water. She sits to the right of Dad, in her usual spot, and hands him the drink. As I take a seat, I look at the table before us to see the food: thick hamburgers, burnt hot dogs, and crinkle-cut fries.

Dad clears his throat, recites a short blessing for the food and promptly starts eating. Mom is a little slower to eat and I notice her eyes are red.

Faith and I can feel the tension in the air, exchanging a mutual glance of understanding. Neither one of us is going to say a word and we proceed to eat our food as fast as we can. We both finish and get up from the silent table at the same time, grabbing our empty plates and glasses to retreat to the kitchen.

I follow her to the sink and ask, "Are you coming with me tonight?"

"Nah, I don't really feel like it," She replies nonchalantly as she puts her dishes in the sink. "Besides, I'm supposed to go to Elizabeth's soon. She's coming to pick me up."

Annoyed, I roll my eyes and set my dishes down on top of hers. "You really should go to Bible study. We are covering important topics that are relevant for young women."

"I'll go next week," She counters, then skips out of the kitchen.

She needs to go. Honestly, she needs it more than I do.

I glance at the clock on the stove: 5:17 p.m. It's a little early to leave for Bible study, but I can't stand being in the house anymore.

I'll go grab my purse and phone. Then I'll leave.

I go the long way to the stairs so I can avoid the dining room. At the bottom of the stairs, I can tell my parents are discussing something, but I can't distinguish the words in their whispers. I quickly climb the stairs, grab my things, and make my way back down. Halfway down, Faith comes running from behind and almost knocks me down the stairs.

"Watch it!" I snap at her.

"You watch it!" She yells back.

"GIRLS!" Mom's voice overpowers us both, even though she is still sitting in the dining room. We know it's her way of silencing us to prevent further arguing. But with the way this day has gone, I don't want to linger for a possible lecture. Now I run past Faith, who yells out to Mom, "Grace started it!"

I dart out the door and across the yard the safety of my white Jeep Cherokee.

"Dear Jesus, keep me safe while I drive. Amen." I mumble frantically as I buckle my seat belt and back out of the driveway. Thirty minutes later, I arrive at Sister Rebecca's house and park in my normal spot on the street before turning to grab my Bible in the front seat.

Oh crap. I left it in my room! Oh well. I'm sure Sister Rebecca has an extra one I can borrow.

I get out of my car and walk up, knocking on her front door. A few moments later, Sister Rebecca appears with a big smile on her face.

"Grace! It's good to see you again," She exclaims, stepping aside so I can enter. "Thank you so much for coming today, we really are making a difference in the lives of those children. It's something special, don't you think?"

"Yes, it is," I reply, smiling and nodding my head. "I accidentally left my Bible at home. Do you have an extra one I could borrow for tonight?"

"Of course! Come this way." She leads me down the hallway, stepping into their guest bedroom to grab a Bible off the nightstand and hands it to me. "Of course, if it weren't for us, those poor children might not ever be exposed to the greatness of our God."

"I know, it is so heartbreaking," I nod my head solemnly in agreement.

She walks me to the living room where we normally have our Bible study before continuing. "It is a shame what those poor children have to endure. I spoke to Pastor John, and we will probably collect school supply donations to help Welcoming Wings."

"Awww!" I exclaim. "That is such a wonderful idea! I'm sure they will love it."

Sister Rebecca motions to the living room. "Feel free to sit wherever you want Grace. I need to finish up a few things, but everyone should be arriving soon."

"Sounds good, thank you Sister Rebecca," I responded before taking a seat on the corner of her couch.

I love this couch so much, it is so comfortable.

Every week I look around their home in awe. Pastor John and Sister Rebecca have a very nice home, in one of the richer neighborhoods.

I bet they don't even have to worry about the Blacks or Mexicans.

Last year, a Black family moved down the street from our home. Dad was worried they would trash the house and make the property values drop. He spoke so often about it that I envisioned a group of nasty thugs living in the home.

But the first day I saw their children get on the school bus, I was shocked. Their daughter was gorgeous, with thick curly hair and wearing nicer brand-name clothes than what I had on. A little boy trailed behind her, wearing a similar, clean, respectable outfit. I told Dad about it that night and he looked relieved that we lucked out and had a good Black family in the neighborhood.

A week later Mom and Dad bought my Jeep, so I started driving Faith and myself to school instead. Even though we didn't ride the school bus anymore, I did occasionally see the Black girl and boy outside riding their bikes in the front yard.

Dingggggg Donggggggg.

I jump at the sudden ring of the doorbell. Within seconds, I hear Sister Rebecca open the door and usher everyone else in. There are about a dozen women in our Bible study and not all of them attended our Church. Some are old friends of Sister Rebecca's, whose husbands are involved at other Churches.

A few others are nurses with crazy work schedules, so it was hit or miss what weeks they attended. I don't even bother to look for Megan. All summer I had begged her to come with me and every time she refused or found an excuse out of it.

I see Debra come in and I immediately turn away before we can make eye contact. She is an older woman, in her late 50s and who talks nonstop. Despite her age, she is quite slim and active. She has so much energy for one person and knows everyone in town. I'm convinced she could carry a conversation with a brick wall.

She also worked with me at the Happy Mart, and I had developed a love-hate relationship about working the same shifts with her. I loved it because she did all the talking with the customers and took charge of doing all the work I don't enjoy. However, I hate it when she talks to me or tells me what to do.

I sigh with relief when I see Debra sit on the other side of the room. She flashes a smile at me and waves. I see her mouth start to open to say something, but thankfully she is interrupted when Sister Rebecca's sweet smile and cheerful voice fills the room.

"Good evening ladies! It is so good to have you all back again," Her tone changes to a more serious one. "Tonight, I am going to deviate from our normal Bible schedule to talk about something different. By now, I'm sure we've all heard the rumors about the possible abortion clinic opening in our small town."

Murmurs of agreement and head nods silently answer her rhetorical question.

Sister Rebecca takes a breath and continues. "Today, Pastor John was able to confirm that the abortion clinic is opening this upcoming Monday."

A few of the women gasp. One even whispers "no" in disbelief.

"You are all women I know and trust. You know my story, what I have struggled with," Sister Rebecca tears up a little. "It has been so difficult for John and me to conceive a child. We are praying and trusting in God's timing. That is all any of us can do. It is incomprehensible to me how someone, who has been blessed with the gift of a child, could choose to murder their child…" Sister Rebecca's voice chokes up and someone passes a tissue to her.

Aww, poor Sister Rebecca. That is so heartbreaking.

A moment passes before she catches her breath to continue. "There are so many women out there, who are called to be mothers and who are murdering their child to avoid the responsibility. It is a sin. A dirty, nasty sin that the devil is trying to tempt us with. The Ten Commandments forbid murder. Period. Doesn't matter who, it is forbidden to murder. Do not let anyone try to convince you differently. Abortion is murder. It is the murder of little children, those of whom could be the very answers that we have prayed for. They are God's will and are meant to be born - to become doctors and teachers and disciples of our good Lord and Savior."

A few women yell out in agreement, one even shouting "amen!"

"Ladies, we must take a stand. For every unborn child who is unable to speak for themselves, we must be the voice of reason, beckoning them to the light of our Lord!" Sister Rebecca's voice increases with intensity, and she lifts her arms up. "My sisters in Christ. Pastor John and I are organizing a protest on Monday, to stand outside the abortion clinic. Would any of you like to join us?"

I eagerly raise my hand, along with several other women. I notice Debra looks bored to be here and that she doesn't bother to volunteer to attend the protest.

"Wonderful, thank you sweet ladies. I knew I could rely on you. I'll start a text message group for those of you who would like to join us," Sister Rebecca's voice softens, and the tears start to swell again. "These poor women just don't know what a blessing it is to have a child. They don't understand that they are being called to a higher purpose and that all they need to do is trust in our God. While our intention is to protest the opening of the abortion clinic, we also need to remember to be disciples of Christ. Help our pregnant sisters to see the good and to understand that our God is powerful and just."

A woman, who I assume is one of Sister Rebecca's friends, stands up and hugs her. Sister Rebecca immediately burst into tears, and they sway back and forth. The room is filled with awkward silence, and I look around uneasily.

Suddenly, Debra's voice starts belting out *Amazing Grace* and I'm impressed at how beautiful her singing voice is. A few more women join in before I cave to the pressure. Sister Rebecca and her friend join in at the halfway point, encouraging everyone to hold hands. By the end of the song, everyone sings and holds hands as the room radiates with the presence of the Holy Spirit.

This, right here, this is what it is all about. Christianity at its core. Loving and embracing one another, simply how we are. My God is so good and so powerful.

Sister Rebecca apologizes for her behavior and ends our Bible study early. Even though we really didn't talk about the Bible, I walk away feeling better. Lighter. Holier.

It was the perfect evening I needed to boost my mood and confidence to return home. I say my goodbyes, returning the Bible Sister Rebecca let me borrow and promising that I will attend the protest. On the drive home, all I can think about is how heartbreaking it must be for Sister Rebecca. To know that God gave her one purpose in life, to be a mother and she can't get pregnant.

I would feel like a total failure if I was married and couldn't provide children for my husband.

My thoughts shift to the abortion clinic and how terrible it is that our government allows them to operate. I'm also excited about the protest and the chance to make some real change in the world.

If we don't take a stand, then no one will.

When I turn down the street our house is on, I am relieved to see that Hope's Subaru is not there. It's almost 7:30 p.m. by the time I park my car in its normal spot. I walk up to the front door, listening intently for any signs of argument or more serious conversations - both of which I would like to avoid.

I am relieved to enter a silent house and cautiously retreat to the safe haven of my bedroom. After a shower, I climb into bed and scroll through my phone, exhausting all my favorite apps.

I don't remember falling asleep or how my dreams started. Soon, I am mesmerized by the peaceful scenery of a meadow with wild-flowers and trees. It looks like springtime, and I watch as new flowers bloom around me. The wind blows my hair, sending goose bumps down my right arm, so I turn away from the breeze.

I want to be in the warmth and sunshine, but the cold creeps closer to me. I start to run, away from the cold and towards the shelter of the trees. Panting, I rest beneath one and watch as the cold wind blows the leaves down. A big one swirls in front of me, each turn getting closer to me and fading from its bright green to golden honey to dark brown.

I reach out to grab the falling leaf to save it from hitting the ground. But when I touch it, the meadow fades away to a stark white room. I try to move, but I am restrained to a medical bed.

Fear overwhelms me and I try to scream for help, but no sound comes out. I can't even move my mouth, and my breathing comes in short rasps. I hear footsteps enter and standing over me is the shadowy outline of a doctor. He has a long sharp needle in one hand and forceps in the other.

Suddenly I realize I am propped up, with my legs spread like I was at the gynecologist's office. A subtle part of my mind becomes more aware of the dream.

NO! This can't be real… It's just a dream, wake up…. It's just a dream.

I jerk up wide awake in my bed sweating. My heart is pounding so hard in my chest I can hear it in my ears and blood is coursing through my body, fueled by my adrenaline. As my eyes adjust to the darkness, I recognize the familiar sights of my bedroom: my music posters, the cross on the wall, my dresser and jewelry stand.

"It was just a dream." I tell myself. Saying the words out loud feels more assuring. In my dream I couldn't speak, but here I can. I place my hand above my heart and take a few deep breaths.

I thought I had gotten over my fear of the gynecologist… I guess not.

Because he does scare me. It feels wrong to let another man, even a doctor, look at my body without clothes on. To touch me and place his fingers inside of me. I shudder at remembering my latest visit and my fingers subconsciously reach for my necklace.

Then I say a long prayer, asking God to help put my mind at ease and to bring me peace. Shortly after saying Amen, I drift off to sleep again.

5

HOPE

It's late when I return to the campus parking deck by my dorm. While I had been back in town for several hours, I had to spend that time working at the campus bookstore. I was supposed to get off later tonight, but it was so slow the manager sent me home early.

Now I am quietly driving into the parking deck and am delighted to find a spot on the main street entrance. During the school year, the parking deck is full of cars, and it is impossible to get a spot. But during the summertime, it was always empty, especially now that finals were over.

I enjoyed parking on the ground floor next to the street while I can, because in a couple more weeks the fall semester will start. My fingers trace the familiar outline of the metal horse keychain as I exit the car and lock the doors.

In the distance, thunder rumbles and lightning flashes across the sky. I hurry across the street, entering the dorm building and flashing my student ID for the security guard at the front desk. He barely looks over to acknowledge me, before turning back to the TV on the wall to watch a baseball game.

I step inside the elevator and click the number four button. As the elevator slowly creaks up to my floor, I stare at my reflection in the doors. My short purple hair is frizzy and sticking out in every direction. Sweat beads along the edges of my face from the intense heat and I regret my decision to wear the baggy pants and V-neck I have on. I am pleasantly surprised that my arm muscles look slightly larger in this shirt though.

Glad my arms are finally starting to bulk up.

Staring at my face, I see a mixture of Grace and Faith looking back. I have the same button nose and blue eyes. Thankfully, I'm not plagued with the acne Grace sometimes struggles with, but I do have the same chubby cheeks. I have always envied Faith with her sharp jawline and fast metabolism.

But I don't envy her name.

It always annoyed me that our parents gave us the most basic-ass religious names in existence: Hope, Grace and Faith. It's wording you would expect to see on home decor plaque from Hobby Lobby.

I rub at the corner of my right eye, where my contacts have been bothering me. Somehow, I am the only one out of the three of us who inherited terrible eyesight.

I can't wait to take these things out.

My dorm is the first door on the fourth floor, right across from the elevators. While it was convenient on move-in day, it has since become inconvenient as loud groups of students come and go. However, on rare days like today, I'm grateful I don't have to walk much further to the comfort of my room.

I shouldn't be surprised they reacted the way they did about my degree change… or my hair.

I enter the dorm room and am relieved to see that Emily isn't hosting any friends tonight. There are four of us to share the common living area that includes a kitchenette, a couch and table for the TV. Then two bedrooms on opposite sides that each share a single bathroom. If the rest of us had known about Emily's social outings, we probably would have found a different roommate.

Saanvi was especially having a hard time with the constant strangers in the dorm and loud noises. She was studying to be a doctor and had zero time for parties or fun.

Emily and Saanvi had argued multiple times about it already and I was grateful that I didn't have to share my bathroom space with either one of them. While I do appreciate how quiet Saanvi can be when she is studying, she has been *very* vocal about how much she despises the trash piling up or the many dishes in the sink. She turned out to be quite the clean freak and was quickly disappointed that no one else was going to follow her daily cleaning schedule.

The joys of roommates, I guess.

I walk past the empty common space and shut the door behind me. Two hands wrap around my waist as Li Mei comes up from behind.

"I missed you," she whispers in my ear. I turn and take all of her in within one quick second. Her long dark hair, petite body, and smooth light-tan skin. She is so small and short, barely coming up to my shoulder. I thought being 5'6 was short until I met her. I stare into her brown slanted eyes and give her a soft-hearted smile.

Concern immediately spreads across her face. "What's wrong?"

I sigh. "I went home to get a few things and as luck would have it, both of my parents were there."

She stares back at me, slightly confused, so I continue to explain.

"They aren't happy I changed my degree. Apparently, the university sent a letter to confirm my degree change, and they opened my mail without my consent."

I brush past Li Mei, as the anger starts to build back up. "They had no right to do that. I have a scholarship that covers almost all my expenses. They have only helped by occasionally buying books for me or food. But you would think they funded my entire education from the way they act."

"Oh Hope..." Li Mei trails off sympathetically.

"And then they wanted to argue about my hair color." I continue annoyed as the fight replays in my head.

"What is wrong with your hair?" Li Mei asks, puzzled.

"They said 'it's an unnatural color and disgrace to god's handiwork.' Ugh, I wish for once they could justify their reasoning without quoting a piece of bible scripture at me," I spit out the words with disgust. Now I'm pacing in frustration and starting to shake.

"All my life they have tried to shove their beliefs down my throat, without ever listening to what I want or how I feel. And to top it all off, I didn't even get my damn birth certificate!"

If I don't get it, I'll never be able to get my passport.

Li Mei reaches out to grab my arm softly to pull me out of my anger.

"Everything will be okay. You only have two more semesters and then you will be graduating, and we can fly away to China, Europe or anywhere else in the world we want to go," Her sweet voice coaxes me, and she stares at me with her slanted brown eyes. She is silently begging for me to calm down and I don't want to disappoint her.

I sigh, taking her face in my hands. "You are too good to me. I don't know what I ever did to deserve you."

A playful twinkle sparkles in her eye. "Oh, I'm still trying to see if you are worthy enough."

I laugh aloud and kiss her forehead. "Come on, I'm hungry and want to grab something before the café closes."

I grab her hand and pull her along. She intertwines her fingers in mine and refuses to let go as we walk out the dorms and across campus. I still get nervous when we walk around campus together, but I'm slowly getting more comfortable with being out of the closet. Ever since I was a little girl, I struggled to find men attractive.

My dad always worried I would get pregnant in high school, but little did he know I avoided boys like the plague. It wasn't until I came to college that I felt comfortable enough to explore my sexuality. I kept it very private though and didn't openly discuss it with anyone aside from the occasional girl I slept with.

That is, until I met Li Mei.

I can't explain it, but everything is just different with her. And so much better. From the first moment I saw her walk through the library, I knew I wanted her. But I was so nervous.

It's risky being a lesbian and trying to find other women who are lesbians too. It's also risky with making friends, as some women didn't want to be my friend simply because they thought I looked at them like a man does. They didn't realize how picky I was and that there are very few women I found attractive.

And Li Mei was one of those few.

I spent months watching her and trying to find the right moment to approach her. Not for a date, but just as a friend. I hoped if we became good friends, I could find out her sexuality and what she looks for in a partner. I tried not to get my hopes up and to face the reality that she isn't a lesbian.

My moment finally came in the coffee shop, when I overheard some guys making fun of her. I called them out for being assholes and told them to fuck off. She thanked me and we talked for a bit.

Turns out we had a few similar classes, but at different times. We spent the rest of the day studying for our upcoming exams and I cherished every moment.

Imagine my surprise when she point blank asked if I was dating anyone. When I answered no, she asked why. I answered her by simply saying I hadn't found the right girl yet.

Immediately after I said it, I panicked. I had exposed what I was and who I was to her. Yet, she remained unphased and responded back that was why she was single too.

That was 6 months ago and ever since we had been inseparable. This summer we chose to be roommates, to see how well we could live together.

I had relished every moment as I learned more about her and yet, she continued to surprise me in the best ways possible. For our 6-month anniversary, she gave me a horse keychain to symbolize the year we started dating. In Chinese culture, the horse is a symbol of strength, freedom, and vitality. It was as if she knew exactly how much those qualities meant to me—how they mirrored the way I felt when I was with her.

Ha, she also gave me the keychain so I would stop losing my keys and student ID…

I look at her and smile as she rattles on about her day.

I couldn't imagine my life without her.

We get to the café in time to grab a few tacos and we go outside to eat on the patio. The storms above us are still billowing in the wind, but so far, no rain has started to fall yet. The breeze feels nice compared to the sweltering heat we had been enduring lately.

While we eat, my phone buzzes from a text message Faith sent and I glance at it quickly.

> Why did you change your major? And why did you dye your hair?

I roll my eyes at how naive she is. Li Mei looks at me confused and I show her the text.

"She's just curious Hope. Explain it to her gently," She advises.

"She is just like my parents and Grace. She will never understand me," I complain back before biting into my next taco.

"You have to give her a chance, Hope," Li Mei pleads, reaching across the table for my hand. "Just try it. Please."

"Okay fine," I say as I give in and smile. "You know I can't resist you."

She takes her hand back to pick up her next taco. "I know," she says and winks.

I roll my eyes playfully and respond to Faith.

> I want to pursue a career in journalism or lobbying, so I changed my major to something that would help me prepare for those types of jobs. And I dyed my hair because I like purple and wanted purple hair.

I can barely take the next bite of my taco before I see the three dots pop up that Faith is typing her response. Then, the dots disappear, and my phone starts to ring as Faith resorts to calling me instead.

"Yes, Faith?"

"Why do you sound so annoyed?" She asks.

"Because I'm trying to eat dinner," I retort.

"Oh okay, um, sorry," Faith spits the words out so fast. "So, what is lobbying? Does that kind of job make a lot of money? Do you think I would look good with purple hair? And –"

"Okay, okay one question at a time," I interrupt her. "You have too much energy for me right now.

"Ugh, fine," She groans, and I can hear her eyes physically rolling. "What is lobbying?

"Lobbying is important in politics. It's where I would work to convince certain senators why they should care and vote for certain laws. Like climate change or healthcare," I explain.

"Does it pay a lot?" She immediately asks.

"Um, well, it doesn't pay high like some other careers, but I'm not going into it for the money. I'm choosing that career to make a difference," I respond.

"Do you think everyone should pay for free healthcare? Wouldn't that be more expensive for the average person?" She asks curiously.

"Don't listen to everything you hear people, or the news say," I caution.

My parents have ruined her with their religious ideocracy.

"We are already paying for it. Large pharmaceutical companies are taking advantage of us and making large profits. They control more industries than just medications and even add dangerous things to our food that they know will cause problems, so then they can profit off us when we need the medication to cure said problem. There are so many things wrong with our healthcare system."

"If that's the case, why doesn't the government change it?"

She is too sweet and naive for this world.

"Because many officials in government are also profiting from it. They are being paid off by the companies to pass certain legislation to protect their profits," I take a deep breath, trying to gather my patience for all her questions. "That's why if I become a lobbyist, I will fight against such policies."

"Well, that's not good," Her voice sounds disturbed by this new issue she didn't know existed. "Do you think Mom and Dad know how that works?"

I hesitate before responding back to her. I don't want to tell her something that will ultimately get her in trouble with our parents. But I also don't want to lie to her.

"I'm not sure," I drawl out slowly.

"I'm sure they would understand if they knew," she says confidently.

I'm not so sure they would understand anything outside their faith...

I hesitate for too long because Faith seizes the moment to rattle off more questions. "So, do you think it is all the companies that do this? I noticed my hair started to fall out more frequently, does that mean they are putting stuff in my shampoo to make me realize I need hair growth products? And what about-"

"FAITH! I'm trying to eat dinner," I snap, interrupting her. "I'll call you back later. Bye."

I don't even wait for her to respond back, and I immediately hang up.

"That was rude," Li Mei scolds. "Why did you hang up on her?"

"Because I'm hungry and she was asking too many questions," I shrug.

Li Mei rolls her eyes, half with annoyance and half playful. "You should be nice to your sister."

"Faith is too energetic. It's the only way to handle her," I reassure Li Mei. "I promise, there is no other option."

Li Mei chuckles and decides to drop the conversation. Now it's my turn to seize the opportunity and I quickly devour my tacos. After we finish eating, we throw the paper plates away and walk back to the dorm.

"Let's take the long way around campus before it starts to rain," I suggest, pulling gently on her arm in the direction I want us to walk.

"Mkay, fine," She giggles back.

The campus is quiet and deserted. It appears no one else is willing to get caught out in the rain. I glance up at the storm, still circling overhead.

A few cars drive down the street and the wind rustles the tree leaves loose as we walk underneath. I start to hear the faint sound of music as we approach one of the other dorms. As we get closer, I am able to distinguish the Christian lyrics and scowl.

"Seriously, they couldn't shut their window and play that shit inside?" I complain, feeling anger rise within me.

Li Mei is unphased. "They are probably enjoying the cool breeze while it blows. It's been a really hot summer."

"It's disgusting and they shouldn't annoy the rest of us with their cult trash." I snarl and look up to identify which dorm room is playing the music.

It's quick to find, as few of the students stayed in that building this summer and only one of the lit rooms has a window open. The music is coming out of a 2nd floor window, which is not that high up. I scan the ground and spot a few larger rocks sitting in gravel.

"Maybe a few thrown rocks will make them stop," I grumble, stepping towards the rocks.

Li Mei jerks me back with a strength I didn't know she had. "HOPE! You cannot do that. That is so rude and mean. They are just playing the music they enjoy, what is so wrong with that?" Her panicked eyes search mine desperately.

"Well, it's shit music, and I don't want to hear it," I snap back, and my body starts to shake with anger.

"Then we will keep walking and go back to our dorm," Li Mei states definitively. "They don't have to turn it off just because you don't like it. And we don't have to stay here either."

I take one last look up at the dorm room then continue walking on our path. Li Mei trots to catch up to my brisk pace.

"What is wrong, Hope? Why are you so angry?" She asks with concern.

"Nothing!" I snap again. My outburst frightens her, and she jumps back. I freeze, finally seeing her eyebrows scrunched and face full of worry.

I realize what I did and pull her to me into an embrace. "I'm sorry. I shouldn't have done that. I shouldn't have yelled at you. I know you are just worried about me. And right now, I feel angry, but I don't know why."

She relaxes in my arms and rubs my back. We hold each other for a long moment, until I stop shaking.

"I really think you should see a therapist, Hope," Li Mei whispers quietly. "I know you are hesitant to, but I think you have some unresolved anger you need to work through. These last few months have been hard on you, and I don't like seeing you upset."

I look down into her eyes to see the worry and pain in them.

She really does care about me. How did I get so lucky?

"I'm so worried to tell my parents about us. But I also don't want to live in fear," I begin. "And I guess I hold some resentment against Christianity because of the way I was raised."

"If you aren't ready for it, I don't have to meet them. We can wait until you feel more comfortable," she says with reassurance.

"No, I want to at least introduce you to them. Even if they don't know we are dating," I stand firm on the decision. "I'm still adjusting to being this open about my sexuality, but I know if we take small steps, I will eventually feel confident enough to come out to them."

"And are you sure you still want us to go see them in a few days?" Li Mei asks cautiously.

"Absolutely. It will be the perfect timing since school is about to start back," I explain. "They will be too busy with Grace and Faith to realize what we are doing."

"Okay, well if you change your mind, it won't hurt my feelings. I know this is a big step," She responds supportively.

"Thank you, I appreciate that. We could..." I trail off as a few drops of rain hit my forehead. Li Mei looked up, so I assume she felt a few drops too. "Come on. Let's get back to the dorm before we get caught in the rain."

We run back to the dorm and as we step into the elevator, we see the rain start pouring down outside. Upstairs, we walk into the dorm and are greeted by several of Emily's friends in our living room.

Oh great, she's having another party.

Emily was known for being an avid host with food, music, and decorations galore. She would also have themed parties, to encourage people to dress up. However, our shared living room was far too quiet and bleak for a party.

"Hope, Li Mei! What have you been up to?" Emily asks.

"We went to the café to grab dinner. The better question is, what are y'all up to and why is your party so lame?" I respond jokingly.

One of the guys chuckles and I recognize his shoulder length hair and vibrant nails. He has attended several of Emily's parties before and always manages to take home a new guy with him. I think I remember Emily introducing us once and that his name is Eric.

"Actually, tonight I am hosting the student diversity club. We are discussing the new women's health clinic that is opening on Monday," Emily explains in a serious tone. "They will provide services and aid to women who need help getting an abortion."

"Oh, that's so great!" Li Mei exclaims.

"Only if the city council allows it to go through," Eric says grimly.

"People have been attending the council meetings to protest its opening. And several Churches are also getting involved."

"Why would they protest that?" Li Mei asks, puzzled.

Poor thing. She really doesn't understand Christian culture.

"They believe it is sinful," I explained solemnly. "It goes against their religion because they believe conception starts when a woman becomes pregnant."

"What does that have to do with the clinic opening?" Li Mei asks innocently. "It's providing healthcare services for women who aren't religious or who aren't ready to have a child. If they don't like the clinic, they don't have to go to it."

"Yes, but the Churches don't think that way," Emily explains. "They see it as an abomination and infringement on their tax dollars."

She looks at me perplexed as other voices start to fill the room.

"I'll explain more later," I whisper in her ear. She glances at me and nods.

"Okay guys! And ladies," Emily exclaims to break up the chatter. "We've already been to the city council meeting to show that as students, we support the decision for the women's health clinic to open. Now, we need to also show our support the day of the opening. I'm worried that some protesters are going to come out and stop women from getting to the clinic."

Murmurs of agreement are heard throughout the small room.

"So," Emily continues. "We need to make sure we are ready and in full force. Signs, T-shirts, buttons, flags, the whole sha-bang. And this is a PEACEFUL protest. We will not act like fools or be disrespectful adults. Understood?"

Several heads nod and respond back with a yes.

"Hope, Li Mei, are y'all going to join us?" Emily asks, turning her attention to us.

"Hell yes we are!" I exclaim.

"Alright then, let's rally the girls, gays, and theys," Emily says enthu-siastically. "We only have 6 days until Monday."

6

DR. MALICUS

Wind tousles my hair as I reappear in my lab, a flash of light announcing my return. I breathe a sigh of relief to be back, before strutting over to the cabinet and putting the empty vial away.

Setting my bag on the table, I retrieve the new blood samples containing the parent DNA. Handing one of the samples to the machine, I click through the prompts, delighted when a new message appears on the holographic screen: *Cloning resumes.*

As the machine hums in the background, I return to my seat to analyze more ICO records and run theoretical scenarios. Hours pass as I sift through the data, until I finally stop at one.

> **Gender: Female**
> **Birth: 12/11/2568**
> **Death: 12/11/2568**
> **Age: -**
> **Sample Collected: Yes**

A newborn. Didn't even live for a day.

My heart pounds and my palms start to sweat as terrible memories resurface.

Ziva and I had a little girl. Shortly after the extinction crisis began, Ziva discovered she was pregnant. At the time, we hoped that our daughter would be spared. The doctors conducted preliminary testing and couldn't detect any signs that she had the defect.

Then we hoped she would live or that a cure would be found in time. I worked relentlessly for months, sometimes going days without sleep, just trying to find a solution. I tried hard not to think about why I needed the solution. How much more personal this work became for me.

I stood in that hospital and watched my baby girl die. There was nothing I could do to save her, and I had never forgiven myself since. Ziva was so strong, never letting me see how much she was struggling, and leaving me alone to focus on my work. I couldn't save our daughter, but perhaps I can help other people save theirs.

Beep, beep, beep, beeeeeeeeeeeeeeep.

I turn to see that the cloning samples are done and ready for evaluation. Glancing at the time, I see that it is past 9:00 p.m., and I immediately stifle a yawn.

Let's just see what the results show and if there are any other samples that need to be made overnight.

I approach the holographic screen to see the new failure breakdowns. The only notable difference in this latest batch is that almost 5% made it to the telophase cycle. None completed the cell life cycle but more made it to that final stage.

"Show me the 5% DNA samples that made it to the telophase cycle."

The holographic screen whizzes around to bring up the data. But 5% of 308 billion still amounts to 15.4 million combinations.

"Remove any known combinations that were previously unable to complete the anaphase cycle."

The holographic screen whizzes again to show the data I requested and is significantly shorter, with fewer than 15,000 combinations. I spend several minutes scanning a portion of it, line by line, and until

I notice a pattern.

"Group the DNA samples based on similar parent samples."

The holographic screen highlights the common samples and reorganizes, so I can see how many combinations came from different people.

"Add percentages of contribution."

The data appears within seconds. I immediately see that over 30% of the combinations came from a single person: 21ABN07.

Now that's interesting...

"Run theoreticals from past experiments against this DNA sample to identify possible combinations that could successfully complete the telophase cycle."

More whizzing and calculations, then a large number flashing back at me.

36 billion.

So not as much as the last batch. But it is still enough to help me to get 1% closer. That's all I really need; if I get 1% better every day then I will always be improving and making progress, no matter how slow.

As I continue analyzing the data to identify any other trends, I feel myself being pulled into the research and losing track of time. It's not until I yawn again and glance at the time that I see it is now after 11 o'clock. I click on a button to process the cloning request and have the computer archive the other results for now.

I don't see Ziva as I walk to the bedroom, but that isn't unusual. She is always doing random things to keep herself busy - cleaning the house, tending to her garden, practicing her calligraphy, or working on the latest puzzle. After a shower, I crawl into the empty bed and fall asleep before my head hits the pillow.

7

GRACE

Sunlight streams through my windows, hitting my face and rousing me from sleep. Still in a daze, I grab my phone and roll away from its bright glare. I groan as I see that it's only 8:30. I'm not ready to get up or start my day yet. I slept better after my nightmare, but I don't feel completely rested like I want to.

Scrolling through my phone, I catch up on everyone's social posts I missed during the night. Smiling faces and life updates are all over my feed.

Eventually, I get up and stumble to the bathroom. I stare at my reflection: dull blue eyes, light brown hair, and pale complexion. Freckles are sprinkled all over my body in various places, but not so many to where it is overwhelmingly obvious.

My boobs feel larger than normal, and I see a few new pimples popping up on my face. Annoyed, I check my birth control pill packet to see how close I am to my period again.

1 more week. Ugh.

I dread being on my period. The bloating, cramps, and mood swings are bad enough without the addition of the clumpy blood or worrying if I'm bleeding through my pants. Then there are the random headaches, fatigue and terrible face acne to deal with as well.

Tampons help me to feel more comfortable, but Megan once told me a story about a girl who died because she left her tampon in for too long. I used to wear pads, but I never liked feeling the slimy blood against my body. It took months to convince mom to let me use tampons instead. I shake my head and push away the dread.

I still have a week to enjoy before it comes back.

I return to my room to read my Daily Devotional. Today's reading focuses on Proverbs 31:30.

Charm is deceitful and beauty is passing, but a woman who fears the Lord, she shall be praised.

Under the scripture, the book continued to explain the meaning of the passage and how I should live according to the Word of God.

As you navigate your teenage years, surrounded by images of beauty standards and societal expectations, it's easy to get caught up in the pursuit of outward appearances. But today, let's explore a deeper kind of beauty, one that goes far beyond the surface.

Proverbs 31:30 reminds us that "charm is deceitful and beauty is passing." This means that physical attractiveness can be misleading and temporary. It's important to remember that beauty is only skin deep. What truly matters is what's on the inside.

The verse also tells us that "a woman who fears the Lord, she shall be praised." This suggests that true beauty comes from a heart that is devoted to God. When we seek to know and love God, we radiate a beauty that is both timeless and eternal.

So, as you journey through life, remember that your worth is not defined by your appearance. Instead, focus on cultivating a beautiful heart that is filled with love, kindness, and a deep connection with God. When you do this, you will truly shine.

I mull over the description and the reflection questions for several minutes, until my stomach growls. I end my Daily Devotional with a prayer and venture downstairs towards the kitchen.

I pass by the dining room, where Dad has his family tree folders and books spread out. It's one of his favorite hobbies to research our family history and find new relative connections to expand the family tree. He looks up as I walk through the room towards the kitchen.

"Good morning Grace," He greets. "Nice to see you finally woke up."

I ignore his sly remark and respond with a simple 'Good morning.'

In a bowl on the counter is an assortment of various muffin flavors Mom must have baked before she left for work. I grab a blueberry muffin and a glass of water, then return to the dining room. Pushing a few papers aside, I sit at the end of the table so as not to disturb my dad's work. I bow my head and mumble a silent prayer before finally eating my breakfast.

With each bite of my muffin, I stare more intently at Dad. His wrinkled face has softened his hard jawline, and I can see small wisps of white hair sprouting around the edges of his light brown hair. Sitting down, it is easy to forget he is over 6 feet tall. His large hands flip through a few pages of paper, occasionally setting one down to write something in his notebook that I know he will add to his online account later.

We don't have enough money to afford a computer, much less internet, so Dad uses his computer at the Church office to access his family tree account and catalog his notes in one place. He has been a full-time deacon at our Church for years to set an example for our family and to help others in our community. Dad is handy with the proper tools and has fixed many broken appliances, mended fences or even cut grass for elderly people who needed help.

Sadly, the deacons at our small Church don't get paid. To make up for the loss of income, Dad drives a bus during the school year. While a deacon position doesn't really require that much effort, Dad took it more seriously than others and devoted his entire career to helping the Church.

We didn't have as much as other families, but we had enough to get by. There were moments growing up when I might have questioned our lifestyle, but Dad would always remind me of Psalms 37:3-5.

Trust in the Lord and do good; dwell in the land and feed on His faithfulness. Delight yourself also in the Lord and He shall give you the desires of your heart. Commit your way to the Lord; Trust also in Him, and He shall bring it to pass.

He would always add that if we just trust in Him, everything will be taken care of, and He will give us everything we need. Dad never questioned how the bills would get paid, or the food would be put on the table; he just trusted in God and let Him do the rest.

"How is your family tree research coming along Dad?" I finally ask between bites of what's left of my muffin.

"Very good," He mumbles trailing off as he scribbles one more item in his notebook before slamming it shut. "I've already found 2 more family members on your great-great-great grandmother's side. The website I have been using recently came out with their own DNA testing process that will connect you to more family members…"

"Oh really?" I ask intrigued.

"Yes, and they will even provide a breakdown of your DNA, where you are from and what traits you inherited from your ancestors," He continues excitedly. "It is all truly fascinating to see how God has gifted mankind with this technology."

"That is pretty cool," I remark before taking another bite of my muffin.

"One day, this research will be valuable for you girls. Especially when you have families of your own. It could be a missing piece a future descendant needs to unlock our family's legacy."

He shuts the notebook he was writing in, stands up and begins stacking his research into a pile.

"I think I'm going to look into the DNA kits to get one for me and your mother," He remarks while grabbing a bag from the other chair and putting his books and papers into it. "Well, I gotta get going to the Church. Do you have to work today?"

"Yup. My shift starts at 2," I answer reluctantly.

"I'm sure I'll see you when you get home later tonight. Try to have a good day," He calls out as he walks away.

Alone at last, I get up to refill my glass with water and go to the living room to watch some TV before it is time for me to meet with Megan.

8

HOPE

"Well, what do you think?" Li Mei shakes her head to show off her new shoulder-length pink hair.

"I love it, very cute baby," I chuckle at her bubbly personality. She just came back to the dorm from the hair salon. I knew she was getting her hair cut, but I didn't expect her to come back with such a vibrant color.

My parents are going to freak out. But I love her so much for supporting me with this.

I continue to pack my clothes for our long weekend away. Standing in front of my small dorm closet, I look over the frilly lace, flowery dresses, and pink shirts I hadn't bothered to wear in months. I start grabbing everything and place it in a trash bag for Faith to dig through later. It just wasn't my style of clothing anymore and I didn't want it taking up precious space in my already small closet.

Even though I worked at the campus bookstore, I didn't make much money to pay for anything besides the occasional date with Li Mei. So, I frequented thrift stores and consignment shops to find "new" clothes that fit my style. Clothes I know my mom would never buy for me. The few clothes I had managed to buy so far went into my duffle bag along with my toothbrush and an extra pair of shoes.

"Are you almost ready to go?" I ask Li Mei, who is still admiring her new hair in the mirror.

"Yes, I just need to grab a few more things," She answers, finally pulling herself away from the mirror.

"Okay, I'm going to pull my car around to pick you up at the front," I tell her, as I throw my duffle bag strap over my head to prevent it from sliding off my shoulder. Then I grab the trash bag of clothes with my free hands.

Ooof, this bag is heavier than I thought. At least all those nights at the campus gym are finally paying off.

Stubbornly, I carry the bag of clothes to the elevator and sit it down briefly for the ride down. I pick it back up when the doors open and exit the dorm building.

At the crosswalk, I shift the bag to one side and quickly turn my head to check for cars. The street is eerily empty and silent for a college campus.

This feels weird.

I quickly cross the street, studying the darker shadows in the parking deck as I approach. Cautiously, I walk into the first level slowly to allow my eyes time to adjust to the darkness. There are a few cars parked on the right side, and I give them a wide berth as I walk towards my car.

I don't want any unexpected surprises here.

When I finally get to my car, I sit the bag down beside it and catch my breath while I unlock the door. The trunk opens slowly, and I throw my duffle bag in the back, before grabbing the trash bag of clothes.

At the same time, I jump at the loud clang of a car driving on the level overhead. Goosebumps sprinkle down my arm as I breathe to calm my racing heart and I am distracted by the sudden vibration of my phone in my back pocket.

I hope that's Li Mei ready to go.

After throwing the trash bag of clothes in the trunk, I shut it and climb into the front seat. In one swift motion, I pull my phone out of my back pocket with one hand and use the other to lock the doors.

I wait until I crank the car to look at the text message from Faith.

> What time are you coming to the house?

I sigh, disappointed that it's not Li Mei, who I imagine is still dancing in front of the mirror admiring her new pink hair. I type out my response but hesitate to send it.

I wish I could say she's my girlfriend... because she is so much more to me than just a 'friend'. But she is too young to understand yet...

I take a deep breath and press send on the message.

> We are about to leave campus now, but I won't be at the house until much later. I want to show my friend Li Mei around town.

I start to set my phone down when I see Li Mei's message coming through that she is coming down the elevator. Instead of responding to her, I put the car in reverse and leave the parking deck to go pick her up outside the dorm.

When I round the corner of the dorm building, she is standing outside with a backpack on and a smaller duffle bag in her hand. I motion for her to open the door behind me to put her bags in the back seat. She obeys, throws her bags in, shuts the door, and walks around the car to get in the front seat.

"Ready to go?" I ask her.

"All ready!" She exclaims, kissing me quickly on the lips. I kiss her back, smile and then hand her my phone.

"You can choose the music if you want," I tell her. She grabs my phone eagerly, shuffling through the songs before she finds one she likes. We ride in silence, blasting the music and counting down the minutes until we are in my hometown. My southern, small, dominantly white, hometown.

The city scenery fades away to quiet, perfectly manicured neighborhoods that display the occasional American flag or yard sign advertising lawn services. A few houses have soccer goals set up in the front yard or a swing from a tree.

Then the picturesque neighborhoods become more spread out with farmland in-between. Now we see confederate flags mixed in with the American flag and signs claiming democrats have ruined the country. We even pass a billboard advertising a call help line for expectant mothers to not abort their un-born child.

The closer we get to my parents' house, the more nervous I get.

Hopefully, no one will give us any problems.

9

GRACE

After several episodes of my favorite food cooking show, I zoned out of watching the TV and drifted into daydreams of being a housewife. Of all the different recipes I could cook my future husband, how beautiful our home will be and the children we will have. A notification from my phone jerks me back to reality.

Leaving my house now! See you in 30.

Oops, lost track of time... again. Oh well, Megan knows I'm never on time anyway.

I turn off the TV and go upstairs to get ready. After brushing my teeth and fixing my hair and makeup, my eyes stare at the hideous work uniform on my bed. I missed working at the boutique so much. They didn't require ugly uniforms or late hours, and I spent each day cleaning up the store or checking people out.

On slow days, when we didn't have any customers, I loved to browse the clothes and pick out what outfits I would like to buy. I never bought any though. All the money I made went towards putting gas in my car or buying the occasional lunch with Megan.

I tried to save money to put towards my car insurance, but as the newest hire, the boutique barely gave me a shift a week. After a month and no improvement in my hours, Dad made me switch jobs.

Even though I had been working at the grocery store since the start of summer, I still couldn't stomach how awful the uniform was. The bright yellow polo shirt has a huge smiley face on it with the words "how can I help you?" plastered above it in the most obnoxious font. The navy pants aren't that bad, but the bulky non-slip shoes are terrible. I sigh, put it on, and grab a light jacket to throw over the ugly smiley shirt.

I say a quick prayer and drive off in my car, already debating whether I want the chicken sandwich or chicken nuggets. Music blaring, I squeal into the parking lot on two wheels at 12:13 p.m. and see Megan waiting in her car.

I park next to her and jump out. A wave of hot July heat blows into my face, and I regret wearing the jacket to cover up my uniform.

I should have just brought a change of clothes instead.

Megan meets me at the end of the car, her blonde hair blowing in the wind. She rolls her blue eyes at whoever she is talking to on the phone. I silently point to the building door, and she nods her head to acknowledge that she is ready to go inside.

As we walk across the parking lot, she unconsciously nods her head multiple times before saying that she has to go and hanging up the phone with annoyance.

"Ugh finally! My mother has been talking to me nonstop since I left my house. I ignored her first two calls, but knew I had better answer the third one," Her sly smile and shoulder shrug indicates she isn't the least bit sorry for ignoring her mom's calls. She opens the door and walks through, holding it briefly for me to follow.

"Did you get in trouble again?!"

"Hmmmm. No, I don't think so," She pauses to think if she has done anything wrong lately. "Aside from the ass-chewing I just got for ignoring her phone calls, I've been well-behaved."

I narrow my eyes and give her a cold stare. She knows I can't stand it when people cuss. Just like her mom's phone calls, Megan ignores me and lunges forward to order her food first. After placing her order, she heads off to find a table while I place my order.

I find her tucked away, on the opposite end from the kiddie playground. I jump at the sudden scream of a child being chased and glare at the absent-minded mother who is scrolling through her phone. I continue walking to our table, popping a fry in my mouth as I sit down.

"Did you see that Courtney and Lindsay went to the Taylor concert last week!?" Megan twists her phone around, so I can see the picture Lindsay posted on Instagram.

I finish chewing and then respond, "I didn't know she was playing here?"

"She didn't. They flew to D.C. to stay with Courtney's sister because her Insta is flooded with pics from around the city." Megan's thumb scrolls on her phone, while her other hand grabs her drink.

"Do you still like vanilla ice cream the best?" Megan's sudden question catches me off guard.

I choke a bit on my nugget and drink deeply to relieve the pressure while shaking my head enough to answer her. Satisfied, she looks back at her phone for a moment and then back up at me.

"You're still going to the thing at the Church tomorrow, right? And on Thursday?"

"What 'thing'?" I ask confused.

She makes a dramatic sigh, then responds with "You know! The reading thing at Welcoming Wings."

"That was yesterday Meg… and you missed it, by the way," I put more emphasis on the last three words to show my annoyance at being left to fend on my own, but not too much to where she thinks I am mad at her.

"No, it's tomorrow. I have it in my calendar," she says definitively.

That explains why she didn't show up... She has mixed up her days.

"Well, you have it on the wrong day, because we went yesterday," I retorted as I opened a ketchup packet and dipped a nugget. "But yeah, I'm going tomorrow too."

Flustered, Megan frantically flips through her phone to find her calendar. I throw my ketchup dipped chicken nugget in my hungry mouth.

"No, I know it is tomorrow because today is Monday. I remember looking at it yesterday to remind myself. See it's right, oh..." She trails off as confusion clouds her face. "No, that can't be right. I remember looking and knowing it was tomorrow."

"I don't know what to tell you, Meg. Seems like you have your days mixed up. I guess I'll forgive you, this time," I wink playfully to reassure her that I'm not mad.

"Sorry Grace, I really thought it was tomorrow," She gives me an apologetic smile and shoulder shrug.

"It's fine. I suffered just fine on my own," I reply casually with a smirk.

Rolling her eyes, she chuckles, then takes a bite of her sandwich. After chewing for a few moments and scrolling through her phone, Megan looks up again.

"Have you gotten your class schedule yet? I want to know if we have the same homeroom," Megan asks, her attention still divided between her phone and our conversation.

"No, Dad says they won't be out for another week," I reply, observing Megan's distracted demeanor. She looks normal – her blue eyes are shinning, her blonde hair is right below her shoulders, whipping about as she turns her head to talk to me. She tucks a few strands behind her right ear and the diamond in her cartilage piercing flashes at me. But something just *feels* off about her.

She is all over the place today.

"Ugh, I wish it was out now so I could know…" She whines, then lights up with excitement. "Have you seen the trailer for that new Inside Out movie? It looks so cute! We should go see it when it comes out, I want to see it." Before waiting for my response, she turns back down to her phone. *Again.*

I eat another fry and study her face closely. Her behavior is unusual, even for her. She seems all over the place and energetic. Maybe anxious? She only gets like that when…

"Have you been smoking pot again?" I demand, my stomach churning with disgust.

She glances up at me, a hint of embarrassment in her eyes and a sheepish smile on her face.

Bingo.

"Meggggg." I roll my eyes and sigh. "You know that is so bad for you."

"But that's the thing, Grace," She pleads. "It really isn't."

"The Bible says to treat your body like a temple, to not put anything harmful in it. You really shouldn't smoke weed," I recite, my voice soft, but firm.

Now she is squirming in her seat, clearly wanting to be anywhere else, but at this booth with me.

"Grace, come on, you're my best friend. You know better than anyone why I need to smoke from time to time…" Megan's wide blue eyes beg me to understand. She's silently pleading for me to let this go, and more importantly, to not tell her mother – who is also my aunt.

A few months ago, Aunt Sharon walked in on Uncle James with another man. A *man*. Apparently, Uncle James had been gay all his life and suppressed it. Until he couldn't anymore.

Now they were going through a nasty divorce, and our entire family was trying to keep his infidelity a secret. It's bad enough to be cheated on, but this is way worse. Especially in a small, Christian town where everyone knows each other's business. I had overheard my mom say on several occasions that she was glad Grandma wasn't alive to witness it.

I also knew Megan was struggling to cope with it all. While the divorce was getting more intense, the custody battle was already done. Her dad forfeited his rights entirely on the grounds that he didn't have to pay for any child support. Her mom willingly accepted because she wanted to keep his sins as far away from Megan and her younger brother as possible.

However, Aunt Sharon did not accept any other terms for how their house, finances and other assets would be divided up, so the divorce had been dragged out for months.

I refuse to answer Megan directly, because I do not approve of her behavior, *at all*. But I don't want to disappoint her. Instead, I opt for the next best option.

"Did you see the football schedule came out? They released it the other day and it looks like our homecoming game might actually be a good one this year!"

Relieved, Megan sighs and picks up the change in conversation. All too quickly it is 1:40 p.m. and I have to rush to get to work on time. On the way, I can't help but think of Megan's situation.

I know when she smokes she is more ditsy, but I don't remember her being forgetful. Usually that's all me… they do say that smoking weed is the gateway drug…hmmm, I wonder what other drugs she has tried or maybe mixed with the weed to make her like that.

I turn down a street, spotting the Happy Mart in the distance, and glance at the clock in my car. It's 2:00 and I'm already late.

I hate the situation she is in, but she has got to do better and be a better example of Christ. The Bible literally says not to smoke weed or do drugs or drink alcohol or any of that other stuff. I wish they would just outlaw it and make all of this so much easier... But I guess for now I can just pray for her and that she will find guidance and strength in the Lord.

I say a quick prayer as I pull into the parking lot. Satisfied with myself, I run inside the Happy Mart to start my shift.

10

HOPE

When we finally arrive, I give Li Mei a tour of the park, shops, and local restaurants. She stares out the window wide-eyed, taking it all in and asking questions. After riding around for an hour, I finally stop at the Happy Mart.

"I need some more deodorant, but we can also grab some snacks here if you want any," I tell her as we pull into the parking lot. I swerve to avoid a pothole and for the first time in years look at the Happy Mart with a fresh set of eyes.

The parking lot is in terrible condition, with potholes everywhere and the lines are so faded most people wouldn't know where to park their car. The building itself had certainly seen better years and one of the Ps in the "Happy" had such a large bird nest that it was hard to tell it is a P anymore. The building's walls were covered in a variety of old posters, from sales and movie promotions over the years.

It's a miracle this place is still allowed to be open.

Yet at the same time, unsurprising. It was the closest grocery store around and much cheaper than ordering anything online. Plus, people valued the consistency of knowing the Happy Mart would have their unhealthy food selection. Don was a dedicated store manager, but he would never venture to stock organic or non-GMO food.

Because anything unknown is such a scary thing to these people.

I parked my car in one of the few spots where you could still see the white lines.

If someone decides to hit my car, that's on them. I did my part by parking correctly.

We walk inside the store and a cold breeze blows over us in the doorway. Inside, the Happy Mart fared no better than the outside. There were places where the floor tiles had broken and been replaced with pieces that didn't match. Several of the overhead lights were out and needed the bulbs to be replaced. It also smelled very chemically for a grocery store, as if to make people think the inside had been cleaned recently.

I glance at Li Mei and motion for her to follow my lead. I don't dare grab her hand though. All it takes is for one person to see us and then the entire town will know we are a couple. Including my parents.

And I am not ready to confront that beast yet.

I quickly find the bath aisle and see that absolutely nothing has changed about the store. We walk down the aisle until I find the deodorant and am dismayed to see I have two options to choose from: a woman's deodorant and a man's deodorant. The woman's smells like flowers and other fruity things that make me gag. The men's is not much better, with a minty ice scent to it. I opt for the men's deodorant since it didn't make me gag when I smelled it.

Besides, it's just for the weekend. Then I can get my normal deodorant.

"Did you want anything to snack on? Or drink?" I ask Li Mei.

"Hmmmm, some chips would be nice," She answers. "And maybe a green tea."

"You got it," I chime, leading the way toward the end of the aisle. When we round the corner, I see Don refilling some packs of meat in the refrigerated cabinets.

"Hi Don!" I call out and wave.

He looks up and smiles at me. "Hope! It's good to see you." Then he promptly turns back to what he was working on, ending our conversation.

I turn my head towards Li Mei to explain. "I used to work here in the summertime before I started classes at the university. Don is the store manager. He's really cool and such a hard worker. He's been the store manager here for years."

Li Mei studies him closely as we walk past. When we get to the chip aisle and out of sight, she whispers, "Is he mentally…"

"I don't know for sure. I know he has several health issues," I answer her, pausing to think.

I mean, everyone thought Don was somewhat autistic. But he functioned completely fine and had been manager of the Happy Mart for years. Surely if he were autistic we would know by now… right?

Li Mei nods her head in understanding. "Either way, it's impressive that he has worked here for so long. He must really love it."

"He does and he is so passionate and kind about it too," I nod my head in agreement. "He was a great manager to work for, so much better than the one at the campus bookstore."

"Ha! I'm sure anyone is better than that jerk," Li Mei scoffs.

She knew I struggled to get along with the campus bookstore manager, as did many people. It was hard to be professional, because if you made him angry, he would just stop putting you on the schedule. He did this to several people until they eventually found other jobs. Lately, he had been decreasing my hours, and I feared I was next on his list.

But that's a problem I can worry about next week.

Li Mei grabs the chips she wants, and we head to the drink aisle to find her green tea. To my surprise, the Happy Mart had two brands of green tea to choose from. Li Mei grabs her favorite and we go to the front of the store to check out.

There is only one register open, so we stand in line behind an elderly man and wait to check out. I recognize the cashier as a girl from my graduating class. We had a few random classes together where we would talk to each other. Outside of those classes though, we had never hung out.

Honestly, I hadn't seen her since graduation, and she had changed quite a bit. She used to be skinnier and tan, even with her dark emo outfits. Her dad owned a house on the lake, but I heard her parents got divorced.

Maybe she doesn't speak to her dad anymore because of the divorce...

The elderly man finishes paying and grabs his bags to leave, so we move up into his place.

"Hey Julie, how have you been?" I ask casually.

She stares at me confused. "Who are-"

"Hope Wilson, we went to school together and graduated in 2012," I explain.

"Oh my god! I didn't even recognize you!" Her face lights up with excitement. "You look fabulous, by the way. How have you been? You know your younger sister works here now. She's a bit of a brat."

I chuckle. "I'm not surprised. She's always been a difficult one. Very caught up in the religious stuff ya know."

I feel a tug on my arm and turn to introduce Li Mei. "Oh sorry, Li Mei. This is Julie, we went to school together. And Julie, this is my friend, Li Mei."

"I love your hair," Julie exclaims. "Very bold, very cute."

"Aw, thank you," Li Mei answers, turning her head side to side as her short pink hair swooshes above her shoulders.

Julie starts scanning all our stuff and doesn't miss a beat. "So, what have you been up to these last few years? Are you still at the college?"

"Yes I am, but I'm going to graduate in the spring," I explain. "Afterwards, I want to pursue a career in journalism or become a lobbyist. I haven't made up my mind yet."

"That's so cool," Julie says, while smacking her gum. "I'm proud of you for getting out of this small town and making something of yourself. I wish I had the grades to go to college. But I am going to beauty school and hope to be a hair stylist by next year."

"That's awesome," I respond, as I put my card in the reader to pay for our items.

"Actually," Julie starts as she pushes the bags to us. "Have you spoken to your sister? Grace's shift starts in a few minutes and she's still not here."

Of course she's running late. She would be late for her own funeral.

"Sorry Julie, I haven't spoken to her," I answer and grab our bags. "But hopefully she will be here soon. We need to go, but it was good seeing you!"

"Nice to meet you!" Li Mei calls out.

"Take care! Hopefully, I'll see you around soon Hope," Julie responds back before returning to her gloomy demeanor.

Outside the store, we look both ways before crossing the parking lot to my car. We are halfway across the pedestrian section, when a jacked up pickup truck comes revving into the parking lot. The driver has to slam on the brakes to avoid hitting us and I see the body of the truck jerk on its uneven axles.

"Watch it asshole!" I yell out.

"Move out of the way freak!" The driver yells out, honking his horn.

We continue walking and when we are safely out of the way, he revs his truck to race past us. The passenger rolls down his window and yells out "slow ass cunts!" as he flashes his middle finger at us. His sleeveless shirt shows off the confederate flag-cross tattoo on his arm with the words "southern pride" below it.

My skin bristles and I can feel the anger brewing underneath. I start to open my mouth, and Li Mei grabs my arm.

"It's not worth it," she says, only loud enough for me to hear.

I close my mouth and watch their jacked-up truck cross the parking lot. There are two flags attached to the back of the truck bed, one is the police flag with a blue line through it and the other is the confederate flag.

So immature. They support a country that doesn't even exist anymore.

We climb into my car and right as I crank it, I see another car come barreling into the parking lot: a white Jeep Cherokee.

Well, there is Grace. Late as usual.

I wait and watch patiently, as Grace parks her car in a random spot that may or may not have lines. She jumps out and runs inside. I look at the time to see it is 2:00 on the dot.

"Do you know her too?" Li Mei asks with a tone of jealousy.

"Yes, I do and before you get jealous, that's my sister," I respond back with a laugh.

"Oh…well then, uh," Li Mei stammers as her face turns red.

I reach over and grab her hand. "I never had a thing for Julie. I'm pretty sure she's straight. We had a few classes together and were friends, but nothing more," I explain.

She nods her head slowly and before she can speak, I continue. "And there will never be anything between me and her. I have you, you're all I want and all I need."

She smiles happily, more reassured with that answer.

Good. I don't want her to doubt for a second that I'm not serious about her.

"Now, are you ready to meet my parents?" I ask her softly.

"Of course. And it's okay to introduce me as your friend," She states. "Because that is mostly true. I am your friend, and I am also a little more than a friend."

"And I'm so grateful you are," I say smiling. I pull out of the parking lot, and we head towards my parent's house.

11

DR. MALICUS

My heavy eyelids open slowly as the alarm fades out.

Morning already?!

"Good morning Dr. M-Malicus. Today is Tuesday, October 24th, 4102. The time is currently 7:15 a.m. Would you like for m-me to continue with your m-morning report?"

"Yes Ziva, please continue."

"Very well sir. The ICO is exploring m-medical engineering m-modification technology that…"

Her morning report fades to the background as I stagger to the bathroom to get ready for the day.

"…an investigation has been opened to find the m-missing…"

I splash water on my face, staring at my reflection. The same haunted look stares back at me, sleep deprived and restless. I grab a fresh shirt and pair of pants to put on, then grab my watch, glancing at the engraving on the back before putting it on my wrist.

Only the strong survive.

"…Dr. Imani Kayitesi, Dr. Hai Văn Xaun, and Dr. Philipe García have been cleared of…"

Downstairs I find my routine breakfast in the same place, waiting patiently for me. I rotate between taking a bite of the whole-grain toast or sipping the fruit smoothie. In the water glass, I see bits of my medication dissolving.

Ziva is good. Too good.

I chug half of the water and finish the food quickly. There isn't any time to waste, and I need to get back to my lab. I take the last sip of my water and barely set the glass down before Ziva walks up to take it. Lips closed, she smiles softly and grabs the empty plate as well.

As she walks away from me, I study her body. Her tall frame is perfectly symmetrical with her athletic body that moves with a fluidness even I envy. Yet, her hips look smaller, and her dirty blonde hair is too short. The hair can be grown out, but the hips... that is another problem entirely.

She used to be so perfect, but losing our daughter took its toll on her. I tried to be a caring and thoughtful partner. I tried to be there for her, in my own way. But I wasn't always at my best.

The stress of the global extinction crisis and my job took its toll on me. It kept me distracted and distant from her. She knew when she married me how dedicated I was to my career. In fact, she used to share that same dedication as a leading genetic technology engineer and developer.

We were the ultimate power couple: I studied and improved genetic modification, while she built and enhanced the technology I used. My research team always had the latest equipment and advantages to put our career advancements far ahead of our peers. It is honestly how I became one of the best genetic modification scientists in the world.

I get up from the table and my feet automatically walk to the lab, while my mind reflects on everything we had endured together the last few years. We didn't just lose our daughter; we also lost our status in the scientific community. Ziva was depressed and unable to work for months. I was left to scramble in the wake of her absence and struggling with the change in our marriage.

When I said those vows, all those years ago, I honestly thought we could handle anything that came our way. Anything that would try to destroy our marriage or weaken us. Little did I know what we were truly up against. I shake my head at how naive I was back then. I glance at my vintage watch, remembering the words inscribed on the backside.

Only the strong survive.

It bothers me to think that our daughter wasn't strong enough to survive. She should have been. I hand selected every DNA trait she would inherit from us. It was some of the best handiwork I had ever done and it should have helped her live. But it didn't.

A faint beep distracts me from my memories.

"Dr. Malicus?"

I turn around in my lab to see Almeta on the hologram. Once again, she is in her lab coat and her brown hair is pulled back into a bun.

"Hello Almeta, what do you have for me today?"

"I was able to secure all your supplies," She pauses, looking around at her surroundings. "And can stop by this afternoon to bring them to you."

"Excellent! That is wonderful news, " I respond, glancing at the screen of reports in front of me.

"Is there a specific time you would like me to bring them to you?" She asks, before continuing. "I do believe I can get there as early as 2:00 p.m."

"Then 2:00 p.m. it is," I answer without looking at her. "I'll be ready and waiting for your arrival."

"Of course, sir. See you soon."

I turn to look her in the eyes before answering. "Thank you, Almeta."

She smiles softly before her hologram disappears and I turn my attention back to the reports. Even though I have been in my lab for several minutes, I haven't focused on what I am actually looking at because I was too distracted by my thoughts.

Of the 36 billion DNA combinations that were processed in the night, less than 3% made it to the telophase cycle and none completed the cell life cycle.

Damnit! I really expected more than this…

I start pacing back and forth, occasionally glancing up at the report.

"Okay, so only 3% of the cells advanced to the final cycle even though 21ABN07 comprised 30% of the previous theoretical results. I expected it to improve in the number of combinations, but instead it decreased. There is a correlation between where the samples are coming from…" I trail off as the realization sinks in. "Pull up the sample file for 21ABN07."

I read the stats for a few moments, then wave my hand to scroll down to the relative's section.

"Show sample files for each relative listed in direct connection to 21ABN07."

Four more files appear next to the first one.

Interesting. All the women related to 21ABN07 have different blood types. I wonder…"

"Run theoreticals from past experiments against the female DNA samples related to 21ABN07 to identify possible combinations that could successfully complete the telophase cycle."

The holographic screen whizzes and I am greeted with 3 error messages: *need sample.*

"Shit."

I don't have their DNA samples in my home system. Which means I will have to go out to get them. But I can't do that until Almeta arrives with my supplies because I don't have any way to carry the DNA back to my lab.

This would be so much easier if I were at my actual lab, with full access to everything.

I glance at the time and see it is barely 9:00 a.m.

Ugh. I don't have the patience or time to just sit here.

My mind races, trying to figure out what I can do for the next five hours until Almeta arrives. I hate it when I have to pause on work that I know is progressing.

Why did they have to send me on sabbatical? I was making such great progress...

I decide to perform routine maintenance checks and prep all the equipment, so it is ready to go when I get the new supplies. At the ICO headquarters, where I worked for years, there are people who work around the clock to maintain the equipment and technology in the lab for us.

Oftentimes, Ziva herself would oversee the maintenance checks, if only to ensure I didn't complain about it to her later when something malfunctioned. Here at my home lab though, I have to do that work myself from time to time.

It was so nice when Ziva did this for me... I wonder if she would be open to trying again.

Maintenance upkeep takes longer than I anticipated because I didn't realize how behind I was on checking the equipment. I check the logs to see when I last checked on things and it was over a month ago, right when I started my sabbatical.

I am going to have to get used to doing this now. I still have several months before I can return to work.

I might not be able to physically return to work, but that sure as hell wasn't stopping me from working on my own. After checking the last item on my list, I check the time: 1:02 p.m.

Still another hour before Almeta arrives.

I spend the last hour checking on my other cloning projects before going upstairs for a late lunch. Ziva already has my protein shake prepared and waiting for me, like always. I gulp it down quickly before rushing back to the lab. I gather all the items Almeta will need to take back with her and organize them neatly on the counter.

A flash of light erupts behind me, and I turn to see Almeta appear.

"Hello sir, it's good to see you again."

"Hello Almeta. I trust you were able to come here discreetly."

"Yes sir," She responds confidently. "And I have everything you need, plus a few additions."

She sets a box on the counter, and I rush forward eagerly. I begin to explore all its contents while Almeta collects the items I laid out for her to take back.

"Excellent. I have been waiting impatiently."

She looks down embarrassed at her feet, so I clear my throat to clarify.

"I've made great progress today, but don't have the DNA sample I need to move forward. I've spent the rest of the day prepping the equipment and doing routine checks."

She nods her head approvingly. "If you don't mind me asking sir, is Ziva still doing well?"

"She is," I glance at Almeta before continuing. "She just needs a little more time to adjust. I'm hoping it won't take much longer because I could really use her help."

"That is good to hear sir. I'm sure she will help to speed things up," Almeta's reassuring voice is more confident than how I truly feel about Ziva's current condition.

We work in silence for a few moments. Even with her limited access and the lab's protocols, Almeta was able to bring everything I needed.

"How is Dr. Kayitesi's research progressing?" I ask nonchalantly.

Even though we just spoke the day before, the technology at the lab is incredible. Scientists on site have access to the best technology and data systems in the world. Months of work can be accomplished in only a few hours, and it is common for the ICO to give daily press releases to the public on the progress being made.

"We are almost ready for preliminary testing," Almeta answers, as she straightens her lab coat. "However, the research team is being delayed because they need an organ reactor for the project to move forward."

"An organ reactor?" I ask, puzzled.

"Yes, an organ reactor," She continues to explain. "After the controlled-clone project was scrapped, Chancellor Fhiachra gave Dr. Kayitesi permission to use it for her project to see if it could be beneficial."

"I mean, I suppose...theoretically, it might work." I struggle to process the logic of using the organ reactor.

It was originally intended to assist military operations with seeing firsthand what clones are doing and to better control their decisions. Its implications were also designed to integrate with a full-grown adult, not a newborn. And certainly not for controlling genes on a microscopic level. The illogicality astounds me.

"Do they really think they can use that to force the genes to function?" My question is rhetorical, as I think out loud at why the ICO would need the organ reactor. "Even if - and that is a big IF - even if it is capable of stopping the organ failure from developing post-birth, there aren't enough organ reactors to sustain our population."

"Yes, I have those same concerns too, because, as you know, they are incredibly rare," Almeta smiles slyly and lays the organ reactor on the counter in front of me. "And it appears that the only one we had at the lab has gone missing."

She is so damn good.

"Well, that's a shame it is missing." I pick up the small organ reactor and spin it around in my fingers.

Hmm. I might could use this later.

I turn back to the new supplies and start organizing them into their proper storage places. Almeta senses that I'm done conversing and ready to get back to work.

"Is there anything else you need before I go, sir?"

"No, I don't think so, Almeta." I pause to make sure there isn't anything else I need. She waits patiently for me to continue. "Thank you. Report back tomorrow at the usual time."

She nods her head respectfully. "Will do, be careful sir."

A flash of light and she is gone from my lab.

Now, I can finally resume my work.

I grab the materials I need to safely bring back the DNA samples and pause to look at my lab.

I think this is everything. Should I tell Ziva I'm leaving? Hmm…no. That might make her suspicious.

A couple of clicks on my transporter watch, and a flash of light whisks me away to my destination.

12

HOPE

I park outside my parents' house on the street. The quaint two-story house had seen better days. The light blue siding is extremely faded, one of the windows is missing its pair of shutters, and there are more dead bushes in the front yard than live ones. Here and there cracks are starting to show in the white brick foundation. One of the brick steps on the porch broke off at the corner years ago and had never been repaired. I was too young to remember when we moved into the house after my grandmother died from breast cancer. It was the only home I had ever known.

Even if I don't feel welcome here.

I'm nervous to walk back in after our fight yesterday. But I need to get a few things from my room that I didn't get yesterday, and I really want my parents to meet Li Mei.

My girlfriend.

Although, they can't know that. They would never be accepting or understanding.

But maybe if they meet her as my friend, they will like her.

It bothers me that I still crave their approval. The rationale part of my mind knows better, knows they will never change how they are. Yet, deep down inside that little girl I was claws at my insides, desperate for them to give me just one word or nod of acceptance.

This would all be easier if I could just let it go…

"Hope?" Li Mei asks, her eyes wide with concern.

"I'm good. Sorry, I just needed a moment to prepare myself," I answer, taking deep breaths. "That's my dad's car, so I know he is here. My mom's car is gone since she is at work. We already know Grace is at work and Faith is too young to drive, so it is hit or miss if she is inside or not."

Li Mei reaches out to grab my hand, rubbing it softly. "It will all be okay. After all, we are just friends, remember?" She winks playfully.

I chuckle. "You're right, I know. Come on, let's get this over with."

My eyes briefly focus on the horse keychain as I turn the car off and pull the key out of the switch.

I have Li Mei with me, that is all I need. That's what she promised when she gave me the horse keychain… Everything will be fine.

We get out of the car and as I walk around the front hood, Li Mei opens the back door of the car to get her bags.

"You can leave your bag for now," I told her. "Let's go inside first. Then, if things go bad, we have a clean getaway."

She nods her head in agreement and shuts the door. We walked up silently to the front porch. My hands are sweating as I knock on the door twice, then slowly open it and we step inside the living room.

The TV in the corner is loudly broadcasting a conservative news channel to the empty room. The news anchor's voice fills sounds disturbed, and I am reminded that some people, like my parents, actually listen to this garbage.

"The border crisis is getting out of hand as more Mexicans continue to cross the border illegally, many bringing drugs and weapons that the border patrol is actively trying to confiscate…"

I cautiously look around, leaning to my left to see if anyone is in the dining room. Aside from the mismatched furniture and remnants of my dad's family history collection across the floor, the house is empty.

He must be in the kitchen or his bedroom then.

Li Mei steps further into the living room to admire the mismatch collage of photos my mom has hung on the walls. Every available space is filled with a frame and in-between are wall plaques of Bible verses, crosses and the multiple variations of "live, laugh, love." Occasionally, one can catch a glimpse of the flowery white wallpaper hidden underneath. A handful of mom's collection had been gifted to her over the years, but the vast majority came from digging through the items people donated at the church.

I wonder how strange this must be for her.

I know Li Mei grew up in a small apartment in a crowded district in China. Her family valued quality time over a quantity of possessions. I haven't visited her hometown, but she's shown me pictures of her simple and functional family home. Not at all like the outdated house I grew up in that had remained almost untouched since my grandmother bought it in the late 70s.

"Conservative leaders continue to criticize the Affordable Care Act, better known as Obamacare, for complicating the healthcare process and making it more expensive for individuals to get…"

Several years ago, Mom got sick of the brown paneled walls in the kitchen and dining room, so we spent a whole week painting them white. We couldn't afford the paint, so Dad managed to collect a few leftover gallons when the church repainted the Sunday school rooms. That was also the same year when he thrifted the dining room table off the side of the road, sanded it down and stained it a faded chalkboard white color.

The mismatched aesthetic was a good distraction from the other defects of the house: the stain on the ceiling where the upstairs tub had leaked, cracks in the wall where the foundation was starting to shift, and a weird smell that I really hope is not mold growing in the crawl space.

"In other news, local legislators are seeking to pass their own state

laws to protect the sanctity of marriage between a man and a woman, after the Supreme Court..."

Growing up, we didn't know anything different. We just accepted that this was our life and that we had to deal with it.

However, when I started college, I became angry at my parents for choosing to be poor. They didn't strive to have higher paying jobs, because they were so content with their simple life. I struggled to adapt to my college courses and almost failed the first year because my public-school education didn't prepare me well enough.

It was hard not to compare myself to my peers, who went to the better schools and were breezing through their classes with perfect grades. I had to bust my ass and spend every day in the library just to get caught up on everything. Dad would always say that "God will provide," but looking around at the house it is embarrassing to see what they settled for.

Thrifted furniture and trash decor.

"Awww you were so cute!" Li Mei exclaims, looking at me and pointing at a picture on the wall. I move closer to see which one she is talking about.

My seventh birthday party.

In the photo, I am sitting on my bicycle wearing a pink shirt with a unicorn and matching shorts. It was the first birthday party where my parents let me invite a few of my friends. It was also the first time I knew I was different.

I just didn't know what to call it back then.

I smile and start to respond back to her but am interrupted as Dad finally walks into the room.

"Hope," he says in a monotone voice. I involuntarily flinch at the sound of his disappointment in his voice. "I didn't expect you to come back home so soon."

He walks into the room, grabbing the remote and muting the conservative news anchor's rant about China and U.S. trade relations.

Deep breath. Everything is fine.

"I-I had a few things I forgot to pick up," I start. "Plus, we wanted to get off campus for a few days before classes start back."

"Oh okay," He responds back with a blank stare.

Ugh. I hate it when he doesn't help encourage the conversation.

"Dad, this is my friend Li Mei," I wave my hand out to introduce her. "Li Mei, this is my dad, Paul Wilson."

"It's nice to meet you, sir," Li Mei responds with perfect politeness.

He raises his eyebrows in surprise, and I can already see the judgement forming in his eyes. "It's nice to meet you as well... Li Mei. Where did you grow up?"

Andddd here we go...

"I grew up in Guiyang with my family, but we traveled all over the world," Li Mei explains. "My parents taught us English at a young age, so it is very natural to me. We have traveled to the States several times over the years."

She's good. She knew exactly what he was getting at with that question.

"Oh, that's very nice," He answers, without bothering to extend the conversation.

This is like pulling teeth I swear.

"Is it okay if Li Mei stays the night?" I ask, trying to hide the emotion in my voice. My right-hand slides into my pocket, subconsciously grabbing the horse keychain and slowly rubbing it. "She's never been this far off campus, and I wanted to show her around our little town."

That perks him up and his solemn expression melts away a bit.

"Of course, that's such a wonderful idea, Hope. Our home is always open to those who need it," He muses.

Don't roll your eyes... I know he just sees this as an opportunity to "save" her.

"That is very kind of you Mr. Wilson, thank you," Li Mei says gratefully.

"Your mom can set up the sleeping cot in your room later, Hope," He commands. "Since she is our guest, Li Mei will sleep in the bed."

"Thank you," I respond respectfully.

Don't want to make him mad again... Now we need to get away before he tries to bring up anything else.

"We're going to grab our bags out of the car and probably ride around town a bit more," I continue. Li Mei glances at me from the corner of her eye but remains silent.

"Oh okay, well have fun! I'm going to have to leave soon anyways to get back to the Church," he says, then his voice takes a sterner tone. "Will you both be joining us tonight?"

Shit, there it is.

"Uhh, we hadn't really talked about it..." I stammer.

"We can see if we can make it," Li Mei chimes in. "We are already meeting a few of Hope's old friends for dinner, because tonight was the only night they were free. But if we finish early, we can try to make it to church."

Very smooth.

"Oh okay, yes I understand," He states, taking the bait. "Which friends are you meeting up with?"

"Julie, Trevor, and a few others," I add in.

Li Mei definitely couldn't have made up names he would find believable.

"Well, that's nice. Maybe you can convince them to come with you to Church too," He presses.

Fucking Christians. Always pushing their own agenda on others.

"Yeah, we'll see," I say quickly, then turn to Li Mei. "Come on, let's get the bags out of the car before your makeup melts in my backseat."

She nods her head and follows behind me as I walk toward the front door. Dad takes a seat on the couch and unmutes the TV.

"Conservative leaders are fighting to protect the second amendment right to bear arms as Democratic leaders propose more gun control legislation…"

Once outside, Li Mei playfully pushes my shoulder. "That wasn't so bad, now, was it?"

"No," I pause, reflecting on the strange conversation. "I guess it could have been a lot worse."

A hell of a lot worse. He could have kicked us out.

"You worry too much," Li Mei chirps, as she opens the back car door to grab her bags. I pop the trunk to pull out my duffle bag and the trash bag of unwanted clothes.

"Let's get inside, it's too hot to be out here," I pant, wiping sweat off my brow.

By the time we get back inside, the TV is off, and Dad is gone. I lead the way up the creaking stairs, passing Grace's bedroom on the right. Faith's bedroom is on the left a little past Grace's door because, for whatever reason, the architects of the house didn't think of putting the doors across from each other, so it was more symmetrical. I can hear music playing on the other side of her door and I knock loudly to make sure she hears me.

Faith opens the door, already rolling her eyes and starts to say "Gra-" but immediately stops when she realizes it is me instead. Her face lights up as she exclaims "Hope! You're here already? I didn't hear you come in, when did you arrive? How long have you been here?"

In true fashion, she spits out all her questions without pausing to wait for the answer. Instead of answering her, I drop the trash bag of clothes on the floor between us.

"Here are my clothes I don't want anymore," I tell her. "You can keep them or get rid of them, I don't really care. I just don't want them back."

She perks up excitedly, grabs the bag and pulls it the rest of the way in her room. "Oh my god it's so heavy!" She pants. "You made it look so easy… Is that one flowery top of yours in here?"

"I believe so," I stammer, unsure of which flowery top she is talking about.

Oh well, she'll figure it out.

I turn to walk away and motion for Li Mei to follow me, which proves to be my mistake.

"Wait, are you Hope's friend? Li Mei? Do you go to college with her? Do y'all have the same degree? Do you want to be a journalist too? Or are you-"

"Faith, chill out!" I snap. "Enough with the questions, geez. Yes, this is Li Mei, and you should know that already because I texted you. She does go to college with me, but she has a different degree. Now leave us alone, we have things to do."

Faith rolls her eyes and says the most dramatic "fine" I've ever seen in my life.

I walk down the rest of the hall to my bedroom in the back left corner. Li Mei follows behind awkwardly. We enter my bedroom and I am glad I cleaned it the last time I stayed. It would have been embarrassing for Li Mei to walk into that mess: flowers, crosses, and clutter had filled my room. I gave most of it away to Grace or Faith.

Now the walls were bare, the dressers were cleared out, and it had more of a minimalistic feel. The only remaining item from my teenage years was the faded flower bed set that I still didn't have enough money to replace.

"You don't have to be so mean to her Hope," Li Mei starts.

"She will be fine. She has a short attention span and will bounce back in half a second with her next fascination," I say nonchalantly. "I promise, by the time this weekend ends, you will be dying to get away from her. Consider yourself spared for now."

Li Mei nods her head subconsciously as she looks around my bedroom.

"Sooo, are we really going to church tonight?" She cautiously asks.

"Hell no. And that was a great excuse by the way," I praise. "I think he actually believed we would try to come."

"But we don't actually have dinner plans," Li Mei counters.

"Sure we do, there's a local bar we can go to and grab a few drinks," I suggest. "We just stay there until church is almost done. Then they can't say anything."

"Works for me!" She chirps with a shrug of her shoulders. "When do you want to go?"

"Hmmm. Well, my mom won't be home for a few more hours," I start. "And there really isn't much to do here at the house."

"Why don't we take a nap?" Li Mei suggests with a sly grin. "We can sleep for a bit until your mom gets here. Or set an alarm so we leave right before she arrives."

Instinctively, I have to fight the urge to yawn when she says the word nap.

"Yeah, we could…" I trail off, looking around my room.

I really want to sleep with her.

"Wait a second," I tell her. I leave my room and go downstairs to peek out the front window to make sure Dad's car is gone.

So that only leaves Faith here. That's easy enough to deal with.

I walk back upstairs, quietly listening outside Faith's bedroom door. She is still blasting her music, and I hear the rustle of the trash bag as she grabs clothes out of it.

Good, she's preoccupied.

I go back into my bedroom and shut the door, locking it softly. For an older house, the one thing I am grateful for is the bedroom locks. Granted, someone could easily bust down the door if they really tried. But the lock would hold for a few hits, which would give us enough time to wake up and separate from the bed.

I turn back to Li Mei, grinning and whisper, "Cost is clear. Dad is gone and Faith is more than preoccupied with her little fashion show right now."

Li Mei smiles back gleefully and climbs into the bed. I pull my laptop out of my duffle bag, turn it on and press play on the first movie I can find. I then put the laptop on my dresser, so if anyone else tries to come in they will clearly hear we are watching a movie. I set an alarm on my phone to wake us up in two hours and climb into bed next to her. It's a little cramped in the full-size bed, but I don't mind that. It allows me to be closer to her.

She lays her head on my chest, and I run my fingers through her short pink hair, absent mindedly staring at the TV.

This is everything.

As I drift off to sleep, my dreams start to take shape.

I'm in a classroom, one that resembles a room from my high school, but the teacher at the front is my college professor. He's watching us intently and when his eyes meet mine, it feels like they are piercing into my soul. He raises an eyebrow and taps the watch on his wrist.

Confused, I look down at my desk to see a final exam in front of me. It is several pages thick, with five staples in the corner trying to hold all the pages together. But most importantly, it is currently blank.

Panic consumes me as I realize I am going to fail my class if I don't complete the exam in time. I frantically fill out the answers for the first page, barely even reading the questions and circling the first answer that I think could be the right answer.

When I turn the next page, the paper transforms into a blanket that wraps around me. The classroom scenery is gone, replaced with the small confines of the college dorm I had my freshman year.

Relieved that the final was over, I relaxed into bed and sighed with content. A strong cold breeze blows under the blanket making me shiver. I pulled the blanket up closer to my face and tighter around my body. Exhaustion consumes me and I close my eyes, wanting to drift off to sleep.

The cold breeze blows up the blanket again, but this time I feel a strong hand grabbing my ankle. My heart starts beating faster and I try to kick the hand away, but it is too strong for me. The hand jerks hard, pulling me out from under the blanket and I see a dark shadow hovering above me.

I open my eyes wide, ending the dream and adjusting to the after-noon light streaming through the bedroom windows. My heart is pounding hard, echoing in my ears, and it takes a few moments to settle down.

It was just a silly dream.

13

GRACE

I sigh as I stare at the long line of people waiting to check out. After restocking the shelves, the general manager, Don, asked me to bag groceries while Debra rings up customers at the register.

Julie was here earlier, but since she worked the morning shift, she left shortly after I arrived. I almost wish I were working with her instead of Debra, who keeps talking to every single person in the line.

At least I don't see anybody I know.

The good thing about small towns, everyone knows each other. Which can also be the bad thing because *everyone* knows each other. I had yet to work a shift where I didn't see at least three people I know come in the store and talk to me.

It can be fun when it is my friends or people I want to talk to, but most of the time it is older people who know my parents and remark about how much I've grown up. Or how they miss my grandmother.

It's so awkward when they say I'm too pretty to not have a boyfriend.

The fading sunlight streams through the front windows, temporarily blinding me. I shake my head, pulling my mind out of my deep thoughts and staring at the long line of people ready to check out.

At the end of the line, I spot an older woman. Her face is nasty and wrinkly, like she's been tanning in the sun every day of her life. Her mismatched eyes are fitting for her equally mismatched outfit: it looks like she pulled the clothes out of a dumpster after someone threw them away. The clothes hang off her body, at least two sizes too big. Maybe even three. Her hair is matted, and when it is finally her turn to be checked out, the smell of smoke and body odor overwhelms me.

She reeks of cigarettes. I bet there isn't a day of her life when she hasn't smoked.

The old woman hands her half-empty basket to Debra, who is talking a million miles a minute.

Debra could literally talk to anyone.

The register beeps as Debra slides each item across the scanner and then down to me. I bag two cans of soup and four cans of cat food. I double up the bag to prevent it from breaking and wait impatiently to hand the items to the old woman, who is still digging through her jacket.

Probably looking for a coupon… or her food stamps. Yeah, definitely food stamps.

She finally finds the little piece of paper and hands it to Debra, who still has not stopped talking about her kids, the weather and whatever else she can think of. I recognize the familiar color and outline for food stamps. There is dirt around her fingernails, and the color of her hand looks significantly darker than her face.

Pathetic. She can't even afford food, but she can afford to take care of a cat?! I bet she has never washed her hands either.

After paying for the cat food, she limps forward to take her grocery bag from me. I extend my arm, as far away from my body as possible to create distance between us. Her dirty hand brushes mine as she tries to get her fingers around the bag. I prematurely let the bag go before she has a grasp of it and the bag falls to the floor.

My cheeks burn with embarrassment as I rush to pick up the bag and the can of soup that rolled out. I inspect the bag to ensure nothing broke. Gripping the sides of it with both hands, I hold it out so she can easily grab the handle without touching me.

"Sorry about that," I apologize half-heartedly.

"It's okay sweetie. Thank you for your help, take care." Her wretched breath hits my face, and she smiles sweetly at me.

Oh, and she's never brushed her teeth either. Disgusting.

"Have a great day." I put on the best smile I can and wait for her to limp away. No one else is in line to check out, so I tell Debra I need to go to the restroom. She silently nods to acknowledge me while continuing to talk to one of her friends who just walked in the store. I walk as fast as I can to the bathroom without drawing attention.

I wash my hands for several minutes, in between each finger and all the way up to my elbows. In the mirror, I stare at my reflection. My dull blue eyes, chubby cheeks, and round button nose. The few pimples along my face are a little less prominent than they were this morning. After seeing that elderly woman, I know this is nothing compared to how she looked.

I will never let myself go like that. Never. It's a shame that anyone would let themselves get dirty like that. She really should take a shower and brush her teeth.

I turn off the water and grab a few paper towels to dry my hands.

Maybe even get rid of the cat so she can afford to buy some clothes that actually fit her...

I take a deep breath before exiting the restroom. As I walk out, I glance at the clock on the wall to see that I only have 30 more minutes left before we close for the night.

Almost there.

Turning down an aisle to head back towards the front of the store, I bump into Don pushing a cart full of various boxed and canned foods to be restocked. He's an older man in his mid-50s, with a balding head and raspy voice from the many cigarettes he probably smokes. His 2X shirt is a little snug around his belly and he waddles around from all the weight his short legs have to carry. We all call him Don, but his name tag says Donald.

He started working at the grocery store when he was 16 and never left. I can't figure out if he just likes the routine consistency of doing the same thing every day, or if he just lacks ambition for anything greater. I, for one, do not want to work here for the rest of my life.

"There you are," He states matter of fact. "Debra is going to handle the registers for the rest of the night, I need you to restock all of these items before you leave."

Ughhhh.

"Yes sir." I grimace.

He pushes the cart to me and waddles off, like Donald Duck from the Disney cartoons.

Quack, quack... Dear God, please help me to never let myself go like that either. I never want to be that obese. The Bible says whatever you eat, or drink should be to the glory of God...Clearly, Don is glorifying something else for him to be that fat.

I take a closer look at the contents in the cart and roll my eyes.

I hate putting up canned foods.

Despite his appearance, Don is quite OCD about how the food is put on the shelves and will double-check everything to make sure it is put up correctly.

Canned foods are the worst though, because you have to pull off the ones currently on the shelf, stack up the new ones in the back, and then put the old ones on the front. This is to help make sure all the older canned foods aren't pushed further to the back and not sold, leading to them being thrown away.

I push the cart to the appropriate aisle and get even more annoyed when I realize this brand of cans is on the middle shelf. Which means I can't sit on the ground to swap these out.

Dear God, I hope one day you bless me with a husband, so I never have to work again. I hate this job, I hate working and I especially hate putting up canned foods. Is that too much to ask for?

I begin the tedious process of taking the cans off the shelf, setting them on the floor, and pushing the newer ones to the back. I don't even bother to turn all the labels to face the same direction because I know Don will come behind me and do it himself. He is such a quirky man.

"Oh, hiya Grace! It's good to see you!"

Startled, I turn to the end of the aisle to see Police Chief Bill waving at me and flashing his bright white teeth. He is a picture-perfect police officer: tall, fit, and charismatic. His short hair is silvery grey, and his trimmed beard is a dark brown, with streaks of gray in it. Today he is wearing his police officer uniform, radio, and handgun, which means he must be on duty. I smile back and start to greet him, but he continues.

"How are your parents doing? These last few weekends I've had to work the night shift, which meant I had to catch the evening service at Church."

"They've been great!" I exclaim, trying to sound more enthusiastic than I feel. "My Dad is getting ready for the school year to start up again and Mom stays busy at the bank, like usual."

Police Chief Bill nods his head. "I've been meaning to-"

"Chief! Did you want me to grab a bag of chips for you?"

I turn to see another police officer walking up with two bags of chips in his hands. He is slightly taller than Police Chief Bill and with a leaner build, blonde hair, and bright green eyes. I also notice he is much younger and *very* handsome.

Whoaaa, who is that?

"Nah I'm good." Police Chief Bill responds back. "Did you get every-thing else you wanted?"

"Yup," the mysteriously handsome stranger answers.

"Great, we ought to-" Police Chief Bill pauses, listening to the radio on his shoulder.

Whoever is communicating through it is speaking too fast for me to understand. All I catch is '10-31' before Police Chief Bill responds back.

"Put your chips down Tucker, we have to go. Now," Police Chief Bill commands before breaking into a run down the aisle. I stand there helplessly as the handsome 'Tucker' takes off after him.

On my own again, I resume putting up the cans and daydreaming about Tucker.

I wonder if he has a girlfriend... and how old could he be?! He can't be that much older than me. Ugh, I hate that he saw me in this stupid uniform. I look terrible right now. Maybe it's almost time for me to go home.

I glance around to make sure no one is watching, then secretly check my phone to see I have a text from Faith.

Heads up! Hope brought a friend home...

I hear footsteps approaching and frantically shove my phone back in my pocket.

Don will write me up if he sees me on my phone again.

I look down the aisle towards the footsteps, and sigh with relief to see a last-minute customer walk by. I don't want to get caught on my phone texting, but I do pull it out carefully to check the time: 8:45.

Only 15 more minutes until we close.

Turning, I evaluate the number of cans I have left and decide to slow down.

I don't want Don to give me something else to do before closing.

I carefully grab each can, turning it in the correct direction and placing it back on the shelf. When I finally finish putting the last can away, I push the cart to the front of the store with the others and finally go to the back office to find my timecard.

Even though there are modern computers and apps to help with timekeeping and payroll, Don still insists on doing things the old way. There is something nostalgic about taking my weekly timecard and physically punching it in that brings a level of satisfaction. It makes me feel official. After I punch out, I scurry to the front so Debra can unlock the door to let me slip out.

I'm so glad it's her night to stay late and clean.

I get in my car and crank it, pausing for a moment to text Faith back.

What kind of friend?

I choose a song and put my phone away. After a quick prayer for safe driving, I fly out of the parking lot to get home. In my rearview mirror, I spot Don rearranging the shopping cart I put back to where he wanted it.

As I turn on the main street, I spot the nasty old woman limping on the sidewalk in the same direction that I am driving.

Should I pick her up? No. She was nasty, and I don't want her in my car.

A pang of guilt rises within me, but when I look in my rearview mirror it goes away. She looks dirty, with one arm on her bag of canned food, and the other holding her orange cat.

Stupid thing probably has fleas anyway.

It's about 9:25 p.m. when I finally arrive home and I am relieved to see that Hope's car isn't parked on the street.

I really hope she hasn't started another fight with Mom and Dad.

Quietly, I unlock the front door and step inside the house. After locking it behind me, I pause to observe the stillness.

Peace and quiet. Thank God.

I go to the kitchen where Mom sat a plate of leftovers from dinner for me. I place it in the microwave and let it heat up for two minutes. My stomach is growling, so I say a quick prayer while it heats up. As soon as it is done, I pull it out and I immediately start to eat. The hot food burns my tongue, and I gulp water to cool down each bite.

My phone vibrates and I look down to see Faith texted me back.

> idk, some girl she met through college. She has pink hair too.

Pink hair? Gross. That's so unprofessional, no one would hire someone with pink hair.

After eating, I take a shower and climb into bed with my phone. I clicked on my Instagram app and clicked through to Hope's profile to see if I can find this new friend she brought over. I don't have to look far; she already has posted 3 pictures on her page. I click through each one to read the captions.

The first is some inspirational quote that must have resonated with her.

'The worst form of inequality is to try to make unequal things equal.'

The second is a picture of a beer bottle at a bar.

Of course she drinks.

The third is a picture of an upcoming rally at her college.

Disgusting! Why would she share this?!

I look closer at the image she shared and see that it is for gay rights. Hope also tagged another Instagram user in the post.

Interesting...

I click on the username and go to her profile to see vibrant pink hair flipping back in a video.

Bingo. Found her.

I see a variety of pictures and videos, messily posted across her account. In her bio, she only has emojis and above that I finally spot her name: Li Mei.

She's Asian?

I click on the first picture I see and zoom in.

Yeah, she is definitely Asian.

There is no mistaking the squinty eyes, soft complexion, or cheesy smile. Hope's new friend is Asian. Our small rural town barely had any Blacks or Mexicans, much less any other ethnicity.

She's probably not even legal.

I stifle a yawn and scroll a little deeper. I don't see any pictures of Hope on her account or in the tagged photos. Satisfied with my search, I plugged my phone on the charger and lay back down to finally go to sleep. My mind wanders into dreams where Tucker notices me and brings me a bouquet of pink carnation flowers.

14

HOPE

"Y'all doing alright down here?" The bartender asks. I meet his gaze, observing his leathery tan skin and the dip in his mouth. He was a rough character, hardened from his years of serving in the Vietnam War and being divorced several times. The scar along his jaw is mostly hidden by the stubble on his face and tonight he has a ball cap on backwards to hide his receding hairline. I had never seen him wear anything but a T-shirt, jeans, and cowboy boots.

"Yup, all good," I answer with a nod of my head.

"Actually, can I get another beer?" Li Mei asks.

He nods his head, responding with a quick, "sure" before turning away to get the drink.

I take another sip of my beer, carefully watching the evening crowd. So far, I don't see anyone I recognize, which is a good thing.

I'm pretty sure he hasn't changed a damn thing in this place for the last 20 years.

The rustic walls are covered in a variety of beer signs, American flags, horseshoes, and race car signs. The barstools are all mismatched and off to one side is a pool table where a few guys are already playing a game. Towards the back right corner is a dart board that has attracted the largest group of people, who all appear to know each other. From the many times they have shouted and taken shots, I have been able to hear that they are out celebrating with some guy named Garrett.

Can't quite tell if they are celebrating the beginning or the end of his marriage.

Despite appearances, the bartender is nice and genuinely doesn't care what people think or believe, so long as they come in and pay. It's not exactly my ideal place to go for a drink, but it is the only bar in town. I had forewarned Li Mei that our options would be limited. This bar didn't carry the normal local ciders and ales we liked to drink, but she didn't seem to mind.

"How are you doing?" Li Mei asks. "You seem distracted and anxious."

"I do feel nervous," I admit. "Every time I come home, I feel like more of an outsider. But I also realize just how backwards and behind they are on the times…Like even hearing that news anchor my dad was listening to was just surreal. Like people actually listen to that shit and believe it. Without researching or reading into the problems themselves. They all get caught up in their so-called righteous religion and then believe they should force others to follow their beliefs."

"Do your…" Li Mei starts but stops as the bartender hands her the beer she asked for.

"Thank you," She directs her statement to him and waits for him to walk away before continuing. "Do your parents really believe everything they hear on the news? Isn't it monitored by the government?"

"Not exactly," I answer. "There are opposing sides that heavily influence what the TV stations cover. And what people hear about topics depends on which station they tune into. For example, my parents tune into a conservative station that will connect a lot of the news stories to religion, individual rights, and traditional values. They emphasize narratives that reinforce their beliefs and often frame issues in terms of moral and religious debates. On the other hand, more progressive stations tend to focus on social justice, government accountability and reform."

I take a sip of my beer while she mulls over my explanation.

"Back home, we know the government dictates what is shown in the news," Li Mei says softly. "Most people don't believe it, at least not all of it. We believe they are reporting the news and events as they happen, but we also know their explanations for government policies are often incomplete or skewed. It's like piecing together a puzzle where some pieces are deliberately left out. We understand that there are always other sides to the story, but getting to those perspectives requires effort and often means seeking information from less conventional sources. So, while we watch the news and take it all in, we know that it's shaped by the government's interests."

"Yeah, unfortunately, the average American isn't smart enough to realize that," I spit out in disgust. "Years of low-quality public education will do that. The conservative stations have a knack for convincing people that policies they could benefit from are bad and anti-religious. That's why everyone in this small town is getting worked up over the healthcare clinic opening. They don't have the capacity to look past it. To realize how these laws could impact the way a business works and therefore how products and services are given. Because, ultimately, a hospital is a business. Healthcare is a business. They aren't doing it just for the good of their hearts, they want money. And a shit ton of it. Restricting healthcare access to abortions will only make it that much harder for people to get the help they need when pregnancies become life threatening."

"The progressive stations aren't that much better," Li Mei points out. "I've seen a few of the news stories you've tuned into. It sounds like they are encouraging discontent with the conservative side as well, instead of finding a compromise."

I hate it when she's so logical about things.

"Yes, but-" I cut off as the bar door rings out. An older man walks through, greeting the bartender by name. I turn back to Li Mei and continue.

"Yes, but it's not as bad as the conservative stations. At least what the progressives propose are things that can make a difference. Things that need to happen."

She must sense the tension in my voice because she takes a sip of her beer and changes the subject.

"Are you still wanting to come to my home for Christmas break?"

"Yes, I would love to," I answered softly. "I just have to get my birth certificate from my parents so I can get a passport."

"Ahhh, so that's why you wanted to come for such a long weekend," She murmurs as it dawns on her.

"Well, yeah," I stammer. "I need to figure out how to get it from them without arousing suspicion."

The door rings out again and I glance over my shoulder to see a familiar face.

"Megan! I call out, beckoning her to join us. Li Mei looks at me confused and I explain. "Megan is my cousin. She's the same age as Grace and they have been inseparable since they were kids."

Megan approaches, her soft blonde hair falling gently down her shoulders. She's wearing cut-off shorts, a t-shirt and flipflops. When she gets close enough to us, she greets us with a first bump.

"What are you doing here?!" I ask her.

"I came for a strong drink," Megan says nonchalantly as she waves down the bartender. He immediately brings a beer to her and walks away.

She must be a regular for him to know her order.

"Wait," I lean close and whisper to her. "Aren't you 17? How the hell did you get him trained to bring you a beer?"

She grins sheepishly. "I have a fake I.D. and I've been in here enough times he doesn't question it anymore."

"Damn girl, that's bold," I murmur, raising my eyebrows at her. "I take it Grace doesn't..."

"No, absolutely not. Grace has no idea," Megan says quickly and takes a sip. She tucks a strand of her blonde hair behind her ear and a new diamond earring flashes in the light. "And honestly, I would prefer it stayed that way, if you know what I mean."

Well, that's new. I don't think she's always had that cartilage piercing.

"My lips are sealed," I move my hand across my lips to emphasize I'll keep her secret.

"Why don't you want Grace to know?" Li Mei asks curiously.

"She just doesn't understand some things..." Megan fidgets awkwardly and takes another sip of her drink.

She's got that right. Grace is stubborn as a mule.

"What have you been up to lately? Is that a new earring piercing?" I asked, changing the subject and pointing to her right ear.

"Oh yeah! I got this at the beginning of the summer," she explains, turning her head to the side so I can see the piercing better. "My mom was so pissed."

"I bet she was. Aunt Sharon has never been fond of ear piercings, she always complains about how trashy it is," I grumble and roll my eyes.

"What is trashy about an ear piercing?!" Li Mei asks in shock.

"Absolutely nothing. NOTH-ING!" Megan exclaims then takes a dramatic drink of her beer.

Sensing her discomfort, I change the conversation. "You're about to start your senior year, right?"

"Yeah, finally. I can't wait to graduate and get out of this place," Megan sighs. "It's been rough since my parents' divorce, and I feel like everywhere I go people are just staring at me because they *know*."

Now it's my turn to squirm in my seat. I had overheard a few snarky comments from my parents about how Aunt Sharon found Uncle James with another man. Since I had been living at college, Faith kept me looped on the nasty divorce and what details she learned from Mom. I can see the pain in Megan's eyes, and a pang of guilt hits me for not checking in with her to see how she was holding up.

I better interject something before Li Mei asks a question.

"I know, and I hate to hear that. This small town jumps at any morsel of gossip," I say sympathetically, then tease. "Especially when people are no good nasty sinners like us."

"Cheers to that," Megan says, clinking her glass to mine. "I'd rather take that over any day in a church."

We all laughed for a moment, and I felt a little pee escape my bladder.

What the fuck? I didn't laugh that hard… Did I?

With my hands still on my beer, I move my legs back, so they are propped up on the barstool instead of dangling in the air. The reposition also allows me to push myself forward to gauge how wet my pants are.

I don't think it's that wet. Besides, these are a darker denim, so no one will be able to see anything.

I tune back into the conversation, as Li Mei explains to Megan about her Chinese heritage and what made her choose to come to an American university. Two more beers later and I developed a good buzz, that finally allowed me to stop thinking about my life.

Eventually, I get up to go to the bathroom and am dismayed to see a small wet spot, mixed with blood.

Well, that explains the 'pee' I thought I felt… And at least I didn't bleed through my underwear.

I don't have a tampon or pad, so I roll a handful of toilet paper together and position it carefully in my underwear.

That should hold me over until I get home. We're about to leave anyway.

Back at the bar, I finish my beer and flag the bartender down for a water. Li Mei and Megan have really hit it off and are talking about their favorite anime shows and books. I sip the water slowly, looking around the bar to see a variety of faces.

It's really gotten packed in the last hour.

The bar door rings out again, and I watch as two more guys come in. Both of them are wearing holey jeans, boots, sleeveless shirts, and ball caps. I catch a glimpse of the tattoo on the one guy's arm and freeze.

Oh no.

I chug the rest of my water and flag the bartender down.

"We need to go," I direct to Li Mei.

She looks at me confused. "Already? We just got here!" She whines.

"We've been here for four hours," I remind her. "Plus, our lovely friends from the parking lot just decided to walk in."

"Really, where?" She practically yells, as she looks around me.

"Who?" Megan asks, turning around confused as well.

"Don't look!" I hiss, but it's too late.

"Hey look, it's our lesbian dumbasses from earlier," One of the guys calls out.

My buzz instantly fades, and I become overly aware of my surroundings as adrenaline courses through my body.

Hell, is it that obvious we are lesbians?!

I turned around to see the two guys approach us. There is a third shorter guy, trailing behind that I don't recognize.

"Take your gay ass shit and get out of our bar," The other one spits out the words and then points a finger at Li Mei. "We don't welcome your *kind* around here."

I feel the anger starting to bubble within me and I jump down from the barstool.

"I welcome anyone who orders beer and pays for it," the bartender is behind us with the tab. "Now shut the fuck up and stop harassing my customers, Brock. Or I will kick you out."

I freeze, waiting to see what *Brock* decides to do.

"Come on, Hank, you can't be serious," the one who must be Brock pleads. "We're your best customers, we come in here every week."

"And every week I have to fight to get you to pay your tab. And to stop you from picking fights," Hank snaps. "These lovely ladies have only been here for the last few hours, and they have already been better customers than any of you. Now take your asses to your normal table or you can get the hell out." He points to the other side of the bar where their table must be.

"It's not worth it Brock, come on man," the other guy mumbles, tugging on his arm.

"FUCK!" Brock screams, slamming his fists at his side and storming out of the bar.

My body is shaking from the adrenaline rush, and I wiggle my fingers to try to work out some of the energy.

"Sorry about that one," Hank says as he hands me the tab.

"It's not your fault," Li Mei says quietly. I look at her and can tell she's a little shaken from the close encounter.

"I think your culture is pretty cool by the way," Hank says with a soft smile. "I always wanted to go to China but couldn't afford the flight."

I hand him my card, and he turns to Megan, who shakes her head no. I look at her puzzled, so she explains, "I'm not ready to go yet. I need another beer before I head back home."

Hank returns a moment later with my card and another beer for Megan.

"Well, it was good to see you, Meg. I hope we see more of you," I say while fist bumping her.

"Oh, I'm sure you will, Grace has been begging for me to stay the night on Friday," Megan chuckles.

"It was nice to meet you, Meg!" Li Mei chirps, giving her a smile.

We step outside and the late-night humid air hits us in the face. It's too warm and sticky for my liking. Around the parking lot shadows linger from the nearby trees and cars.

There isn't enough lighting in this parking lot.

I approached my car cautiously, looking for any signs that Brock came outside to continue his fight. Twisting my keys in my hand, I have my finger waiting to hit the unlock button when we get close enough to my car.

If he approaches me out here, I can stab him with the key to get away...

My car beeps as it unlocks and I climb into the front seat. I put the key in the ignition and shut the door in one fell swoop. After Li Mei's door shuts, I immediately lock the doors and fly out of the parking lot to get us away. We ride home in silence for several minutes.

"Are you okay?" I ask her sincerely.

"I'm fine," she says softly. "I mean, I'll probably never see those guys again... But are you fine?"

I pause for a moment to think.

Am I fine? They outed us without even knowing who we are... But if it were that obvious, my parents wouldn't have welcomed me back home.

I turn briefly to look at her as she stares out the front windshield. I fix my eyes back on the road.

"I'll be fine," I start. "I'm just nervous. I haven't been back home since I came out and it feels weird to be here. To want to be who I am, but not feeling safe to do so... Not even with my own family."

I feel her hand on my thigh, and I switch my hands, so I am driving with my left and holding her hand with my right.

"Well, if you get scared you can just grab my hand," she says reassuringly. "I'll squeeze it to let you know that I'm here for you. No matter what."

I smile and glance at her quickly before turning my eyes back to the road.

"I like that plan."

15

DR. MALICUS

A flash of light and I reappear back in my lab with the DNA samples in hand. I take off the transporter watch then put the new parent DNA sample into my home system and prep the machine to clone the next set of samples.

"Resume my last request."

The holographic screen whizzes to life and within seconds I have the new report I asked for hours ago.

So, 45 billion combinations could potentially complete the telophase cycle. Which means, theoretically, they would complete the full life cycle for the cell.

I click my approval for the machine to create the DNA matches and hope that this time I get a little bit closer to finding the cure. I pause to look at the time: 7:58 p.m.

Hmmm. I could go back upstairs to eat with Ziva…Or I could try to look at other genetic reports.

My stomach rumbles and my decision is made.

To dinner it is.

Upstairs, I found Ziva sitting at the kitchen table. I walk in to take my usual seat, and she jumps up to prepare a plate for me. My eyes follow her gentle hands as she picks up each item, delicately setting the food on the plate. My eyes continue following her hands up her arms and down her smooth waist and small hips. Her empty hips.

She isn't wearing her voice assistant. No wonder she jumped up so fast.

Her voice assistant helps her to speak and without it she will have to use sign language to communicate with me. I know she can't help her disability, but it can be frustrating when I'm in the middle of something and I have to focus on her signing to understand what she wants to communicate. She also knows it can be a hindrance to me and tries to always have the voice assistant on her when she predicts that I might need her.

After she sets the food in front of me, she moves her hands to flash "I'm sorry, I wasn't expecting you to come to dinner so early."

I smile, shrugging my shoulders nonchalantly and smile at her.

"It's fine dear. It's rare that I deviate from my schedule. But today has been full of surprises and unexpected turns. Besides, I thought you might appreciate my company for once."

"Of course! I always enjoy your company. Is the food to your liking?" she signs back.

I recognize the smell of my Tuesday dinner without even glancing at the plate: grilled salmon, brussels sprouts, and dill rice. Years ago, I created the optimal lifestyle diet to help my mind and body to perform in the most efficient way possible. Every meal must be precise to my body's needs to support my work.

"It always is, thank you, Ziva." I finally answered her while adjusting the watch on my wrist.

She smiles back softly before returning to her seat. We continue to eat in silence, and she finishes eating her food long before I do. After she puts away her dirty dishes, she turns to take mine, but I shake my head no.

She fidgets uncomfortably for a moment, before signing. "I'm going to work on a puzzle now. Leave the plate and I'll return in one hour to clean it up for you."

"Thank you, Ziva, I appreciate that." I smile back at her and watch her walk away. However, as soon as she disappears around the corner, my smile fades.

I don't think she will ever be able to work on my equipment again. Her mind is too fragile.

With a heavy heart, I sigh. It is heart-wrenching to see her like this after knowing her for over a decade and seeing who she was.

Ziva was incredibly intelligent, innovative, and ambitious. She never took no for an answer, and she always found a solution. Her contributions to the technological community revolutionized our society, as much as the computer or internet in the late 1900s. She had a way of motivating people and at the same time putting the fear of God in them. Her team never missed a deadline. In fact, they always turned in their projects well ahead of schedule. During the 8 years we worked together, the closest her team ever got to a deadline was two days before it was due.

The first time I met her was at an ICO convention 18 years ago. The convention brought together the four ICO branches from each of the world's hemispheres, to present their findings and to work together to improve the organization. Only the top 1,000 people in each hemisphere were present.

Both of us were speakers representing our respective departments. She quickly rose to a management role for the southern hemisphere engineering division, whereas I was doing the same, but for the genetic cloning division in the eastern hemisphere.

She stood up at the podium and spoke so eloquently. All I could see was her head and hands moving as she presented her vision for creating human clones that could be controlled virtually through another human being. The objective would be to make it easier for scientists to test humans living in various situations - harsher climates, trips to the Mariana Trench, or even other planets - without risking ourselves to unknown elements or dangers. It would provide the hands-on experience the scientists need without the risk.

It was a radical idea, way ahead of its time, so naturally, the ICO never approved the funding for the project. I, on the other hand, immediately fell in love with her insightful mind.

During the next break session, I approached her and introduced myself. Surprisingly, she had heard of my work already and was delighted when I requested that we work together on future projects. If her technology helped my division to make genetic advancements faster than the other divisions, then it would be mutually beneficial to us both. We agreed to stay in touch, and I was satisfied with myself for finding a way to get her contact information.

We didn't know it at the time, but that initial conference wasn't everything the ICO claimed it to be. The organization was also scouting top-performing scientists to establish the new international division. The ICO realized that having the hemisphere divisions was slowing progress and wanted a more cohesive international division to lead the most important projects. The hemisphere divisions would be reallocated to focus on long-term maintenance and sustainability projects.

A few weeks after the conference, the ICO announced the scientists selected for the new division and we were both among them. We celebrated with a long conversation via hologram in our labs, strategizing the new teams we would select and how we would make the world a better place.

I chuckle as I remember it took me months to muster the courage to ask her out for dinner. We had spent months working together and talking about our work, yet I struggled to ask a simple question. Coincidentally, she had the same issue at the time too. A few awkward dates and a night of passion later helped us to overcome our insecurities. Two years after meeting each other at the conference, we got married.

She was so damn beautiful that night.

It wasn't just her looks, but her mind and soul that captivated me. Despite all my technology, experience, and resources, I could never recreate someone as perfect as her. She truly is my soulmate.

Leaving the kitchen, I settled into a dark corner, observing Ziva as she attempted to complete her puzzle across the room. She always enjoyed puzzles and would do them repeatedly to see how fast she could put them together. Once a month, she would host a "competition" where she would make me time her to see if she improved from the previous months' time.

It used to annoy me when she made me do that... I wish I could do it again, just one more time.

The woman I see before me now takes hours to complete a puzzle that I know she has done a thousand times since I met her. Ziva's head twists one way and turns another as she tries to figure out where to put the pieces. She pieces a few together, only to reconsider minutes later, swapping out pieces and trying again. It's like watching a young baby as they first explore the world around them. If I were a stranger, I would never know that she used to be one of the best and smartest engineers of our generation.

Losing our daughter really broke her.

She stifles a yawn, sets aside the two pieces she'd been working on and leaves the room to go to sleep for the night. Instinctively, I yawn in response to hers and chuckle.

After hundreds of thousands of years, our species still reverts back to the basics. Our ancient ancestors used to yawn to signal to the others that it was time to go to sleep and people would respond with a yawn to show they will comply with the leader's order.

Too bad we couldn't warn them that their work was futile. Couple thousand years later and you will still die out anyways...

I stand up and stretch before returning to my bedroom. As I lay back in my empty bed, my mind is racing through calculations and the steps I will take when the latest batch of DNA samples are cloned. Eventually, I drift off to sleep, and dream of my career and life. What it was like before this extinction crisis. I dream of Ziva and our sweet baby girl who didn't survive. The one who should have lived and filled our home with laughter.

Ziva and our daughter are out in the field, running around, chasing each other. They both look so happy, joyful even. I stare mesmerized as their brown curly hair bounces up and down with each step, almost in sync with each other. I start to run to them, but my feet are stuck. The further I run towards them, the further they drift away from me. I watch as my daughter ages backwards into the tiny infant that died, and Ziva cries so much she drowns in the river her tears made.

I jerk up in the bed, shaking. Sweat is pouring down my face, and it takes a moment for my eyes to adjust to the darkness.

It was just a dream. It wasn't real... It was just a dream.

16

GRACE

"Girls come on! Breakfast is ready."

Mom's voice echoes through the house and up the stairs. I crack my eyes open, still in a sleepy haze, and check my phone to see it is 8:00 on Thursday morning. Breakfast on a weekday means that Mom is off because she must work at the bank on Saturday. A sweet, delicious smell hits my nose, waking up my body and making my stomach growl.

Blueberry waffles! Yesssss.

I get out of bed, shivering from the vent's cold breeze. My arm itches and I immediately scratch it, before stretching to pop my back.

At the bottom of the stairs I run into Hope, who grumbles "Watch it!" before continuing to the dining room. Her Asian friend follows behind her with a blank expression. I roll my eyes and proceed to my normal seat at the table.

Faith sits next to me, while Hope and her friend sit across from us, with Mom and Dad at either end of the table. A huge stack of blueberry waffles sits in the center, surrounded by a few syrup options and another plate of bacon. I subtly glance at Hope and her friend. It's weird to see Hope with her short purple hair. Her skin is very pale, as if she's barely been outside this summer, but it makes her blue eyes sparkle. Hope's head starts to move and I glance away quickly so she doesn't see me staring at her.

"Everyone ready?" Mom asks, outstretching her hands for the prayer. I take her hand and grab Faith's as Dad starts the prayer.

"Let us bow our heads to pray…Dear Lord, thank you for this bountiful meal and for bringing all my daughters home safely. Thank you for Hope and her friend, Li Mei, and keep them safe when they return to college. May we continue to be leaders of your faith and share with others the light of your Son, Jesus Christ. Please…"

Faith's hand is shaking impatiently. I open my eyes to peek at her, annoyed that she keeps moving.

Movement across the table catches my eye and I briefly look to see Hope and Li Mei are mouthing words to each other. They don't even have their heads bowed for the prayer. I can't understand what they are saying to each other, and I quickly duck my head back down, so they don't realize I was watching them.

"…bless this food's nourishment to our bodies and our bodies to your service. In Christ's name we pray, amen."

Everyone says 'Amen' except for Hope and Li Mei. Faith lets go of my hand faster than I can and immediately sticks her fork into the waffles she wanted.

Mom ignores her impatient behavior and turns to Hope.

"So, what do you girls have planned today?"

Hope's fork is halfway to a waffle, and she hastily stabs it to bring it to her plate.

"Li Mei just transferred to the university last semester, so I am going to show her around town," Hope explains, stabbing two more waffles to put on Li Mei's plate. "Maybe hike a state park and visit some other local shops. I want her to see what our life is like, here in America."

"That sounds fun!" Mom responds a little too enthusiastically and shoots a glance at my dad to chime in. He coughs to clear his throat before responding.

"Which state park are you thinking of going to?"

"Red Mountain would be the easiest to get to, but Oak Mountain has more trails. If we have enough time, we might visit both," Hope responds nonchalantly.

Ugh. Of course she is such a granola hipster.

I finally seize an opportunity to grab my blueberry waffles and quickly pile two onto my plate. I drown them in syrup and grab a few pieces of bacon before they are gone. Each bite is more delicious than the last and my stomach feels content to finally be fed.

"Be careful of snakes. I'm sure they are everywhere this time of year," Dad cautions.

"We will be very careful Mr. Wilson," Li Mei finally speaks up, in almost perfect English.

"Oh, your English is fantastic Li Mei! I wasn't sure if you would be able to really talk with us or not," Mom's response is full of surprise and wonder. However, Hope's face is turning red with anger.

"Mom, that is rude. You can't say that to her," Hope snaps defensively.

"I don't mean to be rude! We don't have many Asians around here, so I really wasn't sure how good her English would be. I mean it as a compliment dear," She responds sweetly, smiling at Li Mei. "I'm sure Li Mei knows that. It's not often we get, what are you again? Chinese?"

"MOM!" Hope's voice is more exasperated.

Li Mei acts unphased by her comments. "Yes Mrs. Wilson, I am Chinese. My family lives in an apartment in Guiyang."

Big surprise. Hope would befriend a communist.

"You're Chinese? Do you eat rice every day? Do you see Pandas every day? Does it bother you that your eyes look squinty compared to ours?" Faith rattles off all her questions so fast, one can hardly comprehend them.

"SHUT UP Faith! You can't just ask her such racist questions! You are so embarrassing!" Hope is fuming now, and her face is solid red.

"Faith, that is extremely rude and disrespectful. You are old enough to know better. Now apologize to Li Mei," Mom's stern tone makes Faith cower.

"I'm sor-sorry, Li Mei. I've never met a Chinese person before, and it just seems so cool," Faith's apology is sincere, but then she gets a little spark to keep going. "Plus, I like Pandas a lot, they are my favorite animals to see at the zoo. They are so fluffy, and sweet, and lazy!"

Li Mei laughs. "Thank you, Faith, I accept your apology. I actually get those questions a lot and appreciate the opportunity to explain my Chinese culture to others. Our apartment is in the heart of the city, so it is almost impossible to see a Panda in the wild. We do eat rice a lot, but we also eat other foods, like bean hot pot, *si wa wa*, or various types of seafood."

Faith turns up her nose. "What is *si wa wa*??"

Li Mei laughs and shoots a quick glance at Hope. "Everyone here makes that face when I mention *si wa wa*. It is a thin cake made of flour and stuffed with various sliced cooked vegetables. It is a delicious snack. It translates to "baby" in English. We call it *si wa wa* because of the way it is prepared, it looks like a swaddled baby."

"That sounds yummy!" Faith exclaims. "What else do your people do?"

Li Mei smiles again and continues to explain other cultural things her family does. Hope relaxes a bit and finally starts to eat some of the food on her plate. I stuff another bite of waffles in my mouth and tune out the entire conversation.

This is so boring. I don't really care what they do in China.

I set my fork down to drink some water and stare at my half-eaten plate.

I could probably finish this in two minutes and return upstairs. I should call Megan to see if she is going to the Church this afternoon. I do NOT want to go to that alone… again.

Faith exclaims at something else Li Mei said and throws her hand out, knocking my fork to the ground.

"Faith! Look what you did," I grumble annoyed.

"Oops, sorry…" She barely gets the words out of her mouth before turning back to Li Mei.

I roll my eyes and bend down to get the fork off the floor. As I start to come up, I see Hope and Li Mei's hands under the table.

They're holding hands?!

And not in the cutesy, we-are-friends-and-being-supportive way. Their fingers are interlocked, and Li Mei's thumb is stroking the side of Hope's hand.

But that would mean… no. NO!

I jerk up to a sitting position and blurt out, "Why are you holding hands? Under the table?! WHY are you holding hands? Are you a lesbian, Hope?!"

Silence fills the room and Li Mei's face turns bright pink. Hope cocks her head and snarkily says "Thanks a lot for outing me."

She turns to look at Mom, then Dad. I follow Hope's gaze to see Mom is white as a ghost and Dad is thoroughly confused. Faith's mouth is open so wide, I'm surprised it isn't hitting the floor.

Hope is the first one to break the silence.

"I'm gay. Li Mei is gay. And we are dating."

I didn't think it was possible, but Mom's face turned another shade whiter.

"What? But how? We raised you to be a good Christian, you were even saved at 11! I don't understand…" Mom trails off in confusion.

"You brought a lesbian into my house?!" Dad's voice booms across the table at Hope as the realization sets in. He completely ignores Li Mei sitting right next to him. "And slept with her, UNDER MY ROOF?!"

"Dad I…" Hope stammers.

"GET OUT OF MY HOUSE!" I jump at how loud his voice is. I stare down at my last few bites of waffles and decide they aren't worth eating to be in this awkward room. Faith must feel the same way, because we both get up and hastily leave at the same time. Poor Li Mei looks so uncomfortable sitting between Dad and Hope.

"Paul, hang on…" Mom starts to plead.

"Dad you can't do-" Hope starts.

"I am a good Christian Father! I have done everything I can to raise you girls right, and I turned my head more than once on your sinful ways, but this is IT. You will not be gay, not in my house, not under my roof. And you will NOT bring in this communist, devilish trash! Get out! NOW!" His rage is filling the whole house as I run up to my room. I turned to shut the door, but Faith comes barging in behind me.

"What do you want?" I sneer at her in a whisper, scared that somehow, dad will hear my voice and turn his rage onto me.

"WHY did you say something?!" Faith looks upset with me, as if this is all my fault.

"Wait, you knew? You knew and you didn't say anything?!" I am shocked at her for siding with *them*.

"Oh, come on, you didn't see the picture she posted on Instagram and actually think she was straight, did you?" Faith looks at me dumbfounded. "Besides, I like Li Mei, she seems cool."

"Being gay is a sin," I snort before quoting. "You shall not lie with a male as with a woman. It is an abomination. Leviticus 18:22."

"That only refers to men, that doesn't say anything about women," Faith points out, matter of fact.

"It is implied that it goes both ways," I retort.

"Why does it have to be implied? Why couldn't it just say it?" She argues back.

Uhhhhh…. I'm not sure how to answer that.

"You're too young to understand these things. Go to your room or I'll tell mom!" I snap.

She sticks her tongue out at me before running off. I roll my eyes, shut the door and plop down on my bed.

What. A. Morning.

I hear the front door slam, followed by a car cranking, and two more doors shutting. One shuts a lot more aggressively than the other.

I'm surprised her car door hasn't fallen off by now.

I grab my phone to call Megan, and it goes straight to voicemail. I follow up with a text.

> Are you going to the Church event today?

In my closet, I pick out a simple V-neck shirt and a pair of modest shorts to wear. I leave my phone on the bed while I brush my teeth in the bathroom and when I return, I finally have a response back from Megan.

> Ugh, yes. My mom is making me.

I'm taken aback by her response.

She used to enjoy going to these events with the Church...

> Come on, it will be fun! I heard Pastor John tell my dad that we will get ice cream afterwards.

> tbh that is the only thing I am looking forward to.

I hesitated a moment before sending my next text back to her.

> Meet you at the Church at 10! I have so much to tell you.

17

HOPE

"Well, that was a fucking disaster," Li Mei says after several minutes of driving in silence.

No shit.

"They reacted exactly how I knew they would," I sigh. "Cold and heartless. As far as they are concerned, I'm basically dead."

"They can't treat you like this. Hope, they are your parents!" Li Mei sounds exasperated. "You're still their daughter, you're still part of their family. How could they find out one thing about you and just dismiss you like that? Like you're irrelevant?!"

"Not everyone is lucky like you," I say with a grimace. "Not everyone has supportive parents."

"And Grace," She continues. "I really thought I would like her, but she looked disgusted at us. Like we were the plague or something."

"Honestly, that's pretty tame for her..." I mutter as I look both ways before taking a turn. The horse keychain on my lanyard swings wildly from the abruptness of the turn and taps my leg.

She ignores me. "Now what are we going to do? All our bags are still in your room."

Oh, that's right. I'll have to get our stuff and my birth certificate.

"Uhh, I'll figure it out," I say, looking in the rearview mirror.

How am I going to get the birth certificate from them now?

"And what about your birth certificate?" Li Mei presses. "Without it, you won't be able to get a passport to come with me to China."

"I will get it somehow," I tell her.

But how?

"And then what about the holidays when the campus closes? I'll be going back to China for those weeks, and you won't be able to get food in the-"

"I said I'll figure it out!" I snap at her.

She flinches back and we ride in silence for several minutes.

"Are you okay?" Li Mei asked suddenly.

Am I okay?

I stare at the road for several moments, until the silence in the car becomes painfully awkward.

"I'm not sure," I begin. "I feel... hurt. And stunned by their words, even though I expected it. But I also feel... liberated? Like I am finally free to be myself now. The only reason I held back before was because I was scared for them to find out, but now that it's all out in the open, it doesn't matter. I don't-"

My phone rings loudly, cutting off my train of thought. I flip the phone over to look at the screen and see my dad's name.

I am NOT answering that phone call.

Li Mei sees his name on my phone and looks up at me. I shake my head before she can even ask and set my phone back down. She reaches across to grab my hand and hold it.

"Where are you taking us?" She asks calmly, trying to distract both of us.

"Back to campus," I answer. "I want to change into some different clothes. And maybe even go back to sleep. I forgot how early they wake up to eat breakfast."

"Sleep sounds nice," Li Mei murmurs. "And some cuddles."

"Cuddles are mandatory," I tease back.

My phone lights up multiple times as several text messages come through.

"Ugh, can you read these messages to me while I try to get us on the interstate?" I ask.

I'm really getting annoyed at how much my phone is going off right now.

"Yeah, sure," Li Mei says as she lets go of my hand to grab the phone. "Uh, it's 4 te- no, 6 text messages from Faith. No one else has texted you though."

I nodded my head to indicate I want her to continue.

"Let's see, Faith says…" She trails off as she reads the messages. "She can't believe your mom and dad were so rude to us this morning. She doesn't care that we are gay and that you will always be her sister…"

I feel my heart tingle and have to fight a tear from escaping my eye.

"…She also says if you need help getting anything from the house to let her know and she will bring it to us…"

"She doesn't even have a car or know how to drive," I interject with a chuckle.

Faith is the best.

"Oh, she took care of that too. She said she could get her friend Elizabeth to help bring her to us because Elizabeth 'owes her one'… what do you think that means?"

I shrugged my shoulders. "No idea."

"And she just sent another message about Grace quoting the bible at her about why being gay is a sin. But she told Grace the bible verse she quoted only mentions men, so what is the problem." Li Mei finishes with a giggle.

"Can you believe the 13-year-old is the most mature one out of all my family members?" I ask sarcastically.

"That is really sad. I would have thought- oh here is another text from Faith. Does she always text this much?!" Li Mei asks quizzically.

"YES. She never stops. I think it's because she's so young," I explain. "You just have to put the phone down and ignore her sometimes. She'll stop eventually."

"Won't she think that is rude?" Li Mei asks concerned.

"No, not at all. I don't answer her immediately, but when I'm ready I'll respond to the rest of her messages."

"That's so weird," Li Mei laughs.

Several minutes later we pull into the campus parking deck and I'm able to park in my normal spot. As we walk into the dorm building, the TV in the lobby is blaring the local news. The noise catches me by surprise because normally the security guard keeps on something more fun or exciting, such as the latest baseball game.

"In South Carolina, a federal grand jury has indicted the 21-year-old shooter who attacked and killed nine people at a Charleston Church on..."

Looking up at the screen, I see the footage of the young man on the screen. He had been all over the news since June because he opened fire on an all-Black church. When they got him into custody, he would later admit he did it intentionally to start a race war.

That's so disgusting.

"The recent attack has raised concerns about the state's gun control laws. The question now is..."

"Oh, give me a break!" A voice yells out from behind and startles me. I turned around to see a new security guard standing behind the desk. He's tall, with a medium build and brown hair. Your stereotypical white man. "Can you believe that crap?"

I have had enough with the backwoods ass conservatives today.

"Actually, I can and it's a good thing," I snap back. Li Mei tugs on my arm, trying to pull me toward the elevators.

"More gun control would only make it harder for the good guys to get guns," He counters. "It won't stop guys like him from getting a gun and shooting up the place."

"That is a horrible incident that occurred, and the government should do more to prevent things like that-" I point at the TV with my free arm as Li Mei tugs again at the other arm. "...from happening again. Nine people died. NINE people are gone forever because that asshole didn't like Black people."

"You can't let one bad person ruin it for the rest of us," His voice is starting to raise. "It's our 2nd Amendment right to bear arms and I'll be damned if the Government takes it away from me. They are the last people we should be trusting with anything."

"It's your right to own a gun, but it isn't their right to live safely?!" I am practically yelling at him.

"Maybe they would still be alive if they had a gun to shoot him back with," He yells at me, as if the answer is so clearly obvious.

"So, they're just supposed to carry a gun on them everywhere they go? Out of fear that they might one day be shot at?!"

"Carrying a gun will make sure no one bothers to shoot at you in the first place," He spits.

Li Mei yanks my arm so hard, I almost fall down. She stops me from falling and pulls me into the open elevator, slamming the button.

Oh, I guess I got kinda carried away...

My cheeks are burning, and I can see on her face she is mortified.

"Why Hope?" She asks. "Why argue with him?"

"He's such a fucking idiot if he thinks-"

"HOPE! It's not worth it disrupting your happiness," Li Mei burst out. "I know you are upset with your family right now-"

"That has nothing to do with-" I interject.

"NO!" She cuts me off. "It has everything to do with it. You are upset with your family, and you are taking it out on others, including me. You need to cool off and take some time to relax."

"Okay, fine," I mumble, avoiding her gaze. The elevator dings and we step across the floor to our door. It takes a moment for me to grab the right key and then I push the door open to walk through. Inside, we are greeted with an array of posters, glitter, and music. I see what I assume are Emily's friends since Saanvi is nowhere in sight. Some I recognize from a few days ago, the rest are all unfamiliar faces. Every inch of our common room space is being used by Emily's friends decorating the posters.

"Hope, Li Mei! Back already?" Emily asks startled.

"Yeah, I, um, forgot some stuff," I stammer, still trying to shake off the argument I had with the security guard. "What's all this?"

"We're having a party and making posters for Monday's rally!" She squeals happily. "And they are turning out SO great! Do you want to see what we have so far?"

"Uh, sure," I say cautiously.

"Yay, okay so check it out! We have one section that is your normal pro-choice, 'keep your laws off my body' type messaging," She waves her hand towards each poster, likes a salesman in a store. "But then we found out a church group is planning to attend, so we decided to bring out the big guns."

She shows us a few other posters with graphic uteruses, snipped penises, and fetuses. Each accompanied by their own poster sayings, like 'get out of my uterus' or 'stop it at the source.' I spot one that becomes my immediate favorite:

He who hath no uterus should shut the fucketh up -Fallopians 24/7

I break out into a big grin and pick up the poster. "Emily, these are fantastic! Li Mei, do you see this?" I turn the poster to make sure she can see it.

Li Mei moves closer and stares at it silently. "I don't get it."

"It's making fun of their bible scriptures," I explain. "This is how they normally write them."

"Isn't that kinda rude to mock their religion?" She asks sternly with raised eyebrows.

"Uh, well no. I mean," I fumble to find the right words.

Why would she care?! Fuck them, fuck the Christians. They are trying to take away my bodily rights.

"We have tons of others you can choose from!" Emily chimes in, saving me from the awkward moment.

"Yeah, I think I would prefer one of the others…" Li Mei trails off.

"Or we can help you create your very own sign!" Emily offers. "With whatever colors, glitter or body parts you want to put on it."

Li Mei looks a little uncomfortable right now…

"How about," I interject. "We help in a few minutes. I still need to shower and change clothes. We've had a rough start to our morning."

"That's fine! We will be out here for another hour or so. Help yourselves to whatever you want," Emily says before plopping back down to work on a bright pink poster.

I grab Li Mei's hand and lead her to our side of the dorm. I shut the door behind us and fall back on the bed.

"I am so tired," I murmur, half closing my eyes.

"Do you still think it is a good idea to go to the rally?" Li Mei asks quietly.

I sit up concerned and study her body language. She's holding one of her arms and shifting a little awkwardly on her feet.

"Yes of course," I encouraged her. "Are you worried something will go wrong?"

"I wasn't until Emily mentioned that a church might be there and now, I'm not so sure going is a good idea," She explains.

"Hey, we will be fine. Even if other people show up, we don't have to go anywhere near them." I walk towards her and pull her into my arms, rubbing her back. "Everything will be fine, they would never hurt us. They are just mad that some women will finally get the healthcare they need."

She mumbles something under her breath, and I can see my words don't alleviate her concerns, so I try a different route.

"Besides, if we don't like how it's going, we can always leave early. And go to a movie, or get ice cream, or whatever you want."

She smiles at me, then kisses me softly on the lips.

"I love you." She murmurs.

"I love you too."

18

GRACE

An hour later, I tiptoe downstairs. The house has been eerily quiet since Hope and Li Mei left, but I know better. My parents are huddled in the kitchen, strategizing how they want to address Hope's latest issue.

Over the years, they had come to accept that Hope would be the most rebellious of us three girls. The sneaking out, late-night parties, and alcohol look angelic compared to her latest sin. As I slip out the front door, I overhear one small part of their conversation.

"He's the only one that could help us at this point. We have to try, Paul," Mom says defeated.

"Fine. Have it your way. If he can't help her, then she is truly lost," Dad retorts.

My thoughts race as I climb into my car and crank it.

Hmmm… they are clearly talking about someone to help Hope. Probably someone from the Church. I doubt it will do any good.

"Wait for me!" I look up to see Faith running out the door towards my car. She opens the passenger door, jumps in, and immediately starts texting on her phone.

I roll my eyes with annoyance and snap at her. "I thought Elizabeth was picking you up?"

"No, she is at her grandmother's this weekend, so she can't come," She responds without even looking up from her phone.

"Okay, well buckle up. I don't want to get a ticket for you," I command, sternly.

She rolls her eyes. "Ugh fine!"

I wait until I hear the click of her seat belt before I drive off. Faith is being unusually quiet, especially for her. The silence makes me uncomfortable, so I attempt to start a conversation.

"Did you hear anything that Mom and Dad were talking about?"

"Not really, just that they are inviting some people over for dinner tonight. Do you think Hope will come back?" She asks, her bright blue eyes full of concern.

I wish my eyes looked as pretty as hers…

"She'll have to, they didn't take any of their stuff before they left. I'm sure she brought a bag home with her," I remark.

Probably full of beer or weed.

Faith doesn't bother to respond, so I decide to turn up the music to fill the silence. A few minutes later, we pulled into the Church parking lot, just in time.

I can barely park the car before Faith jumps out and runs off to the minibus. Probably to join Jessica and Ashley as they tend to be her back up option when Elizabeth is gone. I'm walking up as Megan's SUV pulls into the parking lot.

I greet Sister Rebecca and wait for Megan outside the minibus. She comes running up, out of breath.

"I'm sorry Sister Rebecca! My mom lost track of the time. I was helping her clean and had to finish it before I could leave. She didn't realize how much she gave me to do…" Her voice trails off with a hint of annoyance that only I can detect.

"Oh, how nice. 'Children obey your parents in the Lord, for this is right. Honor your father and mother.' Do you girls remember what verse that is?" she quizzes us, raising an eyebrow and waiting for the answer. Megan shrugs and glances at me to respond.

"Ephesians 6:1-2!" I say proudly.

"Correct! Good job Grace. You've been keeping up with your quiet time," she praises. Megan stares off into the distance awkwardly. She never remembers to do our Daily Devotional Bible readings.

Pastor John exits the Church, talking quickly on the phone. Right when he gets within earshot, he hangs up and yells, "Alright, load 'em up and move 'em out!"

I grab Megan's arm and climb onto the minibus. I peer out the windows and see Michael, Christopher and David being rounded up by Pastor John to get on board. I pick a seat as close to the back of the minibus as possible, but put space between us and Taylor, who is brooding in the very back. He makes eye contact with me then quickly tilts his head toward the window and his black hair shifts to hide his eyes.

Yeah, don't worry. I don't want to sit near you either.

Megan plops down beside me and I fill her in on everything that happened this morning at breakfast with Hope. When I'm done, Megan looks just as shocked as I was.

"So, your dad just kicked her out?"

"Yep. Told her to take her 'communist, devilish trash' out with her and to never come back," I quoted, matter-of-factly.

"Oh gosh, poor Hope. And poor Li Mei!" Megan responds sympathetically.

Poor Li Mei?! Poor Hope?!

"What do you mean?" I ask, defensively.

"Come on Grace, have a little heart. It's Li Mei's first time in America, first time meeting your parents, and being surrounded by another culture that she doesn't know anything about. She was so excited to meet your parents and now the whole stay is ruined," She explains sincerely.

She can't be serious.

"Megan, she is GAY. Hope is GAY. That is a sin that will send them both to hell unless they repent," I retorted. "Chinese or not, the fact remains that they both disrespected my father's house by walking in there and sleeping together in Hope's bedroom."

Megan winces at my words but recovers confidently to state. "The bible says to love your neighbor, does it not Grace?"

"Well, y-yes," I stammer.

"It doesn't specify to love only your Christian neighbors or your straight neighbors. It says to love YOUR neighbor. Whoever that person might be," Megan argues. I detect a bit of disappointment in her voice. "As a Christian, I would have expected you to be more sympathetic and merciful to their situation."

Now it was my turn to wince at her words. Even though I know, in some ways, she is right, I don't want to admit it. And I certainly don't want to side with my sister.

"She still lied to my parents. She lied to all of us and made us think Li Mei was her friend," I snap back.

"Grace..." Megan sighs. "How else was she supposed to tell you?"

"I dunno." The question catches me off guard. "I guess as soon as she walked through the door."

Megan chuckles. "You honestly think that would have gone any better? Or different from what did happen? 'Hey mom, hiya dad! It's so great to be home again, oh by the way, here is my new girlfriend, Li Mei. She's Chinese.'...Even that would have been poorly accepted. Your parents are harsh, especially your dad."

Now she attacks MY dad?!?!

"Honestly, you don't have much room to talk, Megan. At least my dad wants me." My rage pours venom into each word as it lashes out from my mouth.

Megan's eyes immediately begin to water, and she looks defeated. I start to regret my words, but before I can say sorry Megan stands up and moves to another seat. I hear Sister Rebecca yell at her to sit down while the minibus is moving, and she slumps into a seat too far in front of me for us to talk to each other.

Ugh. Why is she so difficult!? She used to be such a good Christian...

My fingers reach for the cross around my neck and start subconsciously twisting it back and forth. I look around the minibus cautiously, trying to determine if anyone else heard our argument. It doesn't appear anyone was even phased.

It's so awkward to have to sit here alone.

To escape my discomfort, I pull out my phone and browse Instagram for a few minutes. I see an ad for car accessories that reminds me I need to get an oil change. I open my internet app to search for the oil change coupons and notice my last search result loading.

Why is this in incognito mode? And WHY is it on a page about abortion?!

I think back to the last time I went to my internet app. Besides shopping or looking up the occasional random question, I can't think of why I would search for anything related to abortion.

Exodus 20:13 says "you shall not murder." Abortion should be illegal. I wonder if Faith snuck into my room when I wasn't looking... but surely, she isn't pregnant! She's too young, she can't even drive.

I look up and see Faith towards the front of the minibus, laughing and talking to Jessica and Ashley. I shake my head in confusion. Faintly, I hear a phone ringing and see Sister Rebecca answer it before I look down at my phone.

No. Faith wouldn't be pregnant, but Hope… Maybe. But that can't work if she is dating another girl?!

"Okay, listen up everyone!"

I jump as Sister Rebecca's voice echoes across the minibus.

"We can't go to Welcoming Wings today. They had a terrible lice outbreak and need to get it under control…"

EW! Gross.

"…So instead, we are going to go to the Happy Mart and hand out these pamphlets and talk to people about Jesus Christ's love. It is a shame that some people grow up without ever knowing the love of Jesus Christ. If we remain steadfast and dedicated, we will save them and rejoice when we are in Heaven."

Grrrrreat. This day just keeps getting better and better. Ugh… this is supposed to be my one day away from that place.

Within minutes we pull up in the parking lot and Sister Rebecca pulls out a box from under the front seat. Pastor John takes it from her, and we all file out of the minibus to gather around them. I see Megan and move to be next to her, but she shifts her body away to give me a cold shoulder.

"Alright everyone, partner up and take a handful of pamphlets. Your goal is to hand out each of these pamphlets until you don't have any left. Remember to be good stewards of Christ and that you are representing not just the Church, but God Himself. Be respectful…" Pastor John pauses to look each of us in the eye. "…and behave. If you need anything, Sister Rebecca and I will be stationed at the entrance to catch people as they come into the store."

I turned to speak to Megan, but she had already approached Jessica, Ashley and Faith. I sigh as she walks off with Ashley and Faith pairs with Jessica. Michael, Christopher and David have already taken off after the girls, which leaves Taylor. Moody, broody, grumpy, Taylor.

As if this could get any worse.

"Trust me, I'm not happy about this arrangement either." I turn to see Taylor, more annoyed than ever and holding a stack of pamphlets. He takes half and thrusts the other half at me before spitting out, "Let's get this over with already."

We approach the automatic doors in silence. Each step feels like an eternity. I've never even talked to Taylor before, and I can't remember what he was like before he hit his gothic punk stage. There is an awkward pause as we wait for the sensor to trigger before opening the door. As I step through, I notice Taylor steps back.

I glance over my shoulder at him. "Come on, I thought you wanted to get this over with?"

"That sign says, 'No Soliciting' though," He replies, pointing at the sign.

Now I'm really annoyed.

"So?"

He huffs at me and rolls his eyes. "SO, that means we can't hand these out to people in the store."

The automatic doors start to shut, then the sensor detects Taylor, and reopens.

"That's only if we are selling a product. We aren't selling anything. We are just telling people about Jesus, so they can be saved and not go to Hell for eternity," I retorted.

"Yeah, well to some people that will be considered '*selling*' in their eyes," He counters and stares back at me.

"Well, those people are the ones that need to be saved the most. Now come on, you're wasting time." I wave my hand out, clearly motioning for Taylor to come inside the store with me.

Again, the automatic doors start to shut and again the sensor goes off to reopen them.

"No. I am not doing that," Taylor says flatly. He then turns around and dumps his pamphlets in the trash. "You do what you want. I, for one, am not breaking their rules. It's disrespectful."

"FINE! I didn't need your help anyways," I yell and stomp off into the store.

Why is he so difficult?!

I walk around for a few minutes to cool down until I see an elderly man in the produce section.

Now here's my chance to do something good.

I approach him, my arm outstretched with the pamphlet to hand it to him, but he shakes his head.

"I don't want it."

"It's just a pamphlet about God's love for His people and how to be saved, so you don't go to Hell for eternity," I plead, earnestly.

"He doesn't love me. If he did, my wife would still be alive," He snaps back.

"But you want to see her in Heaven, don't you?" I ask, sweetly. "Because I-"

"She didn't believe in that nonsense either!" His voice progressively gets louder with each word he says. "Now, go away! I don't want your stupid pamphlet or your stupid god or your stupid heaven."

What a mean old man. I'm just trying to help him.

I close my lips, duck my head and step away from him. I see another woman and her toddler at the other end of the produce section. We make eye contact, and I smile at her. She scowls and walks away, dragging her child with her.

I try to approach two other people. The first is a young businessman who takes the pamphlet to make me go away and then drops it on the floor of the next aisle in the store. The second is an older lady who won't stop talking to me about the weather, her kids, the local football team, the meat on sale or anything else that is on her mind.

Geez. She could give Debra a run for her money.

When I finally escape that woman, I go down a different aisle and spot the nasty old woman who checked out the day before. The one who bought cat food and canned soup with food stamps.

She's back again? As if she could afford anything else.

Her back is to me, but I see her feet start to move and immediately back track the way I came. I'm in such a hurry to hide from her that I run into someone at the end cap.

"Oooof..." My head is ducked, so I watch my pamphlets go flying across the floor before I look up to see who I bumped into.

Oh, it's Don.

"Sorry Don! I didn't see ya there," I apologize quickly.

"I saw you. There. On the cameras," He looks down at me and it isn't until this moment that I realize how tall he is compared to me. "You need to leave, Grace."

"What? Why?" I stammer, as I bend down to pick up the pamphlets.

"You aren't allowed to solicit store customers, Grace. That is the rule. It is posted on the sign at the front entrance," He states, matter of fact.

"Oh Don, we aren't soliciting. We are just telling people about God and Jesus and how to go to Heaven," I explain in my nicest voice as I stand back up.

I don't want to be the reason we get kicked out.

"No. You are soliciting. I already spoke to John and Rebecca. All of you have to leave. If you want to purchase food or other products you can. But you cannot harass my customers," His voice is stern and solid.

I've never heard him talk like that.

"Oh, we weren't harassing anyone Don," I say back defensively, with a bit of a chuckle.

Seriously? Of all the things a person can do in America, THIS is considered harassment?!

"That's not the point. The sign states no soliciting. You need to leave. Now," The tone of his voice raises a bit, indicating that his mind is made up.

Oh, he's actually mad...

"Okay yes, I'm sorry Don. We didn't mean to upset anyone... I'll leave now." It takes everything I have to keep a nice smile plastered on my face.

"Good." He turns on his heel and takes a half step away, but reels back around. "And I'll take those too." He jerks the pamphlets out of my hand and waddles off, dumping them in the first trash can he passes by.

What. A. Jerk...Well, Donald Duck does have anger issues. Quack, quack.

I exit the store to see Pastor John has pulled the minibus up front to collect us quicker. I climb up the steps and am dismayed to see Megan sitting with Ashley. I ignore her as I walk past and sit in the very back seat, opposite from Taylor, who appears quite smug and giddy.

When everyone is accounted for, Pastor John speaks to all of us.

"You guys did great today! You went out and made a stand for God.

For Jesus. For Christianity. Just think of all the people you helped save by bringing them the Word of Jesus Christ."

He's right. I did something good. Even if they didn't want it. God saw that I was trying to help them.

Sister Rebecca nods her head in agreement. "Y'all were great leaders for Christ. It's okay that we were kicked out because it shows that we are truly doing something great. It means the Devil sees what we are doing, and he is trying to stop us."

Maybe I need to work harder to save Don…

"Exactly. It's not easy being a Christian. If it was, everyone would be one and Jesus wouldn't have had to die for our sins," Pastor John is beaming. "We will continue to work to share the good Word of Jesus Christ with those who are not yet saved. You should all be proud. Now who is ready for some ice cream?"

The minibus fills with cheer for ice cream and Sister Rebecca takes a final head count to make sure no one is missing. Pastor John gets in the driver seat, cranks up the minibus and whisks us away.

"Hmph. We can't save the people if they throw all the pamphlets away."

I glanced at Taylor just quick enough to see a small smirk on his face.

Maybe I need to work harder on Taylor too…Nah. Someone else can do it. He isn't worth the trouble.

19

DR. MALICUS

"Good morning Dr. M-Malicus. Today is Wednesday, October 25th, 4102. The time is currently 7:15 a.m. Would you like for m-me to continue with your m-morning report?"

I roll over and peek one eye open as Ziva's voice fills the room from the overhead speaker.

The day will start, with or without you.

I sit up in bed before answering her.

"Yes Ziva, please continue."

"Very well, sir. The President of Earth Nations is m-meeting with..."

I begin my usual morning routine, casually tuning in and out of listening to her morning report.

"Tensions are increasing as the President of Earth Nations demands to know when the Institute for Cloning Organics will have..."

In the mirror, the same hollow, exhausted eyes stare back at me. I splash cold water on my face and pat it dry with the towel.

"...Chancellor Fhiachra is pleased to share that the ICO has finally found a solution."

My heart stops and my blood runs cold.

No. There's no way they found a cure without me.

"She is expected to provide a full report on the ICO's developments in her Friday press release."

That's still two days away! I can't wait that long to know... I have to contact Almeta.

I frantically grab the first clean shirt and pair of pants I can find in my closet.

"Ziva, please update me if there are any other developments released by the ICO before Friday."

Her voice rings out over the intercom. "Of course, sir. Is there anything else I can assist you with?"

"No. That will be it for now," I call out as I run out the bedroom and down the hall to my lab.

She doesn't need to know I've been contacting Almeta.

"Contact Almeta: Heard ICO news, need to know..."

Ping, ping.

I glance at the incoming message to see Almeta's name on it.

"Cancel contact. Open new message from Almeta."

Her hologram pops up and begins to play her video message.

"Dr. Malicus. I'm sure you heard the news that Chancellor Fhiachra has a solution that will be announced in more detail Friday. I heard the news this morning as well and am shocked. As far as I know, they haven't made any progress on any projects. I am going to investigate more today and will provide an update ASAP."

Her hologram disappears and a deafening silence fills my lab. I take a deep breath in to calm myself.

It's got to be more political bullshit. I just need to get back to work, I'm so close to having the solution. And then I can–

Another incoming message interrupts my thoughts. This one does not have a name listed for me to know who it came from, and I subconsciously adjust the watch on my wrist.

"Open new message."

The computer wizzes to open the latest hologram message. Dread consumes me as I recognize the familiar pale face, piercing green eyes and dark black hair. Her red long-sleeved dress makes her appear taller than normal and intimidating. She cocks her head before she begins speaking, the only visible indication of her discomfort.

"Dr. Malicus. I trust you are doing well and enjoying your sabbatical," Chancellor Fhiachra says while flashing her pearly white teeth. Years of experience working with her are the only reason I know the flashy smile she is giving me right now is fake. "I am sending my acquaintance, Dr. Hai Văn Xaun to stop by and check in on you. Hopefully, I don't need to remind you of how important it is that you rest on your sabbatical."

She pauses on the hologram to raise an eyebrow. I roll my eyes impatiently.

"Please take care Doctor and know that we at the ICO value your contributions to our community and the world. *Fortis*"

The hologram beeps as the Chancellor's face disappears.

How convenient she didn't tell me what day or time he would be stopping by...

I stare around my lab and sigh. This day is not going at all like I planned. I wave my hand up and the computer whizzes to present options for me to select from. The option I really want to select is to see the results of the latest test. I hesitate for a moment before hitting a different option: *lab clean up.*

The holographic screen disappears, and the lab whizzes to life, moving the tables, test tubes, and other supplies away. As I walk out, I see the lights shutting down, and the noise-deafening walls going up. Once I'm safely outside the lab, the wall goes up where the doorway was, blending in perfectly so that no one would ever know that the lab was there.

It's all safely hidden now.

My stomach growls painfully. I was in such a hurry to speak to Almeta about the latest ICO updates that I forgot to eat breakfast.

I guess I can eat while I wait for Dr. Xaun to show up…

While I'm not thrilled about his upcoming visit, I am relieved Cordelia didn't send anyone else. The scientific field is highly competitive and in my years at the ICO I had been the center of numerous conflicts with my colleagues. Some fought over the latest lab equipment, others critiqued my methods. Most of the tensions usually centered on my colleagues' jealousy of my success.

In fact, I can't recall the last time I did see Dr. Xaun…

My thoughts come to a screeching halt as I enter the kitchen to see my cold plate of food waiting on the countertop: scrambled eggs and avocado toast. Before I can touch the plate, Ziva comes running from around a corner and quickly grabs the plate with one hand to heat it up. She signs with her other hand to apologize. I smile half-heartedly.

"It's fine, dear. I just received an urgent message that we will have a visitor sometime soon. Possibly today." She looks alarmed and I continue to reassure her. "You can return to whatever you were doing, and I will take care of our unexpected guest."

She nods her head solemnly in response, returns my now reheated plate of food and goes back to what she was doing. As soon as she leaves the room, my smile disappears, and I stare at the steam now coming off my food.

This is not my usual breakfast for Wednesday.

But I don't have the energy or time to call her back and request that she fix my food to the correct meal. I eat it slowly, hoping that Dr.

Xaun will arrive in time to still see me engaging in a balanced meal. Even if it is the wrong meal.

At least Cordelia didn't send the other one to check in on me.

I know it is more than just "checking in," it's a test. To see if I'm working and more importantly progressing to where I can return to work at the ICO.

A month ago, the Chancellor forced me to leave on sabbatical, claiming that I needed to rest. She thought I was overworking myself, to replace the guilt and sorrow I felt about everything I experienced with Ziva. Apparently, others were concerned too, saying that I was reaching "burn out." Not once in my entire career did I ever feel overworked or like I needed to take a break, much less a 2-year-long sabbatical.

I was furious when Cordelia told me, and I argued back without realizing the decision had already been made and voted on by the ICO board - all without my knowledge or consent. Cordelia promised that if I agreed to the terms, they would still allow me to come back. Provided I don't work, and I actually take the time to rest. Otherwise, she would cancel my project completely and remove me from the board permanently.

Fucking politics.

But I know the truth. Dr. Kayitesi was threatened by the progress I was making. She is close to Cordelia, and they had known each other since they were children. I know she used her connection with Cordelia to force me out and to take my resources for her own personal gain. Dr. Kayitesi wants to be credited with finding the cure for our global crisis and she has no idea how selfish she is behaving.

I would have had the cure by now if I had all my lab resources at ICO headquarters...

I take another bite of my food as the sudden *ding* fills the hollow house. I glance at the time: 9:21 a.m.

At least I can get this over quickly.

As I approach the front door, I chew and swallow the last bite of my food so I can greet Dr. Xaun. My hand grabs the knob, and I hesitate.

Deep breath in, deep breath out...Oh, and smile.

I open the door to see a sharp, well-dressed man waiting impatiently. His hardened face immediately turns soft, as he smiles and his slanted blue eyes wrinkle at the corners. He has some of the whitest teeth I have ever seen, and I notice speckles of gray splattered throughout his thick, black hair. He steps closer to extend a warm hand.

"Dr. Malicus, it is such a pleasure to see you again."

"Dr. Xaun, thank you for stopping by," I responded happily. "It is exciting to interact with another brilliant mind."

Loosen up. Don't make your smile seem too tense.

Dr. Xaun nods his head towards the front garden.

"Are those pink carnations? How ever did you get them to grow in this zone?" He asks curiously.

"I'm afraid I have no idea," I answer, placing my hands on my hips. "My wife Ziva tends to the flowers and garden, it is a passion of hers. She attracts the bees and bugs, and I help study and collect them."

He leans closer to admire the carnations before responding. "Ah, well I will have to get her to explain it to me because my wife adores carnations. Hers have been struggling for the last few years."

"I didn't realize you lived in this province," I try to mask my alarm and displeasure at the idea of Dr. Xaun living so close to me.

"I don't." He muses over the flowers one last time before turning back to me. "But we live in a zone that has a similar climate and harshness that carnations struggle in."

"Ahh. Well, I wish I knew Ziva's secret! To be honest, I don't really pay attention to how she maintains them. I just notice when the bees stop coming," I chuckle, attempting to give my most convincing heartfelt smile. He meets my gaze and returns a soft smile.

Okay, so far so good...

I step aside to let him in and wave my arm to indicate the direction we will be walking in.

"Come. We can sit in here," I remember my manners and add on. "Would you like something to drink?"

"Oh yes, a water would be great. Thank you," He responds respectfully.

I nod my head and lead the way to the kitchen. I grab a cup and fill it with water.

This silence is a little awkward. I know I should say something, but what?

I open my mouth, hoping the words will just come out for me, but I hear Dr. Xaun clear his throat.

"How long have you lived here?"

Perfect. That's a simple topic I can work with.

"I bought the house a few years ago, as a surprise for my wife. She always liked the idea of living in the country, secluded and alone," I turn around and hand him the glass of water. "...and now I appreciate the stillness of it. It's so peaceful and relaxing." I give him the best smile I can muster and hope it is convincing. He takes the glass, and a sip before responding.

"It's exquisite. I couldn't imagine leaving a place like this for a city like Beijing. Too crowded and noisy."

He walks around the room, so his eyes can take it all in: the curved gray walls, the clean crisp lines, and marble finishes. Our career accomplishments and awards are tastefully hung along the walls in groups as small as three or as large as twelve. I recall Ziva organizing each group together based on the project types that were similar to one another. Our biggest career milestones were front and center, in the most obvious places for our guests to see, while some of the smaller projects were carefully hidden in other corners of the house. Ziva designed the entire home to be energy efficient and stylish, something fitting for two world-renowned scientists. A feat she certainly accomplished with all the compliments we had received from new guests over the years.

But he's not a guest.

My heart is pounding in my chest, and I take a silent deep breath as I study his face. He pauses at one of my collections on the wall.

"It's a shame that our lives are so fleetingly short," He muses, as his finger traces the edge of the frame for a moment before instinctively flinching back. "Can you imagine what all we could accomplish if we could live for 20, 50, 100 years longer?"

He turns to face me, and I hesitate to answer his rhetorical question. When he realizes I won't respond, he continues.

"You have accomplished so much, Dr. Malicus. Throughout your career you have helped to eradicate over 150 known genetic deformities and diseases. You've won countless awards, competitions and even have a few Nobel Prizes to display on your wall."

He motioned towards the frame he was looking at on the wall.

"Many scientists in this world will spend their entire life chasing after these kinds of recognitions that you already have. To make sure their name goes down in the history books, so their legacy lives on. Some will even stop at nothing to achieve it."

He takes another long sip of his water, then sets the glass down on the counter.

I don't like where this conversation is going.

I shift uncomfortably and his voice softens. "There's also nothing wrong with taking a break. Relaxing. Clear your mind. Take it easy for a while."

"We are in the middle of a global extinction crisis." I try to hide my agitation, but I'm sure some of it seeped out anyway.

"Yes, we are. And that is why we need you at your full capacity. Physically, mentally, and emotionally." He pauses, studying me closely. I involuntarily fidget under his gaze. I've never liked to be stared at by anyone. Not even Ziva.

"Have you been relaxing, like you are supposed to Iacobus?" His eyes narrow and his tone is flat, somewhere between accusation and curiosity.

"Yes, I have been. The fresh air has been great for my well-being." I smile curtly.

"Hmph."

He doesn't believe me. I need to sell this.

"Of course, I am a scientist. My mind has never been able to sit still. Do you want to see what I have been working on?" His eyebrow rises and he looks alarmed. He doesn't answer my question, so I continue.

"Come, I'll show you my latest project."

I ignore the look on his face and lead the way to one of the front rooms of the house. I open the door to the study that has the same monochrome gray walls. Bookshelves line the room, with a desk at the center and a table by the window. I lead him to the table and grab one of the samples laid on it.

"I forgot how much I enjoy entomology. It's been refreshing to dabble back into it again and give it my full focus," I explain, holding out a sample for him to see.

He walks towards me, cautiously reaching out to grab it and I notice a small finger prick of blood.

"My favorite insects to study are bees. I've been tending to my hives over there –" I point out the window to the collection of natural hives on the edge of the flower garden. "While the honey is sweet to taste, I also like to collect the bees as they die. I've been working with Ziva to rearrange the garden a bit. I want to see if I can attract new species for my collection. Did you know there are hundreds of different bee species and hundreds more color variations in their patterns? You see, the fascinating thing is…"

I ramble on and on about my bee collection. Then, shift to my full insect collection. I continue until I am fully confident Dr. Xaun wants to be anywhere else on Earth, but with me at this moment.

"…and now that it is the end of the summer season, I am preparing my garden for spring, so I can attract new insects. I expect it will snow here in a few weeks, it usually comes early this time of year and –"

"Thank you Dr. Malicus," Dr Xaun raises his voice to cut me off. "This has been quite, umm, insightful. But I'm afraid I really must be going though."

Yes. Please leave.

"Oh, already? You haven't been here long," I stammer, fidgeting with my watch to pretend to check the time.

"Actually, it's already been over an hour and–"

"Oh my! I do apologize Dr. Xaun, I didn't mean to bore your visit with my endless facts about insects," I exclaim with feigned surprise.

"Not at all. It has been delightful to talk with you, Dr," He smiles curtly, but fails to convince me that he actually enjoyed our conversation.

His voice sounds like anything but delight.

"I really do hate to leave, but I'm afraid I have other items on my agenda for today. And don't worry, I'll make sure to give Chancellor Cordelia a full update on your progress." He pauses before continuing in a playful tone. "I'm sure she will be thrilled to know you have dived back into entomology again."

I fake a chuckle. "It's always been a passion of mine, even as a young boy. In fact, I could –"

"Oh, Dr. Malicus, I really wish I could stay, but I must go now. It was good to see you, and I'll look forward to my next visit, so you can tell me more about…" he pauses to wave his hands over my desk. "Your insect collection." He plasters a smile on his face, and I hear the faintest gulp as he swallows.

"Of course, of course, I really do appreciate it, Dr. Xaun." I move towards the door, and I've never been more relieved to have the library right by the front door. He follows quickly, eager to get away.

Almost too eager.

"Do give my best to Chancellor Cordelia and let her know this sabbatical was exactly what I needed," I smile again as I open the front door, and he steps outside.

"Take care Dr. Malicus, I'll return in a month." He shakes my hand, adjusts the transporter in his hand, and disappears to whatever destination was next on his agenda. I close the door quickly and wipe the smile off my face. The clock on the wall says it's almost 11.

What a waste of a morning… but I think he bought it.

I can't have Cordelia thinking I'm still working while on sabbatical. If she finds out, she'll never let me come back to the ICO. But I also can't afford to lose any progress on my research.

Speaking of…time to check the results from last night.

I go to where the entryway of my lab is.

"Periculum abiit." At the sound of my voice, the wall presses in and slides away to reveal the opening. As I walk in, the lab whizzes to life as everything moves back to where it belongs. I approach the holographic screen.

"Pull up the reports from the latest test results."

The holographic screen flashes to bring up the reports and at the same time, a new message arrives. I see the sender's name: Almeta.

"Open new message."

I ignore the reports on the side to focus my attention on Almeta's written message.

Copies of the upcoming press release are attached. In summary, they don't have a solution and are requesting more time. The engineering team is still trying to find an organ reactor that could provide the connection needed for the project.

I click on the attachment and spend the next few hours reading the 50+ page document. It includes not only the details of the press release, but also all the updates on Dr. Kayitesi's project from the last 72 hours.

Very nice Almeta.

At some point, Ziva calls out on the intercom that dinner is ready, but I reassure her I will be up later. Eventually, I am satisfied with how thoroughly I exhausted the files, and I check the time to see that it is after 8:00 p.m. now.

Okay enough of that, time to move on…

I save copies of the files and close out of the message to turn my attention back to the test results, but another ping stops me.

What now?!

I glance at the second incoming message from Almeta and open it. My heart drops as I stare at one single word in her message: *Captus.*

"Oh fuck."

20

GRACE

"So, how did it go?" Mom's voice greets us as we return home. I look in the living room to respond, but Faith beats me to it.

"We got kicked out," Faith says bluntly.

"Kicked out?" Dad chimes in, slowly peeling his eyes away from the TV. I give Faith an annoyed look and offer a better explanation for our parents.

"We couldn't go to Welcoming Wings today because some kid had lice and gave it to all the other kids. So, we went to the Happy Mart instead to talk to people about Jesus and hand out pamphlets about how to be saved."

"Yeah, and then the manager guy kicked us out for 'disturbing' people," Faith's annoyance is quickly replaced with confusion. "Did we do something wrong?"

"No, absolutely not! You stood up for your beliefs and tried to help share the glory of God with others. There is nothing wrong about that," Mom says comfortingly. "Did Pastor John and Sister Rebecca not explain to you that it was good work you did?"

"They did. It just confused me. Like if it was good work, then why did it feel kinda… wrong?" Her voice sounds naive and distrusting, like she doesn't believe our mom.

Why does she have to ask a million and one questions about every little thing?!

"You did nothing wrong. You hear me? NOTHING wrong." Dad's stern voice fills the room so fast, Faith jumps at his outburst. He takes a moment to breathe in before continuing to explain.

"Faith, there are people in this world who are going to tell you what you should or shouldn't do. They are going to challenge your beliefs as a Christian. And you have to take a stand for God. Even if it means breaking the rules or even the law. The Government isn't religious, and they don't always pass laws that uphold the ideals Jesus preached over 2,000 years ago. It is our job to be the messengers for Christ, to spread the Word of His greatness and to try to save as many people as we can. So, we can all enjoy Heaven together for eternity. Nobody wants to spend an eternity burning in Hell. And it would be a shame if we let someone die and go to Hell when we had the opportunity to try to save them."

"We are proud of you both for staying involved with the Church and trying to live a good life as a Christian. I know sometimes it isn't always easy, but it will be worth it someday," Mom smiles reassuringly. "Are you girls hungry?"

Almost on command, my stomach growls loudly.

Mom laughs. "I'll take that as a yes. Come on, help me cook and set the table. Pastor John and Sister Rebecca will be joining us for dinner tonight."

"I need to shower first and then I'll be right down!" Faith starts to back out of the living room and toward the stairs. "Jessica got a bit of honey stuck in my hair and it's driving me CRAZY."

She is so embarrassing. And pathetic.

"H-How did – Why do you have honey in your hair?!" sputtered Mom.

"Jessica bought honey sticks for us at the Happy Mart, but mine exploded when I tried to bite the end off to open it." Faith shrugs her shoulders, as if it isn't her fault she has honey stuck in her hair. Mom stares at her dumbfounded before rubbing the sides of her head.

I wonder if she ever regrets having Faith. She is SO ridiculous.

She finally mutters a response to Faith. "Just go. But come down after your shower to help us get dinner ready."

Faith scurries off before she even finishes speaking. I roll my eyes and go to the kitchen with Mom. I don't see any food laid out on the counter or meat in the sink.

"What are we cooking tonight?" I ask her.

"Spaghetti, salad, and breadsticks. Can you prepare the salad and get the breadsticks from the freezer? Read the box to see what we need to preheat the oven to and turn it on," Her words are framed as a question, but the tone of her voice is a demand.

"Yes ma'am." I do as I'm told, retrieving the items from the fridge. Preheating the oven and prepping the salad is quick work. When I'm done, I move out of the way so Mom can cook the meat and noodles. I decided to grab the plates and silverware to set the table.

"Grace, can you set the table for seven please?" Mom demands.

"Yes ma'am," I answer automatically.

Seven? I wonder who else is coming over…

I do as she says and take the plates and silverware into the dining room. Then I grab an extra chair from the corner of my parent's bedroom, so we have enough seats for everyone. The table looks crowded, and I shift the plates around as best as I can to give every-one some space. After adjusting the last plate, I hear the doorbell ring, followed a few moments later by loud knocking.

"Grace, can you get that?" Mom calls out from the kitchen.

"I got it honey." Dad's voice rings out from the living room. The front door opens, I don't hear what he says to the person or if he says anything to them at all. What I do hear is Hope's voice yelling out.

"Why did you change the locks on the front door?! You do realize all my stuff is still here, right?!"

What is she doing here?? She is going to ruin our dinner.

I don't hear my dad's response back to her, but I do hear Hope's.

"Really? I find that hard to believe! It's just a little too convenient for you…"

I rush back to the kitchen to avoid their argument. After my disagreement with Megan earlier, I'm not in the mood for another fight.

I should try to text her to see if she will respond.

Mom is rushing in the kitchen to finish up the spaghetti noodles and sauce. She places them in separate bowls and takes them to the dining room table. I see the breadsticks still have three more minutes left in the oven. I grab my phone from my pocket and text Megan.

> Did you hear how Faith got honey stuck in her hair?

I don't plan to apologize for our argument earlier. We both said things we didn't mean. I just want to move on and pretend like none of it ever happened. I wait a moment to see if Megan will respond. When she doesn't, I go to her Instagram to see if she has posted anything recently. To my dismay, she has not. I go to check her location, but it shows that it is unavailable.

Which means her phone must be dead. Great. She probably got grounded again.

I go back to my text to see if she read it.

Beep, beep, beep, beeeeeeeeeeeeeeeeep.

I look up at the flashing oven timer. I slide my phone into my pocket and grab the oven mitts. When I open the oven door, a delicious aroma hits my nose.

For the bread of God is He who comes down from heaven and gives life to the world. John 6:33-35.

I set the tray on the cooktop and use tongs to place each breadstick in the basket. I wrap the ends of the towel around it, to contain the heat inside and take the basket to the table. Inside the dining room, I halt. Hope is seated at the table, in her normal spot.

"Paul dear, what would you like to drink?" Mom calls out as she steps into the dining room.

"Water, please," Dad responds cheerfully from the opposite doorway.

"Hope? Grace?" She turns her attention towards us.

"Sweet tea, thank you," I reply quickly to beat Hope.

"Water," She grumbles. Mom nods her head and goes back to the kitchen. Faith comes skipping down the stairs with a slightly damp head of hair and zero clue what she is about to walk into.

"I finally got it out of my hair! And I didn't even have to cut it. But I did have to use so much shampoo and – oh hey Hope! I didn't know you were coming. Wait, why did you come back?"

She is so A.D.D.

"I was given the opportunity to collect my things. And to discuss my living arrangements over dinner," Hope says snarkily, without taking her eyes off our father. He smiles back at her sweetly. Like he accepts the challenge.

Oh boy.

Before he can respond, Mom comes back in with all our drinks balanced on her hands.

"Faith, I just got you a water since you weren't down here," she says curtly, staring at the wet hair on Faith's head.

Faith grabs the water and sits down in her normal spot next to me. Mom sits down and I look at Dad to see when he will start the blessing. Out of the corner of my eye, I see Hope finally looking at the table settings.

"Why are there two extra plates?" She asks cautiously.

"We have guests who are going to join us tonight," Dad says smoothly.

"Who?" She snaps.

"You remember Pastor John and Sister Rebecca?" He states his rhetorical question before continuing. "They will be here any minute to join us for dinner."

Hope's face pales with instant regret.

Good. Maybe they can fix what is wrong with her.

The doorbell rings and Dad rushes to get it before she can change her mind. Faith's eyes widen with realization, and she quickly jumps up to run into the kitchen.

What is she doing now?!

From the front of the house, I hear Pastor John and Sister Rebecca's voices as they greet Dad. A loud slam of the refrigerator door startles me, and I turn to see Faith running back in the dining room to sit on the other side of the table next to Hope. She looks giddy about whatever she has to drink in her new cup.

"Oh, I forgot the bread," Mom mumbled to herself, before getting up to retrieve it from the kitchen. She returns with the basket at the same time Dad leads Pastor John and Sister Rebecca into the dining room.

"Joan! It is so good to see you."

"It is good to see you too, Rebecca. I'm so glad you and John could make it on such short notice." Mom's face is beaming with excitement and motions to the empty chair between us for Sister Rebecca to sit in. Across the table, Hope is frozen in place, her eyes moving from person to person.

"Paul, I can't begin to tell you how excited I am for the football season to start. It can't get here fast enough."

"I couldn't agree more, it has been too long since we watched the SEC play," Dad responds back enthusiastically to Pastor John and motions for him to sit on the other side of me in Faith's now empty seat.

I watch silently as the two different conversations take place.

"Have you given any thought about joining the choir, Joan?" Sister Rebecca asks.

"Oh, I don't know about that Rebecca. It makes me too nervous to sing in front of people!"

"But you have a lovely voice Joan, you should share it with others..."

Ugh. The choir is boring. Let's see what the guys are talking about...

"You really think Saban has it in him to go a few more seasons?" Dad asks.

"Come on Paul, you're talking about Nick Saban, the greatest football coach in history!"

Ugh. That's even worse...

I take a small sip of my water, waiting impatiently for the adults to finish the conversation and bless the food so we can eat. Across the table, I see Faith whispering into Hope's ear and she returns a knowing look. Faith returns a half smile, that I can only assume is meant to be encouragement.

At least she didn't bring that dyke back here.

"Paul, I think the girls are ready to eat," Mom raises her voice, so she can get Dad's attention. I silently mouthed 'thank you' to Mom, grateful that she finally said something to reel him back in.

"Ah yes, let's bless the food, shall we?" He clears his throat and begins.

"Dear Heavenly Father, we humbly come before You today, grateful for Your blessings. Thank You for guiding each of my girls throughout the day, for protecting them and bringing them back home safely. Thank You for giving me such a dutiful and faithful wife, who cooked this wonderful meal we are about to eat. Thank You for bringing Pastor John and his wife, Rebecca, into our lives as well; they serve as great role models for our girls, keeping them on the correct path and preventing them from falling into the ways of sinners. We thank You for providing a roof over our head, great friends to share our faith with and for dying on the cross for our sins. One day we will be able to rejoice in Your presence, and I only pray that You continue to watch over my family, so that we may all experience Your glory together. We ask that You bless this food to the nourishment of our bodies and our bodies to Your service. In Christ's name we pray, amen."

A round of amens circle around the room from everyone except Hope.

Finally! I'm so hungry.

Mom passes the bowls of noodles, meat, and sauce around. We each take a turn, scooping out what we want on our plate and then passing the bowls to the next person. The breadbasket makes its way around the table too and there is a moment of silence as everyone takes a bite of the hot food. Pastor John is the first one to break the silence.

"So, Hope, how is school going?"

"Fine," Her cold answer rings out, filling the silence.

"We haven't seen you lately at Church," He continues.

"Yes, we've been missing you," Sister Rebecca chimes in. "Have you changed Churches?"

Oh, this should be good.

Hope chews slowly before swallowing her food to answer.

"I don't go to church."

Pastor John glances quickly at Dad who silently nods his head.

They planned this…

"Why don't you go to Church?" He asks.

"Why would I waste my time doing that? I don't believe in church," Her response is a cold sharp warning that she does not want to continue this conversation.

Either Pastor John doesn't hear it, or he doesn't care because he continues pressing.

"Why don't you believe in the Church?"

"I don't owe you any explanation for why I believe what I believe," Hope snaps back, setting her fork on the plate and lifting her chin up, daring him to say more. "What are you really doing here? Neither of you have ever been to our house before, especially for a meal."

"You don't have to be rude!" I feel my voice rising as I speak. "He just asked you a simple question, Hope."

"It's okay, Grace," Pastor John pats me on the back to reassure me. "I've worked with plenty of young women, like Hope, who need help."

"He-Help?! You think I need help?" Hope laughs and rolls her eyes. "You have got to be kidding me."

"Yes, you do need help," Dad's sudden, stern voice scares me as it echoes across the table at Hope. "You have disrespected my house and are threatening to destroy this family…"

"Destroy this family!? You are–" Hope yells out.

"…clearly you have turned away from your faith and need help to repent from your evil ways." He continued, without missing a single word. His jawline hardens and he sets his fork down, waiting for Hope to respond.

"You can't be serious. I am NOT the one destroying this family, it is you! You don't listen to me, you bring in these strangers…" Hope yells, swinging her arm out across the table towards Pastor John and Sister Rebecca. "…without my knowledge or consent to blind-side me! To push your religious cult views on to me. All because you think something is wrong with me!" She looks around the table at everyone incredulously.

"Hope, we just want to help you," Sister Rebecca smiles sweetly at her. "The Bible says –"

"The bible says to 'love thy neighbor' does it not?" Hope cuts her off.

"Yes it does! Well done, Hope," Rebecca praises her.

"Is it evil to love someone? Is it sinful to 'love thy neighbor'?" She mocks back at Sister Rebecca.

WHY does she have to act like this?! It's so embarrassing…

"Mom, she does have a point. Jesus says we should love everyone, no matter who they are or what sins they have done," Faith chimes in, but Mom hushes her. At the same time Sister Rebecca starts to explain, "In certain contexts it is. It is sinful for a woman to love another woman. It is –"

"Then, why doesn't the bible say it? In that specific verse, why doesn't it say it?" Hope drills her questions at Sister Rebecca but looks at Pastor John as well. I notice she is avoiding my parents' gaze. "By that line of reasoning, are you also saying I can't love my own mother? Or my sisters? What about my friends who are girls?

Since it is 'sinful' for a woman to love another woman?"

Pastor John chimes in. "Well, it does say–"

"You teach us that Jesus loves us no matter what," She cuts him off again. "...and that he died for our sins. That all it takes is one sin to prevent us from going to heaven. Just one. No matter what it is, one sin. Did he not also say selfishness is a sin? And pride and hatred? What about deception and lying?" She finally glares at our dad sitting at the head of the table.

"Young lady, that is enough. Do you hear me?! ENOUGH!" Our father's voice booms across the table, creating an eerie silence in its wake. "The Bible also says that children should obey their parents, something you consistently fail to do..."

"Consistently?! I'm the only one actually making something of myself!" Hope snaps back.

"...You don't attend Church, you don't read your Bible, you certainly don't obey me or your mother. I've heard from other people about your drinking problem..." He continues, ignoring every word Hope says.

"Since when does one beer equal a drinking problem?" She counters.

He ignores her again, raising his voice to show his authority. "...And then you brought that Chinese devil into our home and slept with her under my roof. I will not have this anymore. I will not have it in my household, not now, not ever. You were raised better than this. We didn't raise you to be gay and I am giving you one last chance to repent."

"Repent for what? I have done nothing wrong!" Hope snaps.

"Stop being gay or you can get out of my house and never come back," His decision echoes throughout the room.

"You can't be serious. I don't have anywhere else to go!" Hope's voice is shaking.

"That isn't my problem," He shrugs nonchalantly. "When you stop being gay, then you can come home."

"I can't just stop being who I am..." Hope's voice trails off into a whisper. "I knew you would never understand. I knew I wouldn't be able to count on you. Or you." She directs her gaze to the other end of the table, where our mother has been unusually quiet.

She turns her eyes away from Hope's. "A good wife must submit to her husband, for he runs the household."

"Wow. That's all you have to say? Quoting scripture?" Hope's voice is starting to rise again.

Once again, Sister Rebecca tries to intervene. "Hope, there is this lovely passage in Psalms that–"

"I don't want to read your fucking bible," Hope yells out.

"NO!" Dad slams his fists on the table and yells back. "Not in my house, you will not fill these walls with that filthy language. You will–"

"I don't want to be a part of your cult," Hope yells louder, her voice overpowering his as she pushes herself up from the table. I notice her arms are shaking and her face is blood red. "You preach about love and compassion, but what happens to the people who don't follow all your fucking rules?! Huh? Your god sends them to hell! What kind of religion is that?! What kind of god would manipulate people to hate others who are different from them?!"

"GET OUT OF MY HOUSE! NOW!" Dad screams as he stands up. Pastor John moves to intervene, placing a hand on Dad's arm to pull him back.

Hope storms out of the room and upstairs, while Pastor John tries to calm Dad and get him to sit back down to finish eating. Right as he starts to sit down, we all hear footsteps running down the stairs and the front door slamming shut. The noise vibrates through the whole house, somehow sounding louder than it had ever before.

Good riddance. I don't want to be around her sinful ways.

"M-Mom?" Faith's voice croaks out. "If the bible says to love thy neighbor, then why are you kicking her out of the house? Do you not love Hope anymore?" I look up to see tears building in her eyes, threatening to spill over.

Mom's face is solemn and white like a ghost, as she walks out of the room without answering Faith's question. Sister Rebecca tries to answer on her behalf.

"Of course, your parents love Hope. That is why they are trying to help her," She smiles sweetly again, only this time a little less reassuring.

"I was asking my mom, not you," Faith retorts.

"Faith! That is so rude. You can't speak like that to her," I scold.

"You're not my mom either! You can't tell me what to do!" She yells at me and sticks her tongue out before running upstairs. I start to yell after her, but a loud sobbing noise startles me. I exchange a look with Sister Rebecca briefly before she rushes to the kitchen. Through the doorway, I briefly see Mom bent over the counter crying at the sink.

On the other side of me, Dad gets up slowly and Pastor John follows him out the back door. I looked around the empty table and the half-eaten plates of food. What drinks are left are watered down from the melted ice. I stare down at my own plate to realize I hardly ate any of it because I was so engrossed in their fight. I take a bite of the cold food.

I really want to heat this up in the microwave…

I lean back in my seat to peek through the doorway and see Mom and Sister Rebecca are still whispering in the kitchen.

Maybe not. I can eat this how it is.

I eat the cold food in silence, occasionally taking a sip of my watered down sweet tea and staring at the empty seats around the table. I check my phone and am disappointed that Megan still hasn't texted me back yet.

Things are going to be a lot different around here now.

21

Dr. Malicus

"Would you like your m-morning report now, sir?"

Ziva's voice echoes throughout the lab from the overhead intercom. I glance at the time: 5:00 a.m.

Morning already?!

"Are there any updates from the ICO?" I cautiously ask, as my stomach rumbles.

"Not yet, sir."

Okay, good.

"I only want the morning report if the ICO announces any updates or changes," I command.

"Yes sir, I will update you immediately when it is released."

I don't bother to respond to her because I am too focused on the reports in front of me. I had been looking at them all night. My heavy eyes are fueled with caffeine that is forcing them to stay open.

When I finally checked the latest test results, more cells were able to advance to the telophase cycle. I can feel that I'm getting closer to the solution and on the edge of making a breakthrough. Behind me, the lab computer is quietly creating copies of DNA samples that should work.

Theoretically.

While it processes, I am studying the parent sample reports and comparing them to the live samples as they come through. These specific samples have a characteristic to them that the other samples did not have and whatever this characteristic is, it gives this DNA an advantage to combine with our advanced modified DNA. My issue is identifying what that characteristic is and discovering how to replicate it.

I wonder if...

"Sir, the ICO press release is now available. Would you like for m-me to read it to you?" Ziva's voice from the intercom overhead interrupts my thoughts.

I hesitate for a moment. I can feel my mind is on the right train of thought, but I've also been curious about the latest press release. I decided to settle on a compromise. "Are there any mentions of a cure or solution found?"

"No sir, there is not," Ziva responds immediately.

"What are the topics covered in the press release?" I ask.

"Genetic advancements, technological innovation, extraterrestrial communica–"

"No. Ziva," I cut her off, annoyed. "I only want to know the subtopics within the Genetic Advancement category."

"Oh yes, sorry sir. There's only one for today: investigation."

Investigation? That's new...

"Is it anything I am going to like?" I ask, running my fingers through my salt and pepper colored hair.

"I'm afraid not, sir."

I sigh and rub the temples of my forehead.

"Go on and get it over with then."

"Very well, sir. Authorities at the Institute for Cloning Organics have expanded their investigation into missing equipment and now have one suspect in custody. 22-year-old Almeta..."

Oh, this is way worse than I thought.

"...Caprae, has been charged with multiple counts for burglary, non-compliance with Global privacy laws, and for hindering an ICO investigation. Chancellor Cordelia Ni Fhiachra's office made the following statement about the arrest..."

Of course, she had to get involved.

"...'It is truly devastating to know that one of our own has been interfering with the ICO's most important mission. Rest assured that we are leaving no stone unturned and will be opening the investigation further to find all responsible parties in connection with Ms. Caprae. Due to the nature of her global charges, Caprae will be detained without bond for'–"

Okay, I've heard enough.

"That will be all Ziva. Thank you. Please update me if the ICO makes any more announcements," I command. "Or if we have any visitors."

"Of course, sir."

If they captured Almeta and if she didn't cover her tracks properly, then they will be headed for me next... I need to have a backup plan.

I remember Dr. Xaun's visit the day before and everything we talked about. If he had known about Almeta's involvement with helping me, he would have questioned me differently. All he really did was make silent threats, asking how I'm doing and talking about my accomplishments.

Accomplishments. That's it!

I leave the lab and run to the kitchen. I approach the wall that has dozens of picture frames, accolades, and other recognitions I had received throughout my career. The middle frame is made of glass and suspended from the wall to look like it is floating. It is also the frame Dr. Xaun pricked his finger on the day before. Carefully, I grab the side of a frame and take it to the lab. I set it down on a table and back away.

"Scan the frame for traces of DNA."

A small scanner appears from the ceiling, twirling around the frame and highlighting all the places where there are traces of DNA on the frame. It sends the data to my holographic screen for a better analysis. I zoom in on the corner of the frame where there is a small dark blood spot.

It may not be enough…

"Recreate DNA sample."

My command echoes out and the computer whizzes to complete the task. I turn back to the reports I was looking at and try to refocus my attention. On the left-hand side are the results and on the right-hand side are the DNA samples that were used in the latest batch. My heart is racing, my eyes are throbbing, and a small rumble from my stomach reminds me, once again, that I still haven't eaten.

"Ziva."

A moment passes before she returns to the intercom speaker. "Sir?"

"I would like to have my breakfast in the lab. Now please," I can feel the hunger taking over my senses and building up with my frustration. "And I would like for you to join me."

"Very well, sir. I will be down m-momentarily."

A few minutes later, Ziva comes into the lab with a tray of food and two cups. It's my correct breakfast for Thursday morning: scrambled eggs, sausage, and avocado toast, with a glass of water. Ziva has the same plate of food too, but with an orange juice instead. She places the trays on the table and sits down to stare at her plate. After a moment, she glances at me then slowly picks up the glass of orange juice. She takes a small sip and scowls at it.

"Orange juice is good for you," I tell her.

You need it. Your body needs it.

She sighs and adjusts the setting on her voice assistant. "It doesn't taste very good though."

Ugh. Just drink it.

"You'll get used to it," I reassure her.

She takes a bite of her food before her next sip. I study her movements closely. While my food is already perfectly cut on my plate, she prefers to cut hers one piece at a time. I watch as her hand gently holds the knife, carefully cutting the sausage to avoid cutting herself. How she licks her lips, just the tiniest bit, before putting the sausage in her mouth.

She is moving better. Now that Almeta is gone...

"Do you think you are ready to come back to work in the lab?" My question catches her off guard and she stares back at me astonished.

"I've never worked in your lab before."

She's scared to try again.

"It will come back to you dear," I put my hand on hers reassuringly. "You were so brilliant before. I'm sure you'll be back to running the whole thing in no time, I mean you were such a natural at it!"

She focuses on her food again and strands of dirty blonde hair fall forward, covering part of her face. "I was... once. A while ago," She murmurs. "What if it doesn't come back to m-me?"

I smile softly, touching her chin and pushing her face up to meet my eyes. "You..." I push her hair back and tuck it behind her ear. "...will be just fine. It will all come back, with time. Just work hard and be patient. Hmm?"

Her cold blue eyes meet mine. "I will try. For you, sir."

"Good," I let go of her face and lean back to give her some space. "Only the strong survive."

"Yes, you're right sir. Only the strong survive."

We finish eating in silence and Ziva takes the empty plates away, so they don't clutter the lab. My mind is racing to all the various projects Ziva could help me with and how I am going to get supplies now that Almeta is gone.

It will be harder... but not impossible.

When Ziva returns to the lab, I hold my hand out to her. She stares at it cautiously, before placing hers in it.

"Come dear. I could use your help over here." She follows obediently, silently. I lead her to a table that is piled with various pieces of technology and machinery.

"I need all of these pieces cleaned and organized. Ha, I don't even know what half of them are!" I smile cheekily. "You know how I get, all caught up in my reports and data and results. I neglect the equipment and technology that got me there."

I watch as Ziva picks up a small piece. She stares at it curiously, rotating it in her fingers before looking back at me with a half-hearted smile.

"I think I could do that," She finally whispers.

"Good! It would be a tremendous help. Thank you dear," I kiss her on the side of the head and walk back to my reports.

Please let that jog her memory... please, please, please.

I glance to see the time is 6:15 a.m. then look around the lab.

What did I want to do next? I could look at those historical accounts again and try to find a connection or I could –

The sudden beeping noise of the DNA samples startles me.

Wait. It's too early for it to be done. I just started this last batch around 3:00 this morning.

I rush over to the report screen, already dreading what error message will appear. But instead, I am greeted with a different message: *Telophase cycle complete.*

My heart is pounding hard now. "Show analysis and DNA sequence for the successful live sample."

The robotic arm swings around to grab the DNA sample and present it to me, like a proud parent presenting their child.

Did I do it?! Did I finally do it?!

"Wait, don't get your hopes up…" I whisper to myself. "Run full scale analysis on this DNA sample to evaluate for injection."

Within moments a report over 30 pages long is presented to me and I scan through it carefully, reading every single word. Looking for any possible error I could have made or could encounter down the road that would ruin my success. Double-checking that the DNA sample properly connected to our modern day genetically modified DNA.

An hour later, I stood up in shock. I feel lightheaded and euphoric. I see my tired reflection in the glass and a small tear escapes the corner of my eye.

"I did it…Ziva, I have the cure!"

22

HOPE

"I-I just don't understand," Li Mei mumbles. I watch her face squinch in confusion and disappointment.

"They planned the whole thing," I explain. "From the very beginning he was setting me up. I knew his voice sounded too calm in that voicemail!"

After I fled my parent's house, I returned to campus. I had been back for an hour and told Li Mei everything that happened.

"And worst of all, I didn't get the one damn thing I went there for," I sigh, shaking my head. "I honestly could have lived without the rest of my clothes. But I really needed that birth certificate."

My shoulders slouch and I hug my arms close to my body.

I feel so betrayed... They never planned to hear me out. Or accept me.

Now it is her turn to sigh. "I guess I can try to get my parents to come here to meet you... But I really wanted to take you to my home, so I could show you around. Just like you showed me around your home."

Li Mei catches my gaze, and I can see her eyes are starting to water.

I can't let her down. Not now.

"Come here," I tell her gently, pulling her towards me into an embrace. "I'm sure I can get Faith to help me. She is the only one who is still on my side."

Faith is much smarter and more observant than she lets on. Before the disastrous dinner started, Faith promised to be on my side and help support me. While I appreciated her enthusiasm, I begged her to stay quiet, so she didn't get into trouble with our parents.

Yeah, Faith will help me. I'm sure of it.

"I hope so," Li Mei mutters.

I squeeze her tighter, in a comforting way.

I don't want to ever let her go. She's the only person I love that I have left.

"Can you text Faith now?" Li Mei asks cautiously.

"Yeah, I can," I answer her as I let go and pull my phone out to text Faith.

> Can you help me with something please?

"I'm sorry, I'm just worried you won't be able to get your passport in time," Li Mei apologizes, looking at her feet.

"I have time, there's no need to worry just yet," I chuckle.

She gives me a half-hearted smile. "You are too relaxed."

"And you worry too much. But I do have something that will take your mind off all that…" I tease.

"Really? What?" She asks curiously.

"How would you feel if I changed my name? I think it's time I fully embraced being my true self. My gay self."

23

GRACE

"Grace, honey! What time are you supposed to be at work?"

I slowly open my eyes to see rays of sunlight streaming through the window. They barely touch the edge of the bed, leaving me in the darker shadows. I rub my eyes and try to on my alarm clock.

"Grace! It's almost 9:00 o'clock," Mom's voice is louder this time, traveling up the stairs to my room.

9:00 already? It's so nice that I don't have to work today–

"Oh no!"

I spring up in bed immediately.

I'm going to be late.

I jump out of bed and throw on my work uniform before rushing to the bathroom.

The Bible says that on the seventh day God rested and we are supposed to rest on Sundays. I shouldn't even have to work today... but it also says to obey your parents. I had to obey my father and get a job. I'll just pray for forgiveness later.

After brushing my teeth, I grab my birth control packet and start to pop out the next pill, but I hesitate. The packet shows I have another week before my period starts.

I thought I was further along...

I double-check the outside of the pill packet to make sure I picked up the correct one. I reach back into the cabinet to find Hope's, but it is gone.

Oh yeah... she must have taken it with her when she left the other night. And Faith isn't on birth control, yet.

It had been three days since the disastrous dinner Thursday night. Mom and Dad continued to act like everything was normal, but the house felt empty. Even though Hope had stayed on campus all summer and had barely been home. This time her departure feels more permanent.

Faith was also acting strange, being unusually quiet, and avoiding everyone. I barely saw her leave her room and the few times I did catch a glimpse of her, Faith would immediately slam her bedroom door.

It's not unusual for Faith to ignore me, but I am starting to get concerned about Megan. She hadn't responded to any of my text messages, and she didn't come over Friday night like she was supposed to.

"Grace! Are you awake yet?!" I hear my bedroom door open down the hall.

"Yes Mom!" I yell out, as I shove the next pill in my mouth and sip water from the faucet. I hear footsteps approaching the bathroom door and then a knock.

"Grace, don't you have to work today?" I can hear the annoyance in her voice.

"Yes!" I fling open the door. "I have to work today, and I am about to leave. I'll be home later."

"Okay well drive safely! Don't get a ticket," She is dressed in a plain knee length flower dress. It is one of her favorites that I had seen her wear several times over the years and the green colors have slowly faded from the many times she has washed it.

"We're about to leave for Church. I'll let you know what passage of scripture Sister Rebecca assigns for quiet time this week." She reaches out to hug me and I give a quick one-armed hug before brushing her away.

"Mommmmmm! I have to go."

Twenty minutes later, I fly into the Happy Mart parking lot on two wheels and run inside. Once through the doors, I slow down to a walking pace to try to bring less attention to myself and the fact I am late. Debra is at her usual cash register, talking away to someone.

Is there anyone she doesn't know?!

I don't recognize the man she's talking to. She must feel my gaze because her eyes briefly cut to me, and I turn away.

I'm only two minutes late. It's not that big of a deal.

In the back office, I find my time card and punch it in. I place my purse and keys in one of the empty cubbies then turn to exit the office. As I come out of the doorway, I startle at the sight of Don, who is very close to the doorway and waiting for me.

As big as he is, you would think I would hear him walk up.

"Remember you are here to work. Not bother customers. *Work*," His stern eyes are piercing down at me as he says each word and adds extra emphasis to 'work.'

"We didn't mean to bother people. We just wanted to save them, so they can go to heaven one day," I explain, trying not to get defensive.

"What customers do and believe outside of this store doesn't matter to me. As store manager, when they are here, it is my job to ensure they are satisfied with our services and spending money, so they come back. And keep us in business. And ensure we ALL have jobs." He takes a step back, so I can leave the office. "If you bother my customers again, you won't have a job here anymore. Now go bag for Debra, you're late enough as it is and we are getting busier."

I bite my tongue and cut my eyes at him as I walked to the front of the store, my heart pounding and mind racing.

I didn't do anything wrong. Dad even said so the other night. I took a stand for my faith, for God, for Jesus. I am only trying to save people from going to Hell... The Bible says in 2nd Timothy to 'Preach the word! Be ready in season and out of season. Convince, rebuke, exhort, with all long suffering and teaching.' Jesus and His disciples took a stand for their faith. This is no different.

As I round the corner, I see a line of people waiting to check out. It's the Sunday morning rush of people who come to get their groceries before everyone else gets out of Church.

Such a shame. These people should be in Church.

I rush to start bagging for Debra and am grateful for the long line because it prevents her from talking to me. Thirty minutes later, the line is gone, but the doors behind us are opening every few minutes as new customers come into the grocery store. I hear Debra shift her body and clear her throat.

Here we go...

"You know, your Church people really upset Don," She pauses, waiting for me to interject, but I don't. "He takes a lot of pride in this store. It means a lot to him, and he doesn't like it when other people disrespect it."

"Disrespect it?!" I scoff in disbelief. "If anything, we were helping his customers. They are all going to die one day and go to Hell if they aren't saved by Jesus."

She can't be serious, I'm not the problem.

"I get that you believe that, but there is a time and a place for those things. And it's not when people are here at a business trying to browse for their weekly groceries," Her stern eyes are boring into me, and I look away as my cheeks start to burn with embarrassment. She takes a deep breath before continuing her rant.

"See, I go to Church every now and again. I believe in Jesus and pray to the good Lord above. I believe in being nice to people, regardless of who they are or what they believe. I also believe in a good bottle of wine and the occasional smoke to calm the nerves. And every now and again I'll cross the state line to try my luck at winning the lottery. All of those are things the Bible says we ought not do. Does that mean I'm not going to Heaven?" She waits a long time for me to answer, until the silence becomes uncomfortable.

"Well..." I start, but she cuts me off.

"My point is you don't know what those people believe. And you shouldn't assume that because they think and believe differently from you that that means they are going to Hell...I see the way you look at some of our customers. How you act. Like they have leprosy or some disease you're scared to get. If you want to walk around here touting those Christian morals you so believe in, then you better act like it. Show some compassion and mercy, forgiveness, and grace. That is what people need more than anything else. And–"

Debra is interrupted by the loud thunk of a customer placing a frozen turkey on the conveyor belt. In an instant, her entire demeanor changes from scolding mother to welcoming and friendly.

"Suzanne! It is so good to see you and Jimmy again. How's life been? How are the grandkids? My, I saw them last week and they are getting so big! I can't believe..."

I tune her voice out as she scans and slides the groceries to me for bagging.

Thank God she finally stopped pestering me with all her questions. She is so exhausting.

I don't pay attention to anything they say while I bag the groceries and place them back in Suzanne's cart. When everything is bagged away, I look up to see if Debra has any other items to hand to me and am disappointed to see she has passed it all to me. I also don't see anyone else in line, which means that Debra is about to talk to

Suzanne for as long as she can.

"Do y'all need any help at the mission? Ya know Don has me working mornings now so I'm free in the evenings to come over if you need anything."

"Oh, that would be lovely Debra, thank you!" Suzanne exclaims. "There is something else you could help with too. There is this one elderly lady we have been trying to get in touch with. It's such a sad story really..." Suzanne lowers her voice a bit so other people around can't hear, except for Debra and myself.

"Debra, this poor woman is struggling with some type of dementia, I believe. She wanders around town in ragged clothes and sometimes I've seen her with an orange cat."

Orange cat? Are they talking about that smelly old lady with the food stamps?

I stop zoning out and pay closer attention to their conversation.

"Oh, I know who you are talking about! I've seen her around," Debra says, nodding her head in understanding and subconsciously pushing a lose strand of white hair behind her ear.

"Okay good, well if you see her again, please give me a call. We have been trying to reach her to help her and bring her into the mission, but she keeps running from us or agrees to come and then we turn away for a minute and she wanders off. Jimmy–" Suzanne waves her hand toward her husband standing behind her. "He did find out recently from the county coroner that this lady was living with her son. And he was taking care of her, but a few weeks ago they found him dead in the house."

Oh, that poor woman, how awful.

"Oh my, that is horrible!" Debra exclaims as she places her hand on her chest.

"Mhmm, suicide," Jimmy chimes in, to stop Debra from assuming a murderer was on the loose. "The neighbors said he was a veteran who served in the military for over a decade. Apparently, he saw a lot of combat and was struggling with PTSD."

I hope he was saved so he could go to Heaven... I wonder if she is saved.

"Yes, they said he was a little squirrely, very odd," Suzanne explains. "They think he never could adjust to civilian life, poor thing... Anyways, he was taking care of the elderly woman, I believe because she was his mom. But when the rent wasn't paid and the landlord came knocking, they found him dead in a back bedroom. She is far too old and fragile, ya know, in her condition, to be working and she didn't have any money to pay the rent. So, the landlord kicked her out of the house, and she's been living on the streets ever since."

I should have given her a ride that night. The next time I see her, I will help her.

"Well, when I see her again, you will be the first person I call," Debra promises. "I could tell by the way her hands shake when she tries to grab her groceries that she must be struggling with some health condition, the poor thing."

"Thank you, Debra, I knew I could count on you," Suzanne turns as another customer places their food on the conveyor belt. "Alright, well, I don't want to hold you up from taking care of these good folks."

"I'll give you a call later Suzanne! And keep your family in my prayers," Debra promises again.

"See ya Deb!" Jimmy yells, as he pushes the buggy out of the store, following his wife.

I glance at the clock: 10:35 a.m.

Ugh. I still have over four more hours before I can leave.

But the time flies by as the Happy Mart gets busier and busier with shoppers. Before I know it, my replacement arrives and I'm able to clock out to go home.

I sit in my car for a moment to pray, asking God for forgiveness and compassion. It's a scorching summer day and inside the car it feels suffocating. I pray quickly, anxious to get driving, so I can feel the breeze of the wind on my face.

Maybe that is what Hell feels like…Dear Lord, I know I'm not supposed to work on Sundays. The Bible says to rest, but it also says to obey your parents. Please forgive me for working when I shouldn't. Protect me as I make my drive home. And forgive me for judging that old lady so harshly. She needs my help now, more than ever. Bring her back into my life, so that I might be able to save her. Amen.

I take a deep breath after my prayer and allow the comforting warm feeling of the Holy Spirit to fill my body. It's why I pray so much, so I can feel close to God and reassured that I am doing the right thing as a Christian.

Others might not take a stand for their faith, but I will.

24

AVERY

(HOPE)

What is taking her so long?

I adjust the vent in my car to direct more of the cold air on my face. It's not even 10 in the morning and yet it is already a humid day.

I waited for my parents to leave for church before I pulled up outside the house. Faith pretended to be sick, so she didn't have to go to church with them. Grace's car was already gone when I pulled up down the street, so I assume she must have had to work.

Because god knows she wouldn't miss church for anything.

Several more minutes pass by before the front door finally opens. I instinctively tense, even though I know my parents aren't home. Faith comes running out and across the yard with a flimsy piece of paper in hand: my birth certificate.

Hell yes, she got it!

I roll the window down to greet her.

"Got it!" She yells out triumphantly, presenting the birth certificate like an award.

"Thank you so much Faith," I say gratefully, taking the birth certificate from her. I looked it over quickly to confirm that it is indeed my birth certificate.

"Took me forever to open the safe," she pants with annoyance. "I already had the code, but I guess I wasn't turning the little dial correctly."

"Yeah, it can be tricky sometimes," I murmur.

"Where is Li Mei?" Faith asks disappointed as she looks inside my Subaru.

"She wanted to sleep in a bit. We went hiking yesterday and she is still worn out," I explain.

I need to get back to her. And leave before Mom and Dad show up.

"Oh, I was hoping to see her," Faith pouts.

"We'll be back in town tomorrow," I offer while adjusting my rearview mirror. "We could probably meet up to get a snack or ice cream or something."

Faith's face lights up at that idea. "Yes please! I want to see her again and ask about the Pandas."

I glance at my phone to see it is 10:13.

They should be getting out of church soon.

"Okay, I'll call you when we are free to hang out." I put the car in reverse and turned to face her. "I really need to go now Faith, Dad and Mom can't see me here."

"I know," she mumbles. "Call me tomorrow?"

"Yes, I'll call you tomorrow," I promise, as I push the button to roll up the passenger window. "Thanks again. Bye Faith."

She mumbles goodbye and sulks back to the house. I drive down the street before I let myself relax.

I have it, I actually have it!

Now I can apply for my passport. We'll be able to visit Li Mei's family for the holidays and plan other trips we've been dreaming about. A passport also opens the door for job opportunities in other countries.

I turn the corner and see the light ahead change to red, so I gently brake until my Subaru comes to a stop. From behind, I hear the most obnoxious country music blaring loudly. I glance up at the rearview mirror and groan when I recognize the truck pulling up in the left lane.

Great. It's homophobic Brock.

The guy from the bar who tried to pick a fight with Li Mei, Megan and I last week. Cautiously, I watch as he flies up to the light and slams on his brakes. The lifted truck lurches forward before coming to a complete stop. Without even looking at his truck, I can feel his eyes boring into me.

"Hey look, it's the lesbian bitch," He calls out.

Don't look, just ignore him.

"Oh, you're not going to talk to me huh? What are you mad? Is that it? Did I make you mad?" He sneers and revs his truck up.

That country music is so annoying.

I take a deep breath and turn up the music in my SUV, trying to drown out both his music and his words.

"Fucking cunt," He yells out. "You don't have any reason to be mad yet."

I watch the light intently, my foot trembling from not being able to press the gas pedal to escape.

Ignore him, ignore him, ignore him…

The light finally changes, and I slam on the gas to get away. The big truck speeds up, but quickly falls behind my smaller SUV. Eventually, I see in the rearview mirror that he turns down a different road and I finally relax my shoulders.

What a dick.

I drive back to campus, turning my thoughts back to the freedom my future passport will bring. When I pull into the dark parking deck, I'm surprised to see more cars than normal.

I forgot it is getting close to the fall semester starting back.

I circle the ground level and am disappointed to see most of the spots are taken. The few that are left open are on the opposite end of the parking deck, away from my dorm building.

Let's try the second level.

I pull up to the second level and find a spot right next to the elevator.

That's better.

As I get out of my SUV and lock the door, I glance out across the street towards my dorm building. It is eerily quiet for a hot summer day. Usually there are people outside, walking around or throwing a frisbee. I've even seen some students throw water balloons at each other, until a campus staff member intervened.

I hear a noise from behind and jerk my head to see what or who it is.

I could have sworn I heard something.

I peer into the darker part of the parking deck, studying the few cars on the second level and not seeing anything or anyone.

Maybe it was someone on the ground floor.

I cautiously walk to the elevator and tap the button. It groans and creaks as the machinery tries to bring the elevator to the second floor.

Should I just take the stairs?

I glimpse the stairs to the right and look back at the elevator doors that still haven't opened. The scuffle of footsteps from behind convinces me to run down the stairs instead of waiting. When I get to the landing between the flights, I pause to glance back up at the second level and where I had been standing moments before. It's completely empty.

I could have sworn I heard something...

Shrugging my shoulders, I continue down the rest of the stairs and venture out to the street crosswalk below. I look both ways for cars and freeze as one runs through the changing red light. The crosswalk light changes, indicating that I have the right of way now. Still, I look left down the street again to make sure no other cars were coming. As I turn right, I catch a glimpse of a lifted truck several blocks away.

Surely that isn't Brock?!

The truck moves too fast for me to know for certain. I shake my head and run across the street before the light changes again.

I must be losing my mind.

Inside the dorm building, I am relieved to see the security guard at the front desk is not the last guy I argued with. I flash my student ID and take the elevator up to my dorm. Quietly I unlock my dorm room door and walk through the shared living area to my bedroom.

Our bedroom.

Li Mei sits up in bed, sitting down her phone.

"Avery! You're back already?!" She exclaims, before asking nervously. "Did you get it?"

"Yup!" I exclaim, holding up the birth certificate for her to see.

Her face breaks into the biggest grin that forces her slanted eyes to almost look closed. She jumps down and flings her arms around me. "Aww, I'm so glad you got it! Now you can get your passport, and we can take all our trips."

"Yes, we can, and I can't wait to spend every moment of it with you."
I hugged her tightly, not wanting to let go.

You are my family now. You are my future.

"Did you have any issues with your parents?" Li Mei asks as she pulls
back to look at me.

"No, they weren't there. They were at church, and I think Grace was
at work, so it was the perfect time for Faith to help me," I explain.

She nods her head solemnly and her pink hair swishes around. "I
still wish they would be more accepting of you. And of us."

"I know. I wish they would be too," I answer grimly.

But they will never accept us.

It is just as bad as I could have imagined. Not only did they not accept
us, but they also tried to reason and convert me back to Christianity. Then to make it even worse, they banished and disowned me.
Kicked me out and acted like I was never their daughter, as if I don't
exist as a human being.

My stomach twists and I feel that small part of my heart that yearns
for their approval. That same part that still feels like a little girl, who
just wants to know that my mom and dad care for me. My body
starts to tingle, a numbness that is slowly spreading out from my
chest, into each limb, and down into my fingers. I swallow hard and
breathe deep to push aside the empty feeling.

*If they can't love me as I am then that means they never truly loved
me to begin with.*

"But we will be fine, and we will find a way to move on from this," I
continue. "Besides, after I graduate and get a big fancy job, we can
get our own place. And if you're really good, maybe a kitten or two."

Li Mei smiles big and bats her eyes at me. "Oh, could we really?! A
kitten, a real kitten?!"

I laugh at her theatrics. "Yes, a kitten. Or a puppy. I don't really care what, but something. A pet we can love and spoil."

"It will be like our own little family!" she gushes.

"Exactly, our own little family," I agree and kiss her gently on her forehead. "Because while we might be born into a family, we can also choose who we want to be in our family. And I choose you. And our future little kitten or puppy."

She squeals, jumps, and hugs me tighter.

It sucks to lose my family, but that doesn't mean I can't create my own family one day.

25

GRACE

When I arrive back home, I walk through the front door and head straight into the kitchen to grab a snack.

I find Faith seated on a chair directly under the bright kitchen lights while Mom inspects her arm. Faith is wearing a tank top, pair of shorts and flipflops. As I walk around them, I notice red bumps on the inside of her forearm that look like a cross between a rash and bug bites.

"What in the world did you get into child?!" Mom exclaims in disbelief and applies ointment cream to her rash.

Faith shrugs her shoulders and tries to leave the chair. "I don't know. Maybe it's poison oak or ivy? I did play in the woods behind Elizabeth's house."

"Hmmm, no it can't be that. It would look different…" She pushes Faith back down into the chair. "Now sit still. You need to let this ointment cream soak into your skin before you somehow wash it off."

"Ughhhhhh. It doesn't even itch though," Faith rolls her eyes in annoyance.

"I don't care. You don't need to scratch this and make it worse. After it soaks in, I'm going to bandage it, so you can't touch it," Mom commands.

Faith wiggles a bit in the seat from impatience. I grab a muffin off the counter and a glass of water. Then, move closer to inspect her arm.

"Do you think it could be bed bugs?" I ask Mom, now paranoid that Faith could bring some parasite into the house. I rotate between taking bites of my muffin and drinking water while I wait for her answer.

I wouldn't be surprised if she did bring them in…

Mom's eyes widen at the realization of what bed bugs could mean. "Hmmm. I don't think so, but maybe… I'll take her to the doctor in the morning to get them to look at it closer. I really hope it isn't because it would cost thousands of dollars to get rid of them. And that's money we don't have right now."

"It's not bed bugs! I would know if bugs were in my bed," Faith pouts.

"Grace, strip all the beds of their sheets and throw them in the wash," Mom commands. "Just to be safe. I need to run to the store to get more detergent, but I'll start the washer when I get back."

"Yes ma'am," I respond obediently. "Oh, what did Sister Rebecca say our scripture focus would be this week?"

"She said this week we will be focusing on Exodus 20! The Ten Commandments," Faith answers, while staring at the bumps on her arm.

"I was asking Mom, not you," I snap.

"You didn't address her, so how was I supposed to know?" Faith meets my scornful gaze with a sly smile. "I'm just trying to be helpful."

"Girls, stop," Mom demands. "Faith is just being helpful Grace, don't be rude to her. And she is right, Sister Rebecca said to spend your quiet time this week studying the Ten Commandments, as they are listed out in Exodus 20. Now go get those bed sheets like I asked you to do."

I hung my head ashamed and walked out of the kitchen to do as she asked.

Dear Lord, please forgive me for disobeying my mother. And grant me the patience to deal with my immature sister. Amen.

After gathering all the bedsheets and placing them in the washing machine, I go back up to my bedroom to change for Church. Since I couldn't attend the morning service, I will attend the evening service.

I wonder if Megan will be there tonight...

I type a message on my phone but hesitate to press send. We hadn't spoken since our fight on Thursday and Megan didn't even come over to stay the night with me Friday like we had originally planned. I didn't want to apologize for what I said, but I did want us to go back to talking like normal. I bite my lip and impulsively press the send button.

> Are you going to Church tonight?

While I wait for her to respond, I pick out a dress and change clothes for Church. I can feel my nerves building up, wondering how Megan will respond. She could ignore me or worse still want to fight. My mind prepares for the worst while I put on makeup and fix my hair. I'm putting on my shoes when I feel my phone vibrate from an incoming text message.

> No, thank god. Mom already made me attend this morning.

I roll my eyes in annoyance and slide my phone into my purse. Maybe I'll text her back later.

She acts like it is the worst thing in the world to be a Christian... But at least she is responding to me now. I guess she isn't mad at me anymore.

Downstairs, Dad is sitting on the couch rotating between watching the evening news and looking at his family history notebook. Faith is nowhere to be seen, and Mom walks into the living room with her purse in hand.

"Are you off to Church now?" Her question is directed towards me.

"Yes ma'am. I want to go since I missed the morning service," My response startles Dad, who must not have realized I was standing behind him.

"Paul, do you have to go back to the Church tonight?" Mom turns her attention to him.

"No, not tonight. The Deacons meeting is next week, and Pastor John is doing the evening service," He explains without taking his eyes off the TV. I catch a glimpse of the news segment closing out and it looks like they were covering the Church shooting that happened in Charleston last month.

I couldn't imagine going to Church and someone coming in with a gun to shoot up the place.

"Okay, well I need to run out and grab a few things, I will be back later to cook supper," Mom informs him.

"Mhmmmm, yes, thank you, dear. Some ice cream would be nice too," Dad murmurs back.

Mom fumbles for the list in her purse, pulling it out to scribble down his request. I follow her out the front door and get into my car. I pray for a safe drive to Church, while Mom backs her car out first.

Twenty minutes later, I pulled into the almost empty parking lot. That morning, it was full of cars to the point where people would park on the sides of the road or on the grass. But the evening service is always much smaller.

I hate that I will be the only teenager here tonight, but I do enjoy being able to park right by the front door. Inside I see a small handful of people, mostly older adults who, like me, had to work that morning. One group is still in their scrubs, fresh off their nursing shift. I see them here every other week when they are working their seven on shift. When they have the seven off, they come to the morning service and dress much more appropriately for Church.

They really should be dressed better. This is the Lord's house, and we are supposed to treat it with respect and come in our very best attire...

I see an elderly couple in another pew and Police Chief Bill waves at me from the front pew where he is seated with his wife. I wave back eagerly, then continue my inspection of the sanctuary, spotting another man all by himself in the back corner. I've never seen him before and yet something about him feels vaguely familiar. His face is solemn as he stares blankly ahead, and his fingers absentmindedly play with the watch around his wrist. He looks severely depressed and sickly, as if someone sucked all the life out of him.

What a creep.

I find my usual seat, close to the front, and wait for Pastor John to start the service. A few minutes later, the music starts to play and after singing a few hymns, Pastor John walks out on the stage.

"My Brothers and Sisters in Christ! It is so wonderful to have you here with us this evening. Let us bow our heads in prayer before we begin... Our heavenly Father, we humbly come before You today to ask that You open our hearts to Your Word. That we might be receptive to it, hearing Your intentions, and applying it to our everyday lives. We thank You for sending Your Son to die on the cross for our sins, for the ones we have committed and the ones we have yet to commit. We are not perfect by any means, but through Your strength and glory, we will stand united as a people and bring others into Your light. So that they too can enjoy the promises You have made us and reunite with You in Heaven. In Jesus' Holy name I pray, Amen."

"Amen!" I yelled out with the rest of our small crowd.

"Tonight, we will focus on the importance of Life. How miraculous it is that God made us in His image and continues to bless us each and every day that we wake up. Have you ever stopped to think about that? How each organ in your body is intertwined and functions? How it is the brain that powers the other organs, so that the heart pumps the blood to the lungs, so the lungs can process the oxygen to the cells, so that the cells can carry that oxygen throughout the body to fuel the other organs like the brain? If you truly stop to think about it in detail, it really is miraculous that any of us exists at all."

He clears his throat and takes a sip of water before continuing.

"Every life is precious. In Jeremiah 1:4-6 it says, 'Before I formed you in the womb I knew you; Before you were born, I sanctified you; I ordained you a prophet to the nations'... He knew you. God knew you, each of you. From the first breath you take to your very last, to every accomplishment and failure you have throughout your life. God knew it all. He knew every moment you would struggle and every moment you prayed to Him for guidance, or forgiveness. He knew the very moment you would become saved as a Christian and be able to enter His beautiful kingdom of Heaven... Our God is so good. And just. And powerful. And merciful. It is through His grace that I am able to stand before you today and preach His Holy word."

He takes another sip of water and starts pacing across the stage.

"There is a battle that is raging in our world today. One of Good and Evil. As Christians, we have to take a stand for God and our Faith. We cannot let the evil win..."

He turns a page of his Bible at the pulpit, reads a few notes before continuing.

"We cannot let it win. Every year, thousands of women are laying with men, who are not their husbands, and are becoming pregnant.

They are then seeking out these abortion clinics, which are backed by our taxpayer dollars mind you, to kill their baby. To end that little boy or little girl's life before they have even had a chance to get it started."

I hear a gasp from the elderly woman sitting a few rows behind me.

"It is a shame. A shame that these women are living in sin. A shame that they are laying with men who are not their husbands. A shame that they are resorting to some of the evilest and most vile measures to cover up the consequences of their sins. Deuteronomy 5:17 says 'You shall not kill.' Now think about that for a moment, think about it real hard. 'You shall not kill.' It is implied that in no way, shape or form are we as human beings supposed to kill another human being. Thou shalt not kill the men, the women, or the children. And especially not the little babies that are still in the infancy of their development... I don't care what the Government or the Scientists or the Socialists tell you. Abortion is murder. Plain and simple. It violates the scriptures and is an unholy sin that should be abolished."

Someone yells out an 'Amen' in agreement.

"These things wouldn't be happening if people trusted and believed in our Lord and Savior, Jesus Christ. If they listened to His teachings and followed the Bible, these women would be able to find respectable husbands... Husbands who could care for them and provide for their family. Who could lead their family and prevent these women from turning to abortion as a means to an end. If these men were following the Bible, they too would refrain from laying with women who aren't their wives. They would not put themselves in such a position as to be tempted by sin... It is because they don't have His teachings that they are choosing to live in sin. They are all, the men and women, meek sheep, being led to slaughter by the Devil. As Christians, we must take a stand and fight back. We must tell them about Jesus, how He died on the cross for our sins, so that we can spend eternal glory in the paradise He has promised us!"

A round of 'Amens' and 'Praise Jesus' sound throughout the sanctuary.

"I challenge you to go forth into the world. To stand strong in your faith and if given the opportunity, share the good Word of Jesus Christ with others. Help as many people as you can, save as many people as you can. So that we might all be able to enjoy Heaven together."

Murmurs of agreement and even a 'Hallelujah' is heard echoing throughout the Church.

"I also want to remind you all that the Church is organizing a protest of support. If you don't already know, an abortion clinic is supposed to open in our small town tomorrow. We are gathering outside the clinic to provide support for any women who might try to seek their services and to convince them to keep their children. We will literally be saving lives tomorrow. Should you like to join, please let myself or my sweet wife, Rebecca, know and we can add you to the text message group..."

He pauses to take a sip of his water before continuing.

"Now, let us bow our heads in prayer. Dear Jesus, please come into the souls of each of us. Guide us through our daily lives, reminding us to keep to Your teachings and the scriptures please. Give us the strength to take a stand for Christianity. Give us the patience to explain Your teachings in a way so that others might be able to hear and understand them. Help us to fight against abortion. Help us to save those who desperately need saving. Help us to stand resilient, never wavering or accepting defeat. Strengthen us, oh Lord, so that we can honor Your teachings in everything we do. In Jesus' precious name we pray, Amen."

"Amen!" I yell with the others.

We sing two more songs before Pastor John ends the evening service. I grab my car keys and Bible, looking around for Sister Rebecca. I didn't see her throughout the service, but I know she is here somewhere. Pastor John never comes to Church without her. I finally spot her with Pastor John, thanking people for coming and wishing them farewell as they walk out of the Church.

I walk up and wait in line to speak with them. The elderly couple in front of me shakes their hands, with the man promising to take Pastor John to his hunting cabin when fall comes.

"Pastor John, I really enjoyed the service. It really spoke to me," I compliment him, while shaking his hand.

"That is encouraging to hear from you Grace. It is your young generation that worries me sometimes. It worries me that y'all won't be able to carry on the Christian faith," He sounds dismayed, but quickly puts a smile on his face. "But it is reassuring to hear that I can at least make sense to some people. I haven't spoken to your folks since Thursday night, how are they? Any word from Hope?"

I shake my head sadly. "No. She hasn't been back to the house, and I doubt she will come back. My parents are taking it... it's just hard to accept her condition. Like her choice to choose to live in sin like this."

Sister Rebecca reaches out to place a comforting hand on my shoulder. "It's okay to mourn your sister. She made her choice. Now all you can do is pray and hope she comes back to Jesus. Pray that she turns away from her evil ways and begs for forgiveness. One day she will realize what she has done. Have faith in the Lord, Grace. His will always prevails. He will bring her back to us, one day."

"You're right. Thank you, Sister Rebecca," I smile softly back at her.

"Are you joining us at the protest tomorrow? We plan to meet at noon," Sister Rebecca asks.

"Yes! I wouldn't miss it," I exclaim. "Pastor John is right. We have to take a stand for our faith. Because if we don't, then who will?"

Sister Rebecca smiles back at me. "You are such an obedient Christian, Grace. I pray that every teenager who walks into our Church has the same faith and dedication as you do."

I feel my face turning red with excitement, beaming with pride.

She is so nice. I do work hard to be a good Christian. To be the best Christian.

26

DR. MALICUS

"I'm so proud of you!" Ziva exclaims as she rushes across the lab to where I am. I see the excitement in her face, her eyes starting to glimmer with tears. Pulling her into an embrace, I savor the moment, not wanting to let her go.

"I did it… after all this time. Ziva, I did it!"

I knew I could figure it out. And now for the next steps…

Holding her out at arm's length, I gaze into her cold blue eyes.

"Okay dear, we have to get back to work," I say as I let her go. I start pacing my lab, thinking out loud. "With Almeta's recent arrest, it is only a matter of time before the ICO comes here to investigate…"

"Investigate? Why would they come here?" Ziva looks alarmed and scared.

I continue without even noticing her question. "…I need to have everything ready. To present to them. But there isn't enough time. I need to hide everything for now. Their investigations can be rather thorough, and I can't risk them finding my results before I'm ready…."

"Sir, why would they investigate your lab?"

"…I'm sure Dr. Kayitesi is just waiting to make a move on my solution. She has always despised how great my work is. Oh, it is going to be so great to be back in my normal lab, my real lab, with full access to everything, and–"

"WHY would the ICO investigate YOUR lab?" Ziva yells, grabbing my arm to pull me to face her.

"Ziva…" I touch the side of her face, staring into her wild, strange eyes. "Everything will be fine dear. They won't catch me. Especially not now that I have the cure. The solution."

Her eyes flicker from side to side, studying my face and not wanting to believe what I'm saying. I twirl my fingers through a stray piece of her dirty blonde hair.

"I can end our global extinction crisis. I can save the human race. Whatever wrong I have done up to this point will be forgiven when they know what I have to offer." I give her the best reassuring look I can muster.

She takes a half step back, putting distance between us.

"What have you done?" Even with her voice assistant, the words come out in a mere whisper.

"Ziva. There isn't time to discuss this. We have to work quickly now," I can feel my temper rising.

She shakes her head in disbelief and grabs her left arm at the inner elbow. "I thought you had changed your ways. I thought you had learned your lesson. I thought…"

She looks up at me, with those cold, piercing blue eyes, then walks out of the lab. I take a deep breath and run my hands through my hair.

She'll come around. Eventually… she always does.

I survey the lab around me and start barking out orders for the computer to start moving my lab to the underground bunker. I can't be too careful, especially now.

Stepping outside the lab door, I watch from the hall as everything I worked on quietly disappears below. In its place is another room, one that to any outsider looks as if it belongs in the house. It's a quiet sitting area with a big window overlooking the backyard.

I turn to walk to the kitchen when I hear it: a knock on our front door.

27

GRACE

I jerk out of my deep sleep, alarmed at the sudden yelling I am hearing. I rub my eyes a bit and scratch my arm, trying to process what I am hearing.

"FAITH! Wake up, NOW!"

I glance at my phone to see that it is 7:30 a.m.

I'm not supposed to be awake yet...

I roll my eyes and shift my head on my pillow. The sweet scent of the fresh laundry detergent fills my nose.

I love the smell of clean bed sheets.

In the hallway, I hear Faith's bedroom door open and her sleepy feet stomp down the stairs.

"What Mom?"

"Don't 'what' me. Get dressed, now! We are going to the doctor straight away. Whatever nasty rash you have, you gave it to me." Mom's infuriating voice travels up the stairs, making me cower in bed.

I guess I can wait a little longer before I eat breakfast.

I grab my phone off the nightstand at the same time it starts ringing from an incoming call. My heart leaps excitedly when I read the name: Megan.

I click to answer the call as I vaguely overhear Mom scolding Faith downstairs for contaminating her.

"Meg!" I exclaim.

"Grace! I just overheard my mom talking to yours," Megan exasper-ation transitions to disbelief. "I can't believe Uncle Paul and Aunt Joan kicked Hope out of the house. That's so horrible."

I sigh and rub the temples on the side of my head.

Why does she care?! Hope is a horrible sinner.

"Are you going to the protest today?" I ask, hoping the change of subject will save what is left of our phone call.

"What protest?" Megan asks puzzled.

"The abortion protest, remember? Sister Rebecca said we are meet-ing up at 12:00 to go."

There is a long uncomfortable pause in the conversation before Megan finally speaks up. "I am not going to that."

Seriously?

"And why not?" I ask with annoyance.

Some friend she is.

I hear a long sigh on the other end of the line. "Why would I Grace? Some women need access to abortions. We shouldn't be protesting to take that away from them. It is their body, their choice."

Their body, their choice?!

I can feel the anger that has been building up inside me starting to boil over.

"I thought you were a Christian. How can you support those whores who are willingly trying to kill their baby?" I yell into the phone.

"It is not our place to judge another person's life choices Grace,"

Megan answers defensively.

"I can't believe this. You are supposed to be a Christian. You are supposed to be my friend," I plead with her.

She has to see she's wrong in this, right?

"Grace come on. I am your friend. But even you have to admit this is getting a little out of hand, right?" She waits for me to answer, but I don't. My lips are pursed, in a ridged line and my entire body is tense.

We never used to fight this much.

"Jesus preached about love and understanding," She reasons. "Tell me where the love is when you are standing outside a healthcare clinic slut-shaming women? Calling them whores, begging them to raise a child they probably can't even afford..."

I roll my eyes at her ridiculous logic.

Maybe if they didn't spread their legs this wouldn't be an issue.

"...You say you are religious, that you care about other people, that you are 'pro-life'. Is it right to condemn that mother to a lifetime of raising a child she can't afford? Is it right to force that child to live, even if they have serious medical complications? I'll tell you right now, Christian or not, we don't have the right to tell people what they can and cannot do with their bodies. That is up to them and them alone."

"No real Christian would EVER say that!" I yell into the phone.

"A real Christian would show love and compassion, not hatred, Grace," Megan says calmly. "You need-"

Her voice cuts off as I hang up the phone.

I don't owe her an explanation... She'll go to hell for thinking that.

I check the time to see it is almost 8:00 a.m. and sigh.

I'm definitely not going back to sleep now.

I lay around in bed, browsing on my phone for a bit longer and trying to calm my nerves. I see on Instagram that Megan posted an image of beautiful flowers that spell out *'Pro-Choice is Pro-Life'* with text under the flowers saying *'Protect Women's Health'.*

I quickly scroll past it, to see the next post from a Christian page I follow with a Bible scripture on it: *'Because He lives, I can face tomorrow.'*

That's better.

I scroll again and am dismayed to see someone I follow posted a picture about the abortion clinic opening today. But I don't recognize the profile picture or the username.

Why do I follow this person?

I click to view their profile and am shocked to see who it is: Hope.

Only, it's not Hope anymore. She changed her name to Avery and her profile bio includes an assortment of rainbow and other gay appropriate emojis. I see she posted another picture and click to view it closer. It is a picture of her and Li Mei at their college with the caption: Celebrating 7 months with this cutie. So happy to be with you babe, love you! #pride

Gross.

I click back and view her latest picture about the abortion clinic opening. The caption with it is extremely long and I only read bits and pieces of it. Enough to get the gist: Hope is praising the abortion clinic for opening, how it is a step closer to healthcare rights for women and the freedom it is going to bring.

Freedom? She can't seriously think that killing babies means America is more free.

I put my phone down on the bed. Between my argument with Megan and now Hope's recent posts, it is just too much.

I feel like I am losing everyone. Is that what Pastor John meant? When he was talking about taking a stand for your faith in God?

It's too overwhelming for me to comprehend. So instead, I do the one thing I know: I pull out my Bible and read our weekly scripture that Sister Rebecca said to read. It's my quiet time with the Lord, something I look forward to because it gives me peace of mind and reassurance.

I am a good Christian. I am doing the right thing. I will just have to pray that those around me turn away from their sinful ways.

I end up reading and praying longer than I anticipated. When I finally go to the bathroom to take my medicine and get ready for the day, it is almost 11:00 a.m. While I brush my teeth, I stare at my reflection. Tangled brown hair, dull blue eyes, and wrinkled oversized T-shirt stare back at me. Then I spot something on my arm and my heart freezes: red bumps. I spit out my toothpaste and rinse my mouth with water before staring down at my actual arm, not the reflection.

You have GOT to be kidding me!!!

I see the little red bumps like Faith had on her arm. The same ones I imagine my mom has on her arm.

UGH! I have the protest at 12:00 and then work at 4:00. There isn't enough time to go to the doctor today, so I guess I'll just have to go tomorrow... I cannot believe Faith gave me her rash. What in the world did she get into?!

Back in my room, I throw on a pair of shorts that come down to my knees, a clean T-shirt, and sneakers. I grab a clean uniform and throw it into my bag for later. I have no idea how long I will be at the protest, and I want to be prepared to go to work if needed.

I'm about to walk out of the house when I get a text from Sister Rebecca in the group chat. Within seconds, several more come flying in as people respond to her message or react to it. I opened the chat to read her initial text that started the conversation.

> Church bus won't crank and is in the shop for main-tenance. Everyone meet at the address below and park in the lot. We will walk over to the clinic to-gether for the protest.

I click the address, and my phone pulls up the directions. It's about halfway between my house and the Happy Mart, which will make it more convenient later if I need to go straight to work after the protest. I drive to the designated spot and am relieved to see that I am not the first one to arrive. Pastor John is waving people down as they pull up and pointing where he wants each person to park. Following his direction, I park my car and hop out to greet him.

"Grace! I'm so glad you could join us today. Come, Rebecca is over there finishing the posters now." His warm greeting is refreshing compared to how I woke up this morning. "Oh, and don't worry about your car, I have good Christian friends who own this business and said we were more than welcome to use part of their parking lot for today. They even provided fresh doughnuts! Make sure you grab one by the pack of waters." He shoos me away as the next car comes up to park.

I walk over to find Sister Rebecca, writing Bible scriptures on posters. "What do you need me to help with Sister Rebecca?"

"Grace! Thank you for coming today. We need to write Bible scrip-tures on all of these posters, as well as encouraging messages for the women," She explains and hands a marker to me. "We want to remind them that there are other options besides abortion and that we can help them."

"Does it matter what scriptures I write?" I ask as I take the sharpie from her.

"Nope! Totally up to you," Sister Rebecca encourages. "Write whichever ones you like the most and think a woman might appreciate hearing."

I get down on my hands and knees and go to work. Several Bible verses immediately come to mind, and I scribble each one on the poster boards. As people from our Church group walked up, Sister Rebecca or I would hand them a poster. I save my favorite one for last because I want that to be my poster board.

Where would we be today if Mary had killed Jesus in her womb?

When I finally finish my poster board, I stand up and look around. My heart is pounding, and my body feels energetic. There are so many people from our Church gathered in protest.

There has to be at least 30 of us here!

Pastor John gathers everyone around, says a quick prayer that our protests will be heard and then we march across the street. When we round the corner and I can finally see the clinic with my own eyes, I am astonished to see crowds of people already assembled around it. We cross the road carefully and join them, lining the sidewalk and blocking the entrance into the parking lot. We have only just arrived and already I am sweating under the scorching sun.

I should have brought a hat… at least I put on sunscreen before I left the house.

Someone, somewhere, has a guitar and microphone. They start to sing Amazing Grace and everyone joins in. I hold my sign up proudly, watching as cars drive by staring at us. One even tries to turn into the clinic, and we all stop singing. The person with the microphone starts repeating John 3:16 and we all join in the chant. I feel proud to be here, with my Church and taking a stand for my faith. I let the words pour out of me, lifting my spirit higher and feeling closer to God.

Through the crowd, I can barely make out the look of scrubs and then I catch a glimpse of the woman's face. I recognize her as one of the nurses from the evening Church service the night before.

Does she actually work here?!

She is trying to get into the lot and is honking her horn at the pro- testors to move. Instead, we move closer together, linking arms and further blocking her entrance. Frustrated, she backs her car up and drives off. A round of applause goes up and the person with the microphone congratulates us on standing strong for the Lord.

Suddenly, a round of commotion happens off to my right. I see more protestors coming to join and I get excited. I've never seen so many Christians gathered in one place outside of Church. I study the new protestors as they get closer.

Wait, they aren't with us.

The new protestors are carrying different signs. Chanting different words. Singing different songs. They are pro-choice and they look angry that we are there. I'm too short to count all the heads, but it appears that they have just as many people as we do.

They are coming in hot… like the devil.

As they get closer, I see an array of posters with genitals drawn on them. Along with the graphic images, there are a variety of slogans such as "pro-choice is pro-life" and "my body, my rights" plastered on the posters. The new protesters wiggle their way in, pushing us back to create a safe tunnel for people to walk through to the clinic.

Someone from behind me pushes forward, attempting to pass through, but ends up pushing me along with them. The two women in front of me part ways, leaving me on the edge of a small gap that has emerged between the two groups of protestors. On the other side, almost directly across from me, I spot Hope and Li Mei a few places behind their front lines.

Of course they are here protesting.

The person who pushed me continues pushing forward, and I realize it is Pastor John. Some of the protestors on both sides are engaged in a heated debate and Pastor John steps in between them. In the background, the guy with the microphone is yelling Bible scriptures into it so fast, he sounds like an auctioneer trying to sell off his prize-winning item for the day.

My arms are getting sore from holding the poster up and I let them down for just a moment. Sweat drips down the center of my back and occasionally the sunlight blinds my vision as I look around at all the people. Someone else from behind shoves me forward into the pro-choice protesters.

No, no, no, I can't touch them!

I try to stop myself from lunging forward, but that same person pushes me harder, and I lose my balance. My poster goes flying and a guy from the other side steps forward to stop me from falling. After catching my breath, I look up into his soft brown eyes for a moment before I realize he is wearing mascara, glittery eyeshadow, and a pink unicorn tank top. He appears to be a few years older than me and as he helps me up, he yells "are you okay?"

"Yeah!" I yell as I stumble back to my group away from his sinful grasp. He gives me a sad smile. As if he knows something about me that I don't realize yet.

I look around me, seeing the mob of angry people on both sides. Total strangers, yelling at one another. Pastor John is holding his arms out, trying to stop a fight from happening. I'm in the middle of it all and smaller than most of the adults present. I could easily be knocked down or lost in the crowd. I don't even have my poster anymore to wave around and show people I am here. Suddenly, I'm scared and full of doubt.

I wish I hadn't come... Lord give me the strength to see this through.

I hear a scream and jerk my head to see Pastor John staggering backwards with blood spewing from his nose. The two people he tried to stop fighting are going at it. Down the street, I hear a police siren and catch glimpses of the car's lights between the crowd of people as it moves closer.

I'm looking around at the chaotic scene in disbelief and my fingers grasp the cross on my necklace.

Is this really what it means? To be a Christian?

I turn to face the pro-choice protestors and see Hope's purple hair bobbing up and down. She's pushing her way through the crowd, trying to get to me.

"Grace! Grace!" is what I believe she is yelling, but I can't hear her over all the other screams. Another fight breaks out on the other side, and I get shoved to the ground as people try to run away.

Fear consumes me as I try to push myself up. Another person trips over me and sends me crashing back down. I try to shove myself up again and this time I see Hope's hand stretching out towards me. I grab it and she pulls me up with a strength I didn't know she had.

"GRACE! What are you doing here?? Are you okay?!" She exclaims, as she looks me up and down for injuries.

Oh, don't act like you care about me now sister.

"I could ask you the same thing!" I snap, jerking my hand back from her. She shrinks back, hurt.

"How could you?!" I yell at her.

"Grace, what are you–" She stammers.

"HOW could you tear our family apart?" I am screaming at her, even though she is close enough to me that she could hear me without my raised voice. "How could you just walk away from us, from your faith, from God?! How could you just be gay?!"

She winces at my words yet lifts her chin with determination to hold her ground. "Grace, that life is not for me. I don't believe in it. I never have. I just did what I had to do to please Mom and Dad. I—"

"No. NO! I refuse to believe that. I saw you, growing up, I SAW you. At every Sunday service, at every Easter play and Christmas parade. You used to love Jesus," I argue back.

"No, Grace. I am telling you right now, I didn't believe any of it. I never have. And I've always been gay. I just never knew how to express it and myself. I never felt comfortable," She explains coolly.

More police cars show up and officers with barricades work their way through the middle to separate the protestors.

"Grace, come on," Hope holds out her hand. "Come with us and we will help you get to your car. You shouldn't be here."

"You don't get to tell me what to do! It is my right to be here. My religion, my faith, my mission," I yell back.

"You have the right to be here and yet you think other women don't have the right to go into that clinic for an abortion?" Hope retorts.

I open my mouth to respond back, but a police officer pushes his way between us to set up the barricade. Another officer follows, setting up a second one next to it. Hope takes a step back towards the pro-choice group and I take a step back towards the pro-life group.

"I'm here to represent the Christian faith. The will and testament of Jesus Christ. I am trying to save those babies from dying. To save those women from committing the ultimate sin and going to hell," I hiss back while leaning on the barricade, making sure she hears every word I say.

"I thought Jesus gave his life to forgive us of all our sins? Hmm? It only takes one sin to stop you from going to 'heaven' Grace. By that logic, all sins are equal. There is no sin better or worse than others," She states matter of fact. "What a blessing it must be, to believe in your faith so much that you ignore all reason and logic. Because if you did open your mind to it, for even just one idea, it would completely shatter the fake reality you have created for yourself to thrive in."

I stare back at Hope in disbelief. Before I can respond, the officers line up behind the barricades, two to each one. They pick up the barricades and push the groups further apart. I step back with the Christians, distancing myself further from Hope. This continues until neither group blocks the parking lot entrance.

She is going to spend an eternity in hell and there is nothing I can do to save her.

I turn my attention back to the rest of the pro-life protesters and see Sister Rebecca fussing over Pastor John on the edge of the group. His nose is still bleeding profusely and someone hands him a wad of napkins. A few other people are beaten up with bruises, but overall, no one is seriously hurt or in need of an ambulance.

I turned around to see how many of their protesters were injured and see the nurse in her car driving between the barricades. She looks at us in disgust before pulling into the parking lot to park her car. When she steps out, someone throws a tomato at her and screams. A police officer yells at the guy who threw it and the nurse rushes to get inside the safety of the clinic.

Sister Rebecca yells trying to gather everyone from our Church together. Once we are all together, she helps Pastor John get up and we walk away in defeated silence. Back at the parking lot with our cars, Pastor John pushes his bloody napkins aside to thank everyone for coming.

"Today might have been a loss, but it is not a complete one. Because now they know we are here, they know we will not stand meekly by and let this corruption in our city. We will keep trying my Brothers and Sisters, and one day we will eradicate this evil from our beloved country."

28

AVERY

(HOPE)

"Okay people, clear out!" The police officer yells.

"Ho-I mean, Avery, come on," Li Mei tugs at my arm.

I follow her lead in disbelief, my body floating along and my mind trying to process everything that just happened.

Grace was here. At the rally.

Of all the places?!

She was here and she was very upset with me, blaming me for ruining the family. For being gay.

But she looked so hurt too. And upset. As if she cared about me, for once.

The police officers stand guard by the barriers, watching the crowd carefully on either side. A few other officers stand between the crowd and the clinic, yelling out for people to go home. I can see the pro-life Christians hanging their heads in shame as they walk away defeated.

On our side of the barrier though, everyone is smiling, and cheers ring out as we shuffle away from the clinic.

Out of the corner of my eye, I see Megan approach us and yell out "What did I miss?"

"A whole bunch of shit," I mumble.

"We have to go-" Li Mei starts but is interrupted as a police officer's voice rings out through a megaphone.

"Go home now! This is your final warning. Anyone who is still lingering around will be arrested for loitering."

"Well damn, I missed the whole thing," Megan pouts.

"Quick, let's get a pic," Li Mei suggests as she steps forward to avoid someone. "Then it will look like you were here for the rally."

Megan pulls out her phone quickly and taps the shoulder of a guy who is standing near us. When he turns around, it is immediately obvious that he is gay: he has on a hot pink unicorn tank top, knee-length shorts that were cut off from a previous pair of jeans, rainbow-colored nails, and glittery eyeshadow.

And to think I was worried about looking gay.

I chuckle softly and turn towards Li Mei, wrapping my arm around her lower back. Megan gets on her other side, and we all look at the phone to smile.

"Alright ladies!" He sings out, as he lowers the phone and hands it back to Megan. "I took a ton of photos, so you will have options to choose from."

"Thank you so much!" Megan answers gratefully, grabbing her phone. "Hey, I really like your eyeshadow. It looks freaking gorgeous!"

"Aww thanks girl," He answers back, pretending to flip his hair. "It took me all morning to perfect. I couldn't show up here and let those bitches think I'm anything less than fabulous."

We all laughed at his comment until a dark shadow loomed over us. I turn to see a tall police officer glaring down, his lips twitching his blonde mustache and green eyes piercing daggers at us. His uniform is tight across his chest and arms, as if he intentionally asked for it to be a size smaller. Dread consumes me as I recognize who he is:

Tucker Wood.

Ugh, I haven't seen him since high school graduation...

"You won't be laughing so much when I arrest you for loitering," his rough voice threatens.

Oh good, he doesn't recognize who I am. I wasn't ready for a reunion yet anyway.

"Calm down, we are going," our photographer friend snaps back. "Don't get your panties in a wad Tucker."

"I'm this close to arresting you, Ethan," Tucker threatens.

Ethan? Maybe he was a few grades above us in school... I don't recognize him at all. And he doesn't look like an Ethan either.

"Ew, that's not even my name anymore," Ethan-not Ethan says with disgust.

Now Tucker looks him up and down.

I don't like the way he is looking at him.

"I always knew you were a faggot," Tucker sneers back.

Li Mei gasps and Megan mumbles "what the fuck" under her breath.

"What the hell is wrong with you?" I yell loudly, stepping closer to Tucker and catching him off guard as he backs up.

Who does he think he is?!

"It's fine, let's get out of here," Ethan-not-Ethan says, turning away from Tucker.

"You better watch your mouth girl," Tucker spits the words out with hatred. "You're speaking to a police officer."

"Oh please Tucker! Everyone knows you're just a washed-up jock who peaked in high school and couldn't handle becoming an adult.

So, you settled on the easiest occupation you could find that would allow you to assert power over others," Ethan-not-Ethan snaps with defiance over his shoulder.

The comment must hit a nerve, because Tucker's face turns red and his eyes start to bulge. I catch my breath when I notice Tucker's right hand move on top of his gun.

Shit, is he about to pull his gun on us?

He uses his left hand to point into Ethan-not-Ethan's face.

"You always were a little shit Ethan-"

"TUCKER!" A loud, angry voice booms out.

We watch Tucker's red face as it immediately fades to white fear.

"Tucker let them leave already before you create more trouble for us to clean up," The voice yells out.

That voice sounds so familiar…

Tucker gives us one last glare before stalking away. I watch him weave through the last few stragglers and approach another police officer, who immediately starts yelling at him. The bulky muscles and silvery hair look strangely familiar, then it hits me.

That's Police Chief Bill! I knew his voice sounded familiar.

Growing up, I had seen him at our church several times with his own family. He was a tall, quiet man, very reserved and had always been nice to us. We always enjoyed seeing him and hearing about his police officer stories. I had never so much as heard him say a negative word to anyone, much less raise his voice. To see him outraged and yelling at Tucker right now is quite a surprise.

"We need to go," Li Mei says as she grabs my arm and gently pulls me along.

The crowd of people has almost vanished, and the people left behind are the ones who were hurt when the fighting broke out.

We walk away from the clinic to cross the street towards our cars. It's not until we step up on the sidewalk that I realize our new friend, Ethan-not-Ethan is gone.

"What are y'all going to do for the rest of the day?" Megan asks.

"We are supposed to meet Faith for ice cream, but I think I'm going to bail on her," I answer nonchalantly, stepping around a small tree outside one of the stores.

"What, why?" Li Mei asks confused.

"I just don't feel like it," I remark, looking away. I pause and scratch my arm before turning back to Megan to explain further. "Grace came to the rally today and we kinda got into a fight."

She doesn't need to know that Grace blamed me for tearing the family apart...

"Oh, no. I'm sorry to hear that," Megan says sympathetically. "She's been in a mood lately, we were arguing on the phone this morning."

"About what?" Li Mei asks curiously.

Megan gives Li Mei a knowing look. "She was upset I didn't want to attend her little 'protest' today. And now that it has ended early, I have no idea what I'm going to do now."

Am I selfish? For choosing to be who I am? Who I've always known I am?

"Honestly, I just want to go back home and sleep. This day has been exhausting," I say quickly to prevent Megan from trying to get us to hang out longer. My answer disappoints her, so I offer an alternative solution. "I can let you know the next time we come to town though?"

I can't handle anything else today.

"Sure, that's totally fine. I understand," Megan nods her head supportively before stopping next to a car. "This is my car right here. Take care and I'll see you around!"

"See ya Meg," I call out.

"Bye Megan!" Li Mei yells after her.

I grab Li Mei's hand and gently nudge her to follow me. "Come on, let's get out of here."

We climb into my hot Subaru, and I crank it quickly to roll down the windows. I hand my phone to Li Mei, silently indicating that I want her to pick out the music. She shuffles through the playlist while I back up the car and pull out into the street.

Music starts to play softly, and Li Mei continues to scroll on my phone for a moment before setting it down.

"You know, you can't help people who don't want to be saved," Li Mei says quietly.

"What do you mean?"

"Your sister. Grace. If she wants to continue to create her own problems, then there is nothing you can do to help her," Li Mei explains. "Same thing for your parents. I know you still love them all, as you should. They are your family."

"They *were* my family," I correct her.

"No, they ARE your family," she says firmly. "Angry words don't change the fact that they are your family. The ones who loved you and raised you. And you can still love them and miss them while recognizing that you want to live a different life."

I look out the window and press my lips together. When I don't answer her, she continues.

"You did nothing wrong, Avery. In the short time that I've known you, it has been wonderful to watch you embrace your sexuality and your love for me. I wouldn't trade that for anything in the world."

She puts her hand on my thigh and rubs it softly. I shift my body a bit, so my left hand can take control of the wheel, and my right hand can rest on top of hers.

"I'm scared to do this on my own," I start. "Even if we didn't see eye to eye, all my life my parents have been there for me. In their own, weirdly religious way. It's scary to break away from that."

"Is it scary-" Li Mei starts as a truck cuts us off. I slam on the breaks and swerve to not rear-end them, cussing at the stupid driver.

"What the fuck!"

The quick force of motion jerks our heads back and forth. Adrenaline surges through my body and I check all my mirrors. The horse keychain hits my leg as it swings back and forth violently from the momentum.

Is that who I think it is?

Sure enough, the truck speeds up until it is riding right next to us in the right lane.

"What the fuck is wrong with you cunt!?" Brock yells out. "You almost hit my truck!"

"What the fuck is wrong with you!?" I yell. "You did that on purpose!"

I speed up, trying to break away from him, but he is also speeding his truck up.

Is the speed limit 50 or 60 through here? I can't remember.

"Avery -"

"No I didn't! You stupid ass lesbian whores don't know how to drive!" He taunts.

"No, you learn how to drive! You stupid inbred redneck!" I scream back.

The speedometer creeps over 60 and towards 65 as we both continue to race down the street.

I can't let him get back in front of me... He will try to brake check me again and then we really will wreck.

"Avery!"

"If you think that is redneck, you haven't seen nothing yet! Wait until I get my hands on your stupid bitch ass!" Brock threatens. "Then you'll wish your gay ass had never been born!"

"Now you want to threaten me?!" I scoff. "You dumbass motherf-"

"HOPE!" Li Mei screams, shaking my arm. "Enough! Stop arguing with him. Roll up the windows and drive somewhere else."

I roll my eyes, slow down driving and take the first left hand turn I can find.

"Why must you argue with everyone?!" Li Mei yells exasperated.

I don't argue with everyone.

"You do realize he could have killed us, right?" I snap defensively. "He is the one who pulled out in front of us. He is the one who intentionally braked. Fucking moron."

I continue driving through the neighborhood, until we loop back to the main road.

"And you were the one who yelled back at him in the Happy Mart parking lot," Li Mei snaps.

"Yeah, another time he almost hit us!" I yell. "I fucking hate this country and all these so called christians and conservatives. They are ruining everything and it's a shame they are allowed to walk around."

I turn the Subaru on to the interstate and slam on the gas. The Subaru speeds up quickly, matching my rising anger.

"That is so hypocritical of you. To demand freedom to be yourself but want to take it away from others just because they believe something different from you," Li Mei scolds. "And I can't believe you would seriously wish harm to another person just because they are different."

"There should be an exception! They are all stupid and ignorant and trying to push their stupid bullshit religion onto everyone," I yell back.

The Subaru is flying down the interstate now and I am weaving around cars to get to campus quicker.

"I didn't see him throwing a bible at you," Li Mei snaps back.

"He only did that to me because I'm gay!" I yell.

How can she be so blind to this?!

"You need to let it go. Stop getting so angry over the smallest things," She states matter-of-fact. "You are holding onto your anger and resentment from your parents and projecting it onto other people. It's making you more miserable to be around."

"Oh, so now I'm miserable to be around?!" I yell back incredulously. "What the fuck Li Mei? He almost caused a wreck, and you want to lecture me?!"

She can't be serious right now.

"I didn't mean it like that," she says defensively. "But it never fails, any time we go anywhere, you get mad and want to start a fight with someone. Like you have something to prove or some anger to unleash. It is infuriating and embarrassing. You have got to stop-"

"If I'm so bad to be around, then why don't you just leave?" I yell.

"For fuck's sake Hope, please slow down before you get us killed,"

Li Mei complains. "You're almost going 100!"

I pause to look at the speedometer, not even realizing that after getting on the interstate I had only continued to press the gas pedal deeper. I pull my foot off the pedal and let the Subaru slow down to 75 before putting on the cruise control.

For the rest of the drive, we ride in silence. Neither one of us daring to bring up the words we said nor offering an apology.

When I finally pull into the parking deck and find a spot, Li Mei jumps out of my car and slams the door hard. She storms off to the dorm building, not bothering to wait for me or check on me.

"Fucking great," I mumble to myself.

I hang my head down and stare at the floor of my car.

So much for creating my own family... I'm pretty sure I just destroyed any chance of that happening with her.

My eyes start to water and I let the tears flow freely.

I'm trying so hard to be strong, but I'm not sure how much longer I can keep it up.

29

GRACE

"GRACE! Where have you been? Did you go to that protest at the abortion clinic? Are you okay? I heard on the news a fight broke out and people got hurt!" She is rattling off the questions faster than I can answer them.

I sit the phone on my lap so I can switch to driving with my dominant hand. I pick it back up to answer her questions.

"Yes, Mom. I went but I'm fine. I didn't get hurt or into a fight. Someone did punch Pastor John in the face though. And a few people got some bruises, but overall, we are all okay."

She breathes a sigh of relief. "Thank God! Every time you didn't answer the phone, I prayed that He would keep you safe. Praise the Lord!"

"I'm fine Mom, but I'm on my way to work now. I have to be there at 4:00 and stay until closing. I'll be home later tonight."

"Okay sweetie be careful. I love you!"

"I love you too Mom. Bye." I click to hang up the call and just in time as I pull into the parking lot. I grab my bag and walk into the store, heading for the bathroom so I can change clothes. Debra immediately greets me as I enter. I wave to acknowledge her but continue on to my destination. Finding the rundown hallway at the back of the store, I begin to pass the office door but pause. Peeking through the door, I see Don sitting in his chair, injecting a needle into his arm.

Is he doing drugs?!

I hear footsteps approaching from behind and scurry off to the re-stroom. While I am in the stall changing my clothes, I hear another woman come into the restroom. The water faucet is turned on, and it sounds like she is washing her hands. I stuff my other clothes back into my bag and exit the stall to check my reflection, only to see that the other woman in the restroom is Debra.

Surely her shift is over now...

"It's rude to spy on people, Grace," Her cool voice echoes throughout the bathroom and she watches me in the mirror.

"Well maybe he shouldn't do drugs. It is no wonder he has worked the same job for over 30 years. This is the best he could do with his pathetic life," I snap back.

"Now you listen here young lady." Her voice changes to a stern scolding, and she turns to face me. "You're speaking about things that are quite frankly, none of your business. You need to stop turn-ing your nose up at people and start looking on them with com-passion, like that Bible you read says you should. I've seen the way you've looked down at the people who walk in this store, and more importantly Don. You have no idea what he has gone through in his life, and it is honestly a miracle that he is still here."

"I didn't–"

"You didn't what? Didn't know? Didn't mean to be rude?" She muses over her words. "The poor man has crippling diabetes. He has to take insulin shots several times a day. He first found out about it several years ago and his wife at the time couldn't handle it. She couldn't handle how expensive his medications are, how his med-ical condition affects his daily life, or how he had to adjust the foods he eats. How it makes him gain weight and sucks the energy out of him to do anything else. One day he came home to see a note on the fridge - she cleaned out everything in their little 2-bedroom house and took off with it. Even took their son with her. That was over 20 years ago, and he has yet to find her. He became so severely depressed from it, he's been a shadow of a ghost ever since."

"I'm sorry–"

"Don't tell it to me. Tell it to him. You might laugh and mock him for taking pride in this small-town grocery store, but for that sweet man, this is all he has left in the world. This job is the only thing that keeps him getting out of the bed each morning," She stares me down, letting the words sink in. Then she walks around me to open the restroom door.

"I'm going to give you one last bit of advice Grace – you need to stop judging people so harshly. You have no idea what some people are dealing with or the types of decisions they had to make because of where life put them... Sometimes, it's all a person can do to get through the day and try again tomorrow. But not everyone will get that chance. Some people will go home tonight with dark thoughts in their head that prevent them from waking up tomorrow. And I can promise, you never want to find out that you are the reason those dark thoughts happened...Now go on and clock in. You're probably late for your shift."

I walk past her in silence and enter the empty office room. I set my bag in its usual cubby hole and catch a glimpse of Don on the cameras. He is bending down to pick up some food boxes that fell on the floor. He struggles to grab the boxes and stand up with them in his hands. Normally I would have laughed at the sight of it, but now I just feel pity and sorrow.

Debra is right. That wasn't very Christian like of me.

I exit the office and walk to the front of the store to bag for Julie. Unlike Debra, Julie doesn't talk to anyone unless they speak to her first and even though I have worked at the Happy Mart all summer, I had yet to see her smile. By this point I am convinced she is incapable of smiling at all. Her hair is much longer than Debra's and always pulled back into a low ponytail. She usually smells like minty gum and wears a mismatched assortment of necklaces, bracelets, and rings. I think back on what Debra said.

Maybe there is something else going on in Julie's life that causes her to be so sour all the time.

I smile at Julie the few times we make eye contact. She never once returns the smile though. After a while, the evening rush is over and Don walks up to tell me what aisle he wants me to restock tonight. I obey his command without objecting and even line up all the little cans and boxes up exactly how he wants them. It actually takes more time than I thought it would and soon enough he is locking the doors. Julie rounds the corner and waves me down.

"Don said it's time for you to go home. You have a lot of hours from this past pay period and he doesn't want you to work more than the 18 required," She informs me.

I nod my head in response and push the food cart I had to the restock room in the back. In the office, I grab my timecard and punch out. For a brief moment, I scanned the camera screens, trying to see where Don is in the store. Finally, I spot him at the front of the store grabbing the cash drawers from the registers. He disappears into the front office.

He'll be in there for a while counting the money and putting it away… I could just apologize to him on my next shift. Yeah, I'll do that.

I grab my bag, and head to the front of the store, where Julie is cleaning up while she waits for me. She turns the lock so I can slip out and she goes back to closing up the Happy Mart. I drive home in silence, pondering everything that happened today.

I can't wait to get home and go to sleep.

I pull into my usual parking spot at the house, quietly open the front door, and proceed upstairs. My arm itches and I briefly scratch it before remembering that Faith gave me her rash.

Ugh, I bet it has gotten worse.

I see my reflection in the mirror and am pleasantly surprised that the rash has not gotten worse yet. After a fresh shower, I put new ointment and a bandage around the little bumps to help it heal. I walk downstairs to get a cup of water and pull my phone out of my pocket. On Instagram, I see that Hope posted another picture from the protest today and tagged Li Mei and someone else. I look closer at the picture and recognize Megan.

She was there? But I didn't see her with us!

I stare at the picture harder, looking in the background and trying to pinpoint where exactly Megan was and why she was with the pro-choice protesters.

She must have shown up after we left... I can't imagine Aunt Sharon would be happy to know that she was on the wrong side at the protest.

I replay our argument from earlier and wondered how I could ever talk to her again.

I don't want to lose her as a friend. But I don't want to lose my faith either.

The holidays between our families were awkward enough now that Grandma had passed away and Aunt Sharon was divorcing Megan's dad. I decide to respond later and slide the phone into my pocket. After refilling my glass of water, I retreat up to my bedroom. I take a final sip of water, then take off my necklace. The silver cross glistens in the moonlight, reminding me of every sacrifice Jesus made for us.

I guess the protest today was nothing compared to being crucified on a cross.

The thought sits with me as I climb into bed, but exhaustion quickly consumes me, and I fall asleep before my head even hits the pillow.

30

AVERY

(HOPE)

My stomach growls as I wait in line at the campus café. In my pocket, my hand traces the familiar outline of the horse keychain Li Mei gave me. My shoulders feel heavy, and my chest tightens at the last words I said to her. A pain erupts in my chest, and I wish I could go back to the day she gave me the keychain. When we were both happy and together.

I glance around the café in a haze, incapable of absorbing what I see. My body feels numb and hollow, as I wait patiently in line.

I'm so glad this place is almost empty tonight.

I'm pretty sure my eyes are still red and puffy. Even though it's still 95 degrees outside, I am wearing sweatpants and a hoodie. I wanted something comforting to wear and difficult for people to recognize me because I am not in the mood to socialize.

After crying in my car for an hour, I finally made my way back to the dorm, but Li Mei was gone. I moped around and watched a few TV shows before finally coming to get food.

Now, I stare blankly at the food options before me: chicken parmesan, pizza, a hamburger, and Thai wraps.

Thai wraps… That was what we both ate for our first campus café date.

I smile bitterly as the memory swarms my brain, taunting me with the happiness I used to feel. I'm not even sure if we are still dating or not and I hadn't seen Li Mei since she stormed off.

I wish she were here with me.

My heart aches with a physical pain I've never felt before.

I really am alone now.

I grab two of the Thai wraps to take back to my dorm. Outside, the sun starts to set, and some students are laughing as they play a game of soccer.

I'm halfway back to my dorm building when I hear footsteps from behind. I freeze and slowly glance over my shoulder.

Oh, it's just students.

I relax as I realize it is two students I have seen frequently on campus before. Coffee cups in hand, the students are in a deep conversation about the upcoming fall semester and the engineering courses they will be taking. I continue walking and eventually make it back to my dorm room. Inside, I see Saanvi studying quietly on the couch. Her dark tan skin looks darker in the white V-neck she is wearing and her long black hair is pulled up into a messy bun on the top of her head. She doesn't bother to look up or speak to me as I walk in and grab a bottled water from the fridge.

When I walk into our shared bedroom space, I peak in Li Mei's room to see that she is still gone. Disappointed, I go into my bedroom and shut the door. I sit on the bed, eating my Thai wraps in silence and watching the TV show I had started earlier.

After eating, I throw the wrappers across the room, trying to ring the garbage can. The first wrapper makes it in, but the second wrapper hits the top and falls on the floor. I stare at it for a moment, then turn my attention back to the TV.

I'll pick it up later.

I watch in silence, occasionally scrolling through my phone to see if Li Mei posted anything online. Each time I checked, I was disappointed again. She hadn't posted anything recently.

Five lengthy episodes later, I am struggling to stay awake and decide it's time to turn off the TV. I make a quick trip to the bathroom and check once again to see if Li Mei is back. Her bedroom is still empty and lifeless.

Where could she have gone?

I return to bed and plug my phone in to charge. Crawling under the covers, I put the lanyard with my horse keychain around my neck and shift the pillows around to create a makeshift body in the bed. I pull the blankets tightly, wrapping one arm around the fake body and using the other to stroke my horse keychain.

I don't recall falling asleep or when my dreams begin. It's a variety of mismatched scenes that my brain has recreated. None of it makes sense and I'm not even sure what it is I am dreaming of when it starts to feel cold.

Suddenly, a hand jerks my body out of my dorm bed and my eyes fly open. In my sleepy haze, I can barely make out the shadow of a person when a cold mist hits my face. I feel rough hands pick me up and I catch a glimpse of the Thai wrapper I forgot to throw away before my world turns black.

31

DR. MALICUS

"Hello Dr. Xaun! What a lovely surprise, I didn't think you would be coming back to visit so soon." Normally I would struggle to make my greeting sound pleasurable. But with the recent discovery of the cure, I am bursting with happiness.

"Ahem, yes. I didn't expect to be back so soon either." He shifts uncomfortably and just enough for me to see two other people standing behind him. "Dr. Malicus, as I'm sure you may already know, the ICO recently arrested Ms. Almeta Caprae for interfering with a global investigation. As such, we have a warrant to search your home for the missing organ reactor we have been looking for, as well as any communication you have had with Ms. Caprae."

He shoves the paper forward, into my hand.

"Of course, come on in. I'm afraid I don't have what you are looking for, but you are welcome to search to document it for the investigation." I smile and step back, waving him in.

"Thank you Dr. Malicus, we appreciate your cooperation." Dr. Xaun steps in and motions with his head for the other two men to begin their search. They each pull out of their pocket a tiny device. I've seen them before, when Ziva's team first worked on them over a decade ago: micro scanners.

Each device will fly around to each room, scanning the room in its entirety and providing an in-depth three-dimensional view of it. The scanners can identify over 1,000 foreign objects, penetrate the thickest of walls and show every microscopic molecule underneath.

But it can't penetrate the strongest metal on Earth: Tungsten.

When Ziva and I first designed this home, it was with the intention of being a safe house. We lived in the city, within walking distance of our labs and had no need to be anywhere else. But I was paranoid that we might one day need a backup place to go to, somewhere safe to hide.

Ziva liked the idea of being in the country because the fresh air helped her mechanically inclined mind to slow down and think better. We equipped the house with everything we could possibly need. So that, in the event we were investigated, we couldn't be caught.

I just need a little more time to finalize my research. And then we can move back to our true home.

"Dr. Malicus?" Dr. Xaun's question pulls me out of my deep thoughts.

"Mhmm?" I answer as I turn to him.

"I was asking you how your wife has been. Where is she?" Dr. Xaun tries to keep his tone calm, but there is an undertone I don't like.

Such a skeptic.

"Ziva is just around the corner, probably putting another puzzle together. Come, I will show you the way." I reassured him, motioning with my hand for him to follow. He hesitates a moment before following in silence.

This is an awkward silence.

"Here she is." I wave my hand to encourage Dr. Xaun to walk into the room. Ziva is sitting in her usual spot, putting a puzzle together. Her dirty blonde hair is lazily hanging down over her shoulders and she is sitting in a tight ball on the floor. "Ziva dear, come say hello to Dr. Xaun."

Gleefully, she jumps up and practically dances across the room to say hello to Dr. Xaun. She signs with her hands, and I interpret for her.

"She says it is wonderful to see you again, Dr. Xaun. She apologizes for not having her voice assistant on at the moment, and if you will allow her to, she will go grab it, so she can communicate directly with you."

Something feels off.

"There's no need. We are almost done with our search here." He smiles softly at her. "My, you do have beautiful eyes. I don't remember them being so bright... and blue."

Does he know...?

She smiles and signs back quickly. "She says thank you sir, that is most kind of you."

Dr. Xaun's watch beeps with what must be a message from the other men.

"Ah, I believe my men are done now. It was lovely to see you again Ziva." Dr. Xaun shakes her hand and turns to me. "Can you step outside with us for a moment please?"

"Of course, Dr. Xaun," I answer politely and wave my hand in the direction we need to go to the front door. Ziva waves goodbye and returns to her puzzle.

Once again, I lead the way in silence down the dark hallway. We round the last corner, where we can see the edge of the front door at the end of the hall when Dr. Xaun whispers, "I know what you are doing Iacobus."

There is no way they found it. Impossible.

My blood runs cold as goose bumps go down my body and I slowly turn around to face him. "I'm not sure I know what you are referring to, Hai."

"Cordelia believes there is still hope for you. Even after all your...

transgressions," Dr. Xaun says coolly, eying me up and down. "I'm not buying your bullshit. We might not have found anything in this search, but I will find out the truth."

Anger flashes in his eyes and I let his threat hover in the air between us for a moment.

"I don't know what you are accusing me of, Hai. But false accusations are a serious crime that the ICO does not take lightly." I smile coyly back. "I am a hard-working scientist, who is trying to save our species from extinction. At the end of the day, the ICO will prioritize results over process. Every. Single. Time. No matter what it takes to get them... Now tell me, how has it been working with Dr. Kayitesi?"

"What do you–" He stammers.

"Oh, you know exactly what I mean," I interject. "She took over the project after I left and I read the daily ICO press releases. I know she awarded you with a significant position on her team, that will look quite impressive on your resume. Especially with your background I might add." Now it is my turn to eye him up and down.

"I have worked hard to get here–" He starts.

"No less hard than I have, I'm sure." I glare back at him, daring him to say another word. "Now, I do believe you have overstayed your welcome."

His eyes dart back at me. "Enjoy your freedom for now, Iacobus. We will be back."

He storms down the hall, speaks briefly to his men and walks out the front door. I follow behind, shutting the door as soon as they are outside.

It's fine. I still have time. To compile my findings, my progress, my success. He can come back all he wants, I'll be ready.

I hear the soft whooshing sound of Dr. Xaun leaving and immediately sprint back to my lab. I can't risk reassembling it, so instead I access the secret stair passage that is hidden behind the wall. Once inside, I pull up the reports and analyze them. The gene sequence is successful, and the embryos are developing as they should.

Now I just need to–

The sound of glass crashing fills the silent lab from behind me. I roll my eyes in annoyance.

Not again. She has got to stop doing this.

32

GRACE

I jolt awake from the sudden sound of glass crashing. Blinking my eyes slowly, I take in the room around me. It is still a little dark and I'm not sure what time it is, but it feels really early in the morning. I hear a raised voice in the distance, one that sounds all too similar to Hope.

Why is Hope back home again?

My eyes adjust to the darkness, and I look around in confusion. This isn't my bedroom. Panic starts to consume me as I recognize the bland medical room from my nightmares. The plain walls, where there is no door or window to be seen. The stiff bed shoved in the corner with the scratchy sheets.

It's just a dream. Wake up Grace, it is just a dream.

Only this time, it doesn't feel like a dream. It feels very real. My breath is coming out in shallow whisps, but I force myself to sit up in bed. Groggily, my arms struggle to push up my heavy body and the room spins as I try to find my center of gravity. My bare feet hit the cold floor and shock ripples through my body, clearing my vision.

This is not a dream. This is very, very real.

My whole body is shaking as I struggle to stand up. I feel light-headed, limp, and speechless. When I finally do stand, lights from overhead slowly turn on. The room looks like something out of a horror movie, where they would keep psychiatric patients in a straight jacket. I shiver at the thought and am momentarily relieved I am not in a straight jacket. My fingers reach up to grasp for my cross necklace and pat my empty neck.

That's right. I took it off before I went to bed... I really wish I had it right now.

I look down and see that I'm still in my pajama pants and t-shirt from the night before. My hair is still braided, and my nails are still painted in a soft pink color, but they have grown out a lot.

I just painted my nails the other day... they can't be this long already!

Adrenaline rushes through my body, making my limbs tingle. I can't see my reflection, but I just know that something isn't right. Not just with the fact I am in a room that I have no idea how I came to be in or where I could possibly be. Something is wrong with my body. Something is... *different.*

My body feels larger. My breasts are tender, and my nipples are sore. I feel like I haven't eaten in forever, but also the thought of food makes me want to vomit. I am all too aware of the sterile stench in the room and the body odor under my armpits. And I need to pee really badly.

Yet, this doesn't feel new to me. It feels overwhelmingly familiar.

Oh God, what is happening to me?

My nose itches for a brief second before I sneeze. With the sneeze, I lose control of my bladder and a little pee drips down my leg. I pat my pajama pants on my leg to stop the pee from dripping down further. Until I know where I am and what is going on, I don't want to take my clothes off.

For all I know there are cameras looking down on me. Watching my every move.

Cautiously, I circle the perimeter of the small room.

I don't see the door... How can I get out if I can't find the door?!

Panic consumes me again and makes me forget my fear of being in the room.

I have to get out, I can't stay in here.

Frantically, I start feeling the walls, trying to find the door, a window, a vent - anything. When I can't feel anything with my hands, I start to pat the wall and listen to the vibrations.

I have to get out!

My patting gets harder and harder, until I am hitting the walls and moving all over the room. I flip my hands back and forth, between hitting with my palm and hitting with the side of my fist.

I scream out in frustration and hit the sides of my head. "Wake up Grace, wake up, wake up, WAKE UP!"

Tears start to build up in my eyes as the realization sets in. Someone took me from my home. Without my knowledge. Without my permission.

And the worst part... this isn't the first time it has happened.

33

DR. MALICUS

I walk into the cloning section of my lab, checking on each of the test subjects. I see 21AP17 is waking up from her medical-induced sleep.

Good. She will be awake for her first trimester checkup and then she can go back to sleep.

I walk past 21AN05 and 21ON03 who are still in their medical-induced sleeps. The fetuses are still growing in each of the women's bodies and this time I experimented with implanting twins to see if I can get faster results.

Afterall, two are better than one. Or so they say.

I continue down the hall and see 21ABP06 is wide awake and seething with anger. She only has a few days left in her pregnancy and needs to be awake in case her body goes into labor. I learned the hard way that the test subjects don't do well if they are still asleep when they go into labor.

I almost lost 21ABP05 from that. It would have been worth it if the fetus actually survived.

I peer through my hidden window at 21ABP06. To my surprise, she somehow managed to break one of the overhead lights. Kneeling in the middle of the floor, her purple hair is clinging to her sweaty forehead as she claws at the pieces of broken glass trying to find one sharp enough.

Oh no, you don't.

I wave my hand and press a button on the computer screen outside her room. The matter control light beams down lifting her body off the ground. Her face is full of shock, and I'm sure she wants to scream or fight, but her body is physically frozen in place. A robot appears, cleaning up the glass and clearing away anything else she could use to harm herself.

Once her room is cleaned again, the light beams gently move her feet to the ground before disappearing. She sways back and forth, reaching out for the bed to support her as her feet adjust to holding her body weight again. When she regains her balance, she screams out in frustration. I pull up the scanner to check her and the fetus's vitals.

Heartbeat is strong, vitals look good. She is progressing well. Should go into labor any day now.

21ABP06 suddenly stops yelling and cocks her head to the side. Down the hallway of the lab, I can hear the screams coming from 21AP17.

Why must they always scream?

Irritated, I wave my hand and click on the screen to mute all the test subjects' rooms. Out of the corner of my eye, I see the confusion and fear on 21ABP06's face as she realizes she can no longer hear the screams. I turn away to jog down the hall towards 21AP17.

I need to make sure she isn't trying to hurt herself too.

At the end of the hall, I approach the hidden window and watch 21AP17 from the shadows. She is screaming and banging on the walls inside her room. Her face is full of fear about her new surroundings and agony that she cannot find an escape.

I check her vitals and see that the fetus is progressing behind from where it should be for this checkup. I sigh and decide to let her stay awake for a few more hours to see if the fetus improves.

I would get faster results if I had access to the genetics enhancer in my lab.

Unfortunately, without full access to my lab, I am forced to wait the duration of each pregnancy before I will know if the fetus is viable or not.

It was convenient when I had Almeta to get these materials for me...

Even though I tested the DNA samples in my lab, it is only half the battle. The embryos were developed in test tubes but needed to be brought to life through a surrogate.

Before I left on sabbatical, we had many women volunteer for our research project. Each one was hopeful that with our assistance they could have a child. Yet our efforts were futile. There wasn't a modern solution we could create through genetic modification to prevent organ failure from occurring after birth.

The ICO was so desperate for a solution, that Cordelia sanctioned bringing back Ziva's controlled-clone project that was rejected all those years ago. It only took a handful of clones for us to realize their genetically modified DNA was even worse than ours – the clones were simply copies of our existing DNA. Not an alternative and certainly not an improvement.

After the project failed, I immediately realized that our issue spanned back generations and that a modern woman today wouldn't be able to grow the embryos. The most logical solution was to go back in time to collect live samples of DNA that could be fused with our modern DNA. It was a straightforward process to collect a blood sample from the arm and could easily go unnoticed.

My research team at the ICO was responsible for traveling back in time to collect the samples we needed to test. Another team was supposed to integrate the samples with the embryo to plant into the surrogate's body.

But after hundreds of trials, we were still unsuccessful. I had pleaded with Cordelia for months that we needed a female surrogate from a time period before genetic modification. She was appalled by the idea and refused to approve it for my project.

I did what was necessary. Everything was for the survival of our species.

I look down at my watch that Ziva gave me all those years ago and adjust it on my wrist. The engraving, '*Only the strong survive*' had become my personal motto these last few years. It is the sad reality of life.

The most painful sacrifices occur when a parent must pave the path for their children.

34

AVERY

(HOPE)

I sat on the edge of the bed, terrified. The screams echoing from down the hallway sound too familiar, triggering a hidden childhood memory.

It sounded like Grace.

A shudder runs through me at the thought.

What if that monster has her too? What if she is pregnant like me?

The thought reignites my anger and I scan the room once again to look for any way out. My mind spins, desperately searching for an escape.

What kind of sick fuck would do something like this?!

Stealing women, impregnating them against their will.

But why? Why do they need to do this to me?!

The thought had haunted me ever since I woke up and realized I was pregnant. It continued to haunt me every time I woke up in the same hellish nightmare and realized my stomach was getting larger. The realization that I am alone, fighting a battle against an enemy that I don't even know.

And I am sick and tired of being in this damn room!

The pain of being away from Li Mei and my friends has been unbearable.

Hell, I would even settle for my parents at this point... anything to indicate that I'm back home and free.

Frustration rises in my chest, and my eyes well up with tears. I hate this feeling of being caged, isolated, alone.

I choke on a sob, wiping my eyes, and focus on the broken pieces of the horse keychain in the corner. The one Li Mei gave me. It's supposed to remind me that I'm cared for, that I'm not alone, but now... it's shattered.

I groan as I slowly stand and waddle across the room to gather the pieces. I'd been relieved to find the keychain still around my neck when I first woke up, clinging to it for dear life. It was my only link to the outside world, my only reminder of Li Mei's love.

And now I've broken it...

In a frenzy of anger, I threw the heavy keychain at the overhead light. When I saw it cracked the light, I started throwing the keychain repetitively to break the glass. I wanted a weapon to protect myself or a tool I could use to cut through the wall.

If that is even possible.

I've run my hands over every inch of these walls, searching for a way out. The white walls look stronger than regular sheetrock, but not as tough as metal. Maybe—just maybe—a shard of glass could cut through it.

But then that was taken away from me too.

I don't even know who's keeping me here. I haven't seen a single person. Not one. Not since I woke up in this room that had become my prison.

I don't even know how I got here... or where I am.

After witnessing the strange lights that controlled my body and the weird mechanical robot, I am convinced I am not in my own time period.

Which is so absurd.

Time travel only exists in sci-fi movies and books. It isn't real. This can't be real.

And yet... I'm far from home. My memory is very hazy. And somehow, I've grown a whole-ass baby even though I haven't eaten solid food in what? Months?

My hand instinctively rests on my stomach as I feel a soft kick. I pause, not sure if I'm touching my belly out of instinct or because I remember Mom doing it when she was pregnant with Grace and Faith.

With a deep breath, I finally squat down to grab the pieces of the keychain, my body protesting with every movement. Sweat beads on my forehead as I stretch to reach the broken fragments. I finally managed to pick them up, but even as I hold the pieces in my hand, I know they're beyond repair.

I waddle back to the bed, sitting down with quiet defeat. My body aches, my stomach heavy with life—my life and the life inside me. The baby shifts again, and I can't help but feel the oddest sensation.

That feels so fucking weird.

Each time I wake up, my stomach is larger, and I'm overwhelmed with a variety of emotions. Exhaustion for all the energy my body still needs to grow another human being. Disgust that someone impregnated me without my consent. Fear that I am being held against my will in this nightmarish prison. And pride, that despite everything I have endured I am still alive.

And growing another life.

When I first realized I was pregnant, I didn't want to accept it. I didn't want it at all.

But you didn't ask for this any more than I did, little one.

Every time I thought I reached my breaking point, the baby would kick inside, as if to say we aren't giving up without a fight.

He, or she, is the only reason I haven't tried to kill myself by now.

In its own strange way, the baby gives me hope. That if it can survive all of this with minimal nutrition, then I can too.

I never imagined I would ever want to be pregnant, much less want to keep it.

But a part of me does want to keep it. As odd as it is, given my circumstances.

Or maybe that is just the hormones taking over.

Either way, I am stuck with it and for all the hell I have had to endure, maybe this baby could be something good. Maybe it could help start the family Li Mei wants.

Oh Li Mei.

I hate myself for not trying to find her sooner. For knowing that the last thing I said to her was ending our relationship.

I want her back… I would do anything to get her back.

But it's too late.

My stomach churns, and I take a shaky breath, trying to calm myself. I look over the bland room again, trying to distract myself from the sickness: the plain floors, white walls, and lone bed that had been my prison for who knows how long.

There's no window, no way to tell if it's morning or night. No phone. No clue what day it is.

Or the year.

The only thing I do know, for certainty, is that my due date is getting closer.

A terrifying thought.

I shove the broken keychain under my pillow and rub my aching stomach. My eye twitches and I rub it again to relieve the discomfort. I really needed to change my contacts.

Probably going to get an ulcer from how long I've worn this same pair... I wonder if they miss me? Mom, Dad, Faith, Grace, Li Mei... Does anyone even care that I'm missing? That I've been taken against my will?

They are scary thoughts, I don't want to believe could be true.

Surely someone is looking for me... right?

I remember the last time I saw my parents, at the so-called dinner they invited me to. How my dad disowned me, how my mom turned her head away.

Okay, so maybe they don't miss me. But Faith should, right?

The last time I saw her was when she gave me the birth certificate. She wanted to hang out the next day.

And I bailed on her. I made a promise, and I broke it.

All because of the argument I had with Grace.

Which somehow hurt worse than anything my parents said to me.

She was once my best friend, my sister. We were inseparable. But somewhere along the way, we grew apart. I still feel protective of her, though. I still love her.

Oh, and she's probably here too. That monster has her and there is nothing I can do to help her. Nothing I can do to save us.

My eyes fill with tears, but I blink them away.

"Okay Avery, pull yourself together," I whisper to myself. "A few more days and the baby will be here. And then..."

And then what?

The thought freezes me. I've been so focused on escaping, I haven't even thought about what happens after the baby comes.

What if this is one of those sick-ass-pedophiles who keeps women in his basement? Constantly impregnating them to produce his own offspring?

I recall a few stories and even documentaries I had watched about men doing that. Or even religious cults.

It would make sense, but the robots and futuristic technology doesn't make sense.

I don't know if it is worse to wait and not know, or to wait for what I know will come.

Both options sound terrifying and bring their own set of fears. The uncertainty of the unknown keeps me on edge, my mind racing with possibilities, while the certainty of what's to come feels like a ticking clock, each second pulling me closer to an inevitable end.

It's a paradox of hope and dread—wondering if the worst will happen or if I'm just prolonging the pain of anticipation. In the end, both choices force me to confront my own vulnerability, each whispering that I'm powerless in the face of time and fate.

Either way, I will confront the enemy head on. Because no one can fight my battles for me, and I refuse to give up.

35

GRACE

"Dear Lord, please watch over me and protect me. Deliver me from this evil place. Amen," I whisper to myself repeatedly. I can feel my lips beginning to numb and my tongue rolling in confusion.

I'm sitting on the bed with my arms wrapped around my knees and slowly rocking to the tune of my desperate prayer. I don't know when I started it. I have no idea how long I have been at it. But it is the only thing I can hold on to right now because the waiting is unbearable.

Waiting for some creepy doctor to come into the room. To poke and prod and defile me.

I start rocking again and repeating my prayer. I can't let my mind wander, I can't let it realize what is happening, I can't let it accept that this horror is real.

I need to get out of here.

I look around the bland room again. I've stared up and down the walls at least a hundred times by now, but I still can't figure out where the door is. I don't want to be caught off guard when it finally appears, so the bed in the corner seems like a safe option for now.

At one point I thought I heard footsteps approaching. I ran to the safety of the bed, begging God to spare me. But no one appeared. At least, not yet.

"Dear Lord, please send someone to save me. Please help my captors to realize that they are wrong and to return me unharmed.

Please help me. Amen."

I repeat my new prayer desperately. Pouring every bit of my strength into the words in the hope that I wake up from this awful nightmare.

I hear whirring noises coming from the other end of the room and freeze. My heart races and my palms start to sweat. I want to move back, further away from what I believe is about to be the door, but my body is paralyzed with fear.

A portion of the wall becomes semi-transparent, in the shape and height of a door frame. I hold my breath, waiting for the person to emerge. Some vile, nasty, grubby man who is overweight and likes weird porn. I don't even know what is considered "normal" porn, much less weird porn, but it fits the image in my mind.

I see two blue eyes peek into the room and the soft face of a woman in total shock.

Another woman!

I slide quickly to the edge of the bed, and she jumps back from my sudden movement.

"Who are you?" Her voice sounds odd, distorted.

Maybe the doorway isn't fully open?

"Please don't go! Help me. I don't know where I am or how I got here," I say the words faster and faster, the tears building up in my eyes. I cautiously get off the bed and step towards the doorway, hopeful that she will help me escape. "I just want to go home please, please help me get home. Help me…"

She moves closer to the doorway, placing her hand on it. A light flashes in the doorway and a loud noise answers her back. It sounds like a blaring alarm, rejecting her attempt to help me. I move closer to the doorway, my pleas fading to whispers and the tears falling harder.

My room is too bright to see her in the dark room beyond the doorway. I catch glimpses of her moving and clicking what must be a computer screen on the wall. My whispers are now sobs getting louder and louder while my whole body shakes uncontrollably.

"Shush, I will help you. But you have to be quiet, so Dr. M-Malicus doesn't hear you."

I sniffle and nod my head to communicate I will obey her.

She reappears at the door, allowing me a clearer view, and I am blown away by how beautiful she is. Her soft dirty blonde hair, bright blue eyes, a perfectly symmetrical face, and cute nose catch my attention. She is slightly taller than me with a perfectly proportioned figure.

Yet, something feels off. Her clothing is unconventional, her eyes too large, her movements too fluid, giving her an alien-like quality.

I take it all in, her whole appearance, in one brief second.

"M-my name is Zi-" She starts to say but suddenly gasps. Her eyes bulge and the right side of her body crumbles to the floor. I see the glint of a knife, the outline of the strange man and scream. Immediately the doorway disappears, and I am surrounded by my blank four walls again.

I flee back to my seat on the bed, grabbing my knees and trying to make myself as small as possible. I can't hear anything else over the pounding of my heart.

My gaze focuses on the hidden doorway, ignoring everything else around me. I don't want to be caught off guard again. I don't want to be killed. The tears start falling again as I say a new prayer.

It's so much worse than I thought... That poor woman. Oh God, please let her join you in Paradise. Please, please, please. Whatever sins she has committed, forgive them Lord, she was trying to help me. She would have helped me, she would have, she would...

36

DR. MALICUS

Ziva sets the plate down in front of me before asking, "Is everything to your liking, sir?"

I gaze at my perfectly balanced breakfast: overnight oats with chia seeds, almond milk, blueberries, and a scoop of peanut butter. Arranged perfectly in the bowl, exactly how I like it. And on the correct day of the week too.

"It is perfect, dear. Thank you." I smile back at her, and she beams in return, taking her seat beside me to eat her meal in silence. Her curly brown hair bounces with her movements and I admire her golden bronze skin. She is a little shorter now, with skinny arms and the wide hips I have missed.

She is adjusting much better now and I'm glad that horrible stutter is finally gone. That was annoying to deal with… Her skin is a little too dark, but so long as she remains out of the sunlight it should lighten with time.

I reach for my glass of water and discreetly peek into it.

Good. She didn't put the pills in it today.

I take a long sip before finishing my breakfast. Ziva silently clears the table, and I rush to my lab, eager to begin. Yesterday, 21ABP06 went into labor and birthed a male. She was now fully recovered and ready to undergo her next procedure.

I just need one more blood sample from her… then she will be ready to go back home.

I silently monitor her vitals outside her room. She is still unaware that I am standing outside looking in. Her newborn is cradled in her arms, nursing on her milk.

Good. The injection to speed up her breast milk production worked.

It still baffled me how long it took the mother's milk to arrive.

And time is a luxury I don't have right now.

I click a few options on the screen and the familiar beam of the matter control light immediately surrounds her. Frozen in place, the beam effortlessly pulls the male baby out of her arms and floats him out of the room.

Her eyes remain frozen in rage as she watches the baby leave her. The beam hoists her up, limbs outstretched, as the robotic arms appear. One to take her blood sample and another to drain her breasts of its milk. Her body is still paralyzed by the beam, preventing her from feeling any pain. The robotic arms move away, and the room fills with the sleeping gas. I watch her vitals carefully as her eyes struggle to stay open. More gas has to be pumped into the room before she finally drifts off to sleep.

She's a strong one.

Then the body modification process begins, erasing any evidence of her pregnancy and restoring her hormones to their pre-pregnancy state. It even dyes her hair back to its wretched purple color and cuts it in the pixie style she had when I first brought her to the lab. The final step is wiping the memories, which will further prolong her sleep.

Let's hope it lasts long enough for me to get her back to her own timeline, where she belongs.

The memory wipe could take up to an hour, so I wander down the hall to peek into the newborn's room. He is rocking in the cradle, lulled to sleep by the sounds of classical music.

I wish you were a girl so I could give you to my Ziva. She would really like that.

I continue down the hall, checking on the rest of my test subjects. 21AN05 and 21ON03 are in a state of hibernation, nurturing the growing embryos within them. I monitor their vitals, noting that they require a boost of growth hormone to accelerate the development of the twins.

Dammit. I didn't think about the surrogates needing more nourishment to offset the growth of two fetuses.

As I walk back to the main part of my lab, I pass 21AP17 who is curled up in a ball of fear on her bed.

Ugh. I'll deal with you later.

I roll my eyes at her theatrics and contemplate my choices.

I need results and I need them now. I can't afford to wait nine months. The ICO could have a solution by then… Time to implement plan B.

I weave through my lab equipment to the station where the cloning samples are stored. I knew this day would come when I wouldn't have Almeta to help me and would be forced to get my own resources.

She was a loyal servant, while I had her. Pity she was reckless.

Thanks to Ziva's old files for the controlled-clone project, I had everything I needed in my lab to recreate a clone. But I didn't have an ideal DNA sample I could replicate until Dr. Xaun cut his finger on that frame when he visited.

It's a good thing the ICO didn't approve her project all those years ago…

Even today, the ICO maintained strict rules against cloning projects. While the ICO tolerates cloning organs and body parts, it strictly forbids cloning an entire person. There was a fear that some people might recreate clones for military purposes or to carry out other illegal activities.

And identifying a human clone is impossible...

I punch the code into the holographic screen and wait patiently. The main part of my lab transforms from being an experimental room with tables, test tubes and equipment, to having a raised platform in the middle. The holographic screen relocates to align in front of the platform as I take a step up and move to the center of it.

I take a deep breath, close my eyes, and utter the command.

"Fortis."

Matter control lights beam around the platform, syncing to my body's movements and lifting me up in the air. The screen illuminates to show a black screen until the clone's eyes open. He is laying on a bed, staring up at the ceiling. It takes another moment before my consciousness is connected to his mind, and I jolt from the sensation.

It feels weird to do this again.

With a mental command, I direct the clone to sit up at the edge of the bed, and he immediately complies. I guide his gaze down to his wrist, where the transporter watch already contains the coordinates for his destination.

After a few clicks of the button, his surroundings blur into a spinning vortex, gradually taking shape as solid ground materializes beneath his feet. Through the screen, I see the familiar sights of our other home take shape. A bookshelf, a couch, the awards, and various accolades from our careers scattered on the wall. It's our true home where Ziva and I belong. It's where we built our entire lives, careers, our marriage. It's also a short block away from the ICO headquarters.

A longing pain erupts across my chest as I see our home again.

I have missed it more than I thought.

For a moment I wish I could trade places with him, the clone. I want to be in my home, my true home, not thousands of miles away. Glancing at the time through the clone's eyes, I see that it is almost 6:00 p.m.

I should go now. While they are all still at the conference and distracted.

Still floating in the air in my lab, I put my arm down and start walking in the direction I want the clone to go. He mirrors my movements exactly, opening a closet door to reveal a special lab bag. I make him grab the bag and walk out the front door.

With each step I take, my heart beats faster and I suddenly become overly aware of how fast I am walking. How fast the clone is walking. I slow down my pace to be more leisurely. The clone mimics the new pace as he descends the porch steps and walks toward the ICO headquarters.

One step at a time. Don't want to attract attention. Remain calm.

As he rounds the final corner to the entrance, I catch sight of the three familiar security guards standing before the security gates. The thick wrought-iron gates have a laser beam shield surrounding the entire property and preventing anyone from accessing the headquarters' campus. It's the same technology that Ziva's team designed a few years ago when the global extinction crisis started.

Perfect.

"Dr. Xaun! It's a pleasure to see you sir, are you here for the conference too?"

One of the guards calls out to the clone, awaiting my response.

While my voice rings out in empty echoes within my lab, the clone's voice answers his question in real time.

"Yes, I am and unfortunately running terribly late for it too. Dr. Kayitesi will surely have my ass if I don't get these project files to her before presentation time."

The clone hands over the bag to be scanned. The security guard looks skeptical for a moment. I can tell he wants to ask more questions, but ICO procedures forbid it. There are various levels of clearance in the ICO, and a security guard is one of the lowest. They aren't allowed to know what the projects are, what is going on with the latest developments or anything outside of what the public hears in the daily press releases. Which works to my advantage, as he takes the bag to scan it. While he is looking down, I pull a memory from the clone's mind.

"How is your wife Taraji doing?"

He looks up and his skepticism melts into a smile.

"She's been great, of course she would prefer that I'm at the house with her and the kids," He chuckles. "But I couldn't beat the extra pay for working tonight. Need it to cover all their school supplies and sporting activities. Thank you for remembering her Dr. Xaun." He pauses to wave me forward. "You know the drill."

I nod my head and move my arms into the familiar outstretched position. The clone matches my movements, and the guard moves back to start the body scan.

From Ziva's prior work, I know the security scanners will search various bodily features to ensure they match the biometrics on file for Dr. Xaun. Eyes, nose, fingers, height and even the bottom of the feet, hidden under layers of sock and shoe. Every inch of the outer body is scanned to ensure it matches the ICO's database.

But it does not scan on a molecular level.

I hold my breath for a brief moment, nervous that Dr. Xaun is already on campus and that I'm about to trigger some alarm. Instead, the security guard waves me through and hands the bag back to the clone.

"Good luck Dr. Xaun."

"Ha, I'm going to need it with this bunch."

The clone responds with a chuckle. The guard laughs and nods his head in acknowledgement. I direct the clone to walk away and wait until he is out of earshot to take a deep breath of relief.

I knew Ziva had fixed the issue with ICO security identifying the clone, but I wasn't sure if any other advancements had been made to the security systems since then that would have picked it up. Apparently, nothing had really changed at all.

Marrying her was the best thing I ever did.

I smile softly, my focus shifting to the clone's next steps. The hardest part is over now. I direct the clone to the appropriate building, following the familiar path to the elevator. It transports me to the 5th floor instantly, where I see the hallway is perfectly still and quiet. I sigh with relief and satisfaction, as memories from throughout the years resurface.

I miss these kinds of nights. When everyone is gone and I have the whole building to myself.

The clone walks halfway down the hall, past the private offices and into the lab. I immediately freeze and stare at the strange room around me.

No, no, NO!

Everything is different. The equipment I used every day is gone, replaced by different equipment. The tables are in a different arrangement and even the stools have been changed.

Breathe. It's just the tables and how the room is set up. Breathe. You can put it all back how you want when you return. Breathe. Just find the supplies.

They can change the equipment and layout, but they can't change the actual building. I see the familiar door to the storage room at the back corner of the lab. I instruct the clone to move towards it, winding through the strange lab until he slightly bumps into a table. I back up half a step and move around it.

Just as Almeta reported, they installed a new biometric scanner on the door.

The clone reaches out to touch the screen, lighting up to show three uncolored check marks. I direct him to tap the first one, and a light hovers over his eyes for a retinal scan. A moment passes before the first check mark lights up.

So far, so good.

He proceeds to hit the second check mark, and I am dismayed to see that it is a vocal test.

Well, let's hope I finally figured out how to fix the genetic composition for designing the vocal cords...

A few words appear on the screen, and I direct the clone to say them out loud until there are no words left. My body tingles with anxiety, half afraid I'm about to set off an alarm. Several seconds pass by before the light disappears and the second check mark lights up.

Hell yes! It worked... Now what is the next step?

I have the clone click on the next check mark, which shows a blank screen for a moment and then a statement: *Enter next deadline.*

I smirk.

Almeta, you are the best. The fucking best.

Before she was arrested, she sent me the ICO's full report on the project. Outlining in detail the deadlines, and the passwords to be used on this door, as well as the individuals who had been granted clearance to access the supplies. The clone punches in the date, and

I hold my breath until the third check mark lights up.

He then turns the handle and enters the storage room, shutting the door behind.

It all looks the same… Good, that will make this so much easier now.

Everything I need is all in its familiar places: the growth hormones, the memory wipe and even the vials for traveling back in time. I direct him to move quickly, grabbing everything I need from the back of the shelves of inventory, where it is less noticeable that some are missing.

I can't believe they thought this room would be more secure. Let's see, I think I have room for one more…

His hand reaches out, grabs one more vial, and places it in my bag. I direct his movements to secure all the bottles, being careful to make sure they don't break in transit.

I did it. I got everything I need. This should be enough to see me through to the end.

He opens the door, exiting the storage room and weaving through all the tables again. As he exits the lab and steps into the hallway, he barrels into an unsuspecting stranger. I watch helplessly as the force of the impact sends the clone crashing to the ground. I catch a glimpse of flying vials and hear the sound of breaking glass echoing down the hallway.

37

GRACE

I sit on my bed, and I can't take my eyes off the doorway. Or, at least where it should reappear *if* someone comes back.

I don't know how much time has passed. Several minutes, at least. Maybe an hour? My heart is still pounding, but it's softer now. Almost back to its normal rate.

In school, we learn about the flight or fight response. How in the wild the survival of a species can come down to a single moment, a decision. Where the animal can take flight away from the danger or fight back.

Like anyone else, I've heard the stories. Of young women and children being grabbed in parking lots or gas stations. How they fought back or struggled to yell loud enough for someone to hear them. Then weeks or months later, when their bodies are finally found, the investigators will find the culprit's DNA lingering under their fingernails.

Now I'm questioning my instincts. My capabilities, to take flight or fight back.

When it comes down to it, will I really make the right decision? Will I actually survive this?

I can feel my heart start to race again, and my eyes search the room for any hidden danger. There is nothing but these four white walls, the white floor, white ceiling, and my stiff bed. Satisfied with my search, I take a deep breath to still my heart.

Deep breath in, deep breath out...

I didn't notice it before, but the bed has a dip in the middle of the mattress that is making my butt feel numb from the awkward, uneven cushioning. I release my knees, and my arms collapse at my sides. My whole body feels stiff from the lack of blood flow, as if it's asleep.

Deep breath in, deep breath out...

I wiggle my fingers and toes to try to get movement back to help the blood flow. It tingles painfully for a moment, then the feeling returns. I notice the polish on my fingernails has grown out quite a bit.

Almost time to repaint my nails. Wait, didn't I just paint them the other day?!

The hairs on my arm stand on end as I stare at the fingernail polish harder.

It shouldn't look like that... Not yet. The polish usually lasts a few weeks.

I shake my head in disbelief.

Maybe I mixed up the days I actually did paint my nails. Or maybe I have been here longer than I realize.

I have to survive this. I have to find a way to escape, to get back to my family.

My family! Will I ever see them again? How will they find me? Where will they start the search party to look for me? I was in my bed, at home...HOME.

My eyes widen in fear as the realization hits me.

If they took me from my home, there won't be any clues. We don't have security cameras. They won't have any clues, they won't have a way to find me, they won't know where I've gone...

My shoulders slump, my body shakes, and the tears start falling uncontrollably.

No one is coming to help me. No one is going to save me.

I take a deep breath in, but it smells different. Not the sterile stench I had become accustomed to. It's a faint smell, a new one that I have never smelled before. I look around my room, trying to identify where it could have come from. I don't see anything to indicate the source. No window, no open vent, or hole in the wall. I breathe deeply to confirm that I do smell something different. On the next breath I don't detect it, but when I breathe again, I do.

Suddenly, my eyelids feel heavy and tired. My body slumps down on the bed, involuntarily going to sleep and my mind can't comprehend the dark shadow of a doorway that finally reappeared.

38

DR. MALICUS

In my lab, I jump back at the clone colliding with another person. As I grasp what happened, I start to panic.

THE VIALS!

I direct the clone to stand up, brushing off the shattered glass on his clothes. The force of our sudden collision also sent the other person to the ground, and I glimpse to see that it is a woman I don't recognize. She looks young, almost too young to be working at the lab.

Maybe she won't recognize him…

"Dr. Xaun!"

Well shit.

I freeze and direct the clone's head, so he stares back at her.

"I am so sorry sir, I had no idea you would be here tonight. I-I…" she looks terrified and moves quickly to scoop up the broken glass. I notice a few of the pieces are too big and dirty to be from my bag. My shoulders slump with relief.

I speak to her through the clone. "And what exactly are you doing here tonight?"

"I promise I am working on the project, and I will meet our deadline by tomorrow. I had to take a break earlier, I-"

"Break?! Do you think we have time to waste so you can take a break?!" The clone's sharp tone echoes throughout the empty hall.

"No sir, I-" she starts to respond.

"I want your project on my desk at 9:00 a.m. first thing. Or else."

"Yes sir, you will have it by then Dr." She nods her head earnestly to show how sympathetic she is for her mistake.

"And clean this mess up. Now!" I yell, watching with satisfaction as the clone's words scare her even more. She frantically scrambles to clean up the mess and run away.

Oh, I do miss this too. New recruits were always so easy to scare.

The clone turns and walks toward the exit. I move the clone's hand into the bag to ensure the vials are all still in place and intact.

Good. Nothing broke.

I continue walking, directing his steps down the hallway. As we approach my office door, I glance behind me to be sure no one is around. I open the door, excited to be back where I belong, but panic instantly washes over me.

That's not where my desk should be!

He pushes the door the rest of the way open and enters what *was* my office. As I direct him to walk inside, he spins around so I can take it all in. Anger starts to boil beneath my surface. Everything has been replaced with Dr. Kayitesi's items instead: her achievements, her project notes, her lab coats. Everything is hers. Not mine.

I can't believe this. After everything I did for them, building the international ICO from the ground up and finding the issue to our extinction cris-

I jump at the sound of footsteps approaching from down the hall. They sound too confident to be the young woman I bumped into a few minutes ago. I push the clone forward, towards the closet and hope that whoever is coming will walk by quickly. He shuts the door quietly behind him, backing up and sinking into the lab coats hanging up. I have him continue to move slowly backwards until I feel the wall touch his back.

The footsteps get louder and to my dismay, I hear them enter my office.

There's at least two different people.

"The conference has been great for sure, but it doesn't undermine the fact that we have so much work left to do."

I would recognize that stern voice anywhere. That's Dr. Kayitesi.

"We do too. The plans Dr. García has drawn up for the next phase will require several days of work from our engineers to make the right configuration."

I don't recognize the other one though.

"Please, it is only for two days and only a few hours for each day. We have this conference every year, you both knew this was coming."

I freeze as I recognize the low grumble of the third voice that belongs to the one and only person I do not need to run into at headquarters: Dr. Xaun.

"It's a shame," Dr. Kayitesi replies coolly. "The ICO is falling apart under Cordelia, and she is to busy trying to retain voters for the next election cycle."

For once, I agree with you Dr.

"It is impeding our ability to move forward with the project so we can reach a solution," the unknown voice chimes in with agreement. "My engineers still need an organ reactor or comparable power source to be able to accurately produce this desired outcome Cordelia wants."

The unknown voice must be Ziva's replacement over the international engineering department...

"I know, I know. The investigation is still ongoing. But we will uncover the truth," Dr. Xaun responds exasperated.

"Do you think he did it, Dr. Xaun?" The unknown voice asks curiously.

"Based on his track record… I wouldn't be surprised if he did," Dr. Xaun responded back. "I mean, the man went mad and tried to kidnap young women from other time periods to recreate new babies."

"Didn't your men go to investigate his home?" Dr. Kayitesi cuts in.

"Yes, and so far, it has yielded nothing. However, my men are still running tests to see if there is any other potential connection to Miss Caprae," Dr. Xaun sighs.

Oh no. I thought I was in the clear?

"Surely, he understood the gravity of his actions, right? Maybe he truly is enjoying his sabbatical and taking a break?" The unknown voice says half-hopeful.

"Take a break?! That man would work himself to death before taking a break," Dr. Kayitesi laughs back. "He's involved, I just know it. Someone like that doesn't just quit… You need to investigate him again, Dr. Xaun. He is getting those supplies from us, one way or another."

"Rest assured Dr. Kayitesi we are doing everything we can. We will get to the bottom of this and prosecute those responsible," Dr. Xaun responds reassuringly. "Now if you'll excuse me, it's been a long day, and I still have to go to the main security office for a physical check-in."

"Why do you need to do that? Your clearance level was renewed at the beginning of the year. You aren't supposed to be reevaluated for a few more weeks," the unknown voice questions.

"When I came back this evening, the security guards had multiple issues with my clearance," Dr. Xaun sounds annoyed as he continues to explain. "According to their records, I had already returned to the premises, and they were unsure how to fix the issue. It took several calls before they could get the head supervisor on the phone to manually allow me to enter. Now they want me to go in for another physical check-in to be sure they have the correct one on file. I don't know how on Earth someone could have messed this up so badly."

"Interesting, I wonder..." Dr. Kayitesi mumbles so softly, I almost don't hear her.

"Dr?" The unknown voice asks.

"Oh, never mind. I was thinking of something else," Dr. Kayitesi says. "Go on Dr. Xaun, we don't want to keep you from getting home."

"Yes, those physical check-ins can take a while to complete. Best to hurry. See you tomorrow Dr. Xaun," the unknown voice agrees.

"Good night!" Dr. Xaun responds back as his footsteps disappear down the hall.

I listen hard and almost take a step forward, until I hear the unknown voice again.

"Do you think he will come back? After his sabbatical?"

They are still here, I need to wait longer.

"Absolutely not. There was more than the abduction of young women – even Ziva, his own wife, believed his mental state was too far gone," Dr. Kayitesi replies. "I read the note Ziva left Cordelia, and no one has seen nor heard from her in months. Dr. Xaun claims he saw her at his house, but she seemed different... If anything, he got off too easily for what he did."

What note?! Ziva didn't leave a note. I would have known about it.

"Wait, you actually read it?!" The unknown voice exclaims.

They would have told me. She would have told me...

"Yes, Cordelia asked me too. I was one of the scientists who was consulted on his mental state and if he needed to be removed from the ICO. Honestly, he should have been arrested, but you know Cordelia hand-picked both of them for their positions," Dr. Kayitesi spits out the words in disgust. "And what Cordelia wants, she gets."

"Mhmm, that's such a shame..." The other voice says with sadness. "I thought they were such a happy couple, they were always working here at the lab, staying late and making more progress on their assignments than anyone else."

We were a happy couple! No, we ARE a happy couple!

"Hard times change people. Sometimes for the better, sometimes for the worst," Dr. Kayitesi mumbles. "It was devastating to lose them. Ziva was incredibly talented and innovative. He might have been a pompous ass at times, but he was real competition. Pushing us all to be better."

"Do you think this time we really might have the cure?" the other voice asks.

"I honestly don't know. This time feels more accurate than all the other times before. But I don't know if that is because we are getting closer to the cure or closer to exhausting all our options," Dr. Kayitesi sighs again. "Either way, sitting here debating it for an hour won't do us any good. I'm going to the lab to check on a few more things before I go home."

"Yes, it is getting late..." I hear their footsteps move out of the room, shutting the door behind them. I wait until their voices have completely faded away before I direct the clone to leave the closet.

Back in my lab I am shaking. I never knew Ziva left a note before she died.

But Cordelia knew. And she withheld that information from me.

I can feel the anger rising within me, distracting me from my mission.

Stop. There isn't time to do this right now. Get the supplies, get the clone home. Get the supplies...

I take a deep breath and direct the clone to quietly shut the closet door behind him. He then weaves through the office toward the door. I hesitate for a moment, before commanding him to turn the knob.

Please don't be locked, please don't be....

The knob turns effortlessly, and I breathe a sigh of relief. Instead of turning left towards the elevators, I make the clone turn right.

The security guards at the gate will have been alerted that Dr. Xaun's body metric scans are faulty, so I won't be able to exit the ICO head-quarters the way I came in.

Which leaves only one option...

I'm almost back at the lab door when a voice calls out behind me.

"Dr. Xaun! Dr. Xaun! Wait!"

Shit.

I slowly turned the clone around to see who is calling out his name. I recognize the man as one of the security personnel who accompanied Dr. Xaun to my home.

"There you are! I was hoping I would catch you before you left for the night." He takes a quick moment to catch his breath before continuing. "Do you have a quick moment to talk?"

Can't give anything away. Remain calm.

"Of course," the clone responds. "How may I be of help?"

"Thank you sir, I'm sorry to hold you up from going home. I'm sure you're tired, but you told me to notify you straight away when we received the results back from Dr. Malicus's home inspection."

I feel my body tense, goose bumps going up my arms, and appreciation that I made the clone wear a long-sleeve shirt.

"And?" The clone questions him, and I force him to have as bleak an expression as possible.

"They came up negative. For every single test."

"Negative? Hmmm. That is..." I searched his face for half a moment, trying to gauge if this is the result Dr. Xaun was hoping for or not. "...Unexpected." I pronounce the word slowly, squishing the clone's eyebrows together and glancing away to show confusion.

"I agree, sir. We were all so sure we would finally have the hard evidence to prove his malpractice in the scientific field." His face softens to bewilderment, and he glances away, lost in thought. "I really thought we had him this time. Do you think it is possible he truly is taking a sabbatical?"

I force myself to hold my breath, I can't give away any sign that the clone is not the real Dr. Xaun.

"It might be possible. He bored me to death about his ridiculous bug collection," the clone's voice answers him back with irritation. "Maybe I was wrong, maybe he really did learn his lesson."

"After all these years, do you truly believe that sir?" He looks at me with a mixture of curiosity and shock.

So Dr. Xaun hasn't liked me for a long time...

"It's hard to say. Are there any other tests we could run to prove his guilt?" The clone looks the other man straight in the eye.

"There is only one test left that we haven't done, the FTTS."

The Foreign Time Travel Substances. Damn, they really did try everything to catch me and none of it worked.

I have to bite my tongue to prevent the clone from smiling with smugness.

"There is no way he would have had access to time travel capabilities. The ICO completely stripped him of his access and even took away his travel device." I try my best to make the clone sound skeptical.

"I agree sir, there is no way he could have been able to time travel. But it is the one and only test we haven't run. Do you think it is worth looking into?" He looks at the clone earnestly, waiting for a response.

"No. Don't waste the resources on someone like him. Let's expand the investigation to consider other culprits."

"Very well, sir. We will begin immediately." He nods his head obediently.

He bought it.

"Now, if you'll excuse me, I have a few things I want to accomplish before the night is over."

"Of course sir, thank you for taking the time to speak with me." He nods his head respectfully and begins to walk away. "Have a good night Dr. Xaun!"

"You too!"

I have got to get out of here before anything else happens.

I turn the clone around, pretending to walk further down the hall. When I hear the elevator descend behind me, I have the clone turn into the door past the first lab. The room he enters contains the time travel equipment.

The best, and now only, way I can leave the ICO is to travel back in time. Then, I can use my transporter watch to travel forward in time to my home lab. While the machine would register that Dr. Xaun traveled back in time to a specific destination, it would not be able to track where he traveled to next.

It sucks that I have to use their machine at all. I wish I could just use my watch.

But it would never work within the ICO headquarters. The ICO has too many security protocols in place that prevent my transporter watch from being able to fully function and transport me to a different time period.

I was lucky I could slip past security with the watch on my wrist...

I turn the clone's head around to search the lab. In the center of the room is the platform to stand on to travel and the large metal arms on the side generate the force to create the time travel portal. The computer screen to control it is still turned off and angled to my height.

No one has been here since I left.

I spot the closet door in the corner and make the clone approach it. Cautiously, he taps the screen to unlock the door. The screen populates with the same prompts the other lab closet had and luckily for me, the steps are the exact same.

So much for their state-of-the-art security.

After completing the prompts, the door unlocks, and I step inside the closet to inspect the equipment options. I make the clone grab a tray of time travel serum off the shelf, stuffing all but one in the bag.

Don't want to get stuck in the wrong time period.

I direct the clone to pre-program the transporter watch for the correct destination and time period. If someone checks the logs for the time travel machine, they will see where I go and could try to time travel to a few moments before that to catch me.

I will need to be prepared to time travel again as soon as I reach my first destination.

Well, technically they could jump to the moment before I travel from here... Unless the time travel machine isn't here anymore.

It's a risky thought. Very risky.

It's not any more of a risk than I've already exposed myself to.

I have everything on this floor to place a small bomb to trigger after I time travel.

But if it goes off even a moment too soon...

I swallow my hesitation and breathe deeply. I make the clone put the bag down by the platform and quietly gather all the materials from the other lab. Within a few minutes, I have the bomb set and ready on the time travel machine.

I direct the clone to the time travel computer screen, powering it on and setting my desired destination. While normally the machine would require someone to activate it for the person time traveling, years ago I had Ziva install a special exception just for me. A secret passcode that sets a 30-second timer before the machine would activate.

Okay, I have to do this in one, quick, fluid motion.

The clone reaches down to activate the 1-minute timer on the bomb, then types in the passcode to activate the time travel machine. He quickly runs to pick up the bag off the floor and stands on the platform.

At the same instant, an alarm blares overhead to alert security.

Damn Cordelia!

I breathe deeply, hoping that the bomb I created is strong enough to destroy this entire room and every time travel device in existence. Footsteps come pounding down the hallway and I hear voices calling out. The machine starts to whirl and light up, as it prepares to transport me.

Come on, come on!

I catch a glimpse of a boot in the doorway right as the time travel lights flash the clone to my destination. Within seconds, the clone is standing on the streets of Pompeii. Through his eyes, I see the volcano erupting in the background.

I chose this moment of history to make it even harder for anyone to find me.

Or stop me.

I have the clone ignore the screaming people running through the streets and click the button on the transporter watch. Lights flash again as the clone time travels to the present-day standing behind me in my lab. It's an odd perspective, observing myself from behind, and I direct him to place the bag on the nearest lab table before returning to his sleeping cell.

"Somnum."

The screen before me starts to fade, as my consciousness disconnects from the clone and I am lowered back down to the ground. Finally free to move about my lab, I walk towards the table to examine the supplies. It feels strange to be back in my own body after the last couple of hours. My legs wobble a little, and my arms move too quickly to grab the bag. I take a deep breath to steady myself. It feels even stranger to touch the bag with my actual hands now, after the clone carried it for so long. I open the bag and smile.

These supplies should last long enough for me to develop the cure.

Time to get back to work.

39

GRACE

My eyes slowly open, and I blink a few times to clear away the blurriness. I stare at the strange ceiling above, as disappointment washes over me.

I wish I could go home.

My stomach growls, and I sigh because I'm not ready to move yet. My body aches and feels exhausted, as if it didn't get any rest at all throughout the night. I move my arms and start to roll, but I don't go anywhere.

Adrenaline rushes through my body, and all my senses are alert. The sleepy daze is gone from my eyes, I'm overly aware of how large my body feels, and I can smell the sterile stench of freshly mopped floors. I look down at the large bump that now occupies the space where my flat stomach was.

Panic consumes me, and I jerk up in bed. My arms tremble as I slowly touch my stomach and stare at its massive size.

This can't be real.

My insides are churning from a mixture of hunger and anxiety. I'm trying to convince myself that is what is making me nauseous, because the alternative would be unbearable.

And then I feel it.

A twitch, a jerk, a movement.

From inside me.

I freeze and my eyes grow wide with fear.

I can't be pregnant. I can't be, I haven't even kissed a boy.

I jerk my head up as it dawns on me.

I haven't even kissed a boy, A BOY... I can't be pregnant. If I were raped, I would feel it... right? Isn't that what women report after they have been raped? Incredible pain and discomfort? How could I get pregnant and not know it?! It doesn't make sense, I'm still a virgin. Unless... Could I be the next virgin Mary? Jesus did say He would return one day... Could I really be pregnant and not know it?

My body is starting to shake from the shock, and I feel a cold sweat starting around my temples.

I can't stand sitting on this bed another moment longer, I have to get up.

I roll to a sitting position, taking deep breaths to steady myself, so I don't roll backwards. It takes several attempts before I'm able to get up on my feet and I pause again to catch my breath.

It is only then that I realize I am no longer wearing my pajamas. Instead, I am wearing an ugly, plain gown. A heat wave flashes through my body, and my throat starts to close. Someone undressed me without my consent. They impregnated me without my consent. They violated me without my consent. My head starts spinning as I look around the small room and the pieces start to click together.

All the times I thought I mixed up my birth control pills or when I found the incognito search for abortion or when the nurse at the gynecologist's office thought I had been pregnant before... all those instances were because I *had* been pregnant. I had been here.

How many times have I been through this? And how is that even possible?!

I didn't ask for this. I don't want this. I don't want to be here, I don't want to wear this ugly gown, and I definitely do not want to be pregnant. I can't believe that someone would do this to me, to take advantage of me, to abuse me. The betrayal runs deep, into my core, and I can feel my heart physically hurting from the pain of it.

The anger is rising inside of me, an uncontrollable fit of rage I never knew I had. I look around the bland room suspiciously, ready for an attack. Finally, I know what my answer would be if I would choose to take flight or fight.

I choose to fight. I choose me.

If it comes down to it, I will do whatever is necessary to ensure my survival. I didn't ask for this baby, I don't want it. I don't care if it lives or dies, but I care if I do. Right now, my life is endangered, and I am the only thing that matters.

Now, I finally understand why some women want an abortion.

It's the freedom to choose their life, to define their life on their terms. To not submit to someone else's authority, someone who may not know what is best for them. Someone who could be abusing them.

I had been haunted by that same nightmare for months. Never knowing that it was my body's way of trying to protect me, to save me from this horrible fate. From this monster growing inside me. I can't take it home, I can't be a mother without a husband. Dad would kick me out of the house, just like he did Hope for being gay. I have no idea how Mom will react. Faith will ask a million stupid questions that will make it even worse. Hope would have a smug smile on her face if she ever found out. I would be left to fend for myself and I'm not even a legal adult yet.

I slouch my shoulders in despair and small tears start to fall down my face as my new reality comes crashing down on me.

I'm about to start my senior year, I will be the laughingstock of the whole school. No one will want to be my friend. No one will invite me to the football games, pep rallies, or ask me to go to prom. I'm supposed to have a bright future ahead, find a husband, and choose to have children much later in life. When I am ready for it.

But not now. I can't have a baby now. This baby will ruin my life.

I walk around my prison again, trying to find anything I might have overlooked - a door, a window, a secret passage - anything that might offer an escape from this nightmare or a means to defend myself. And then, I see it on the bed.

My phone! It must have fallen out of my pocket.

I rush forward eagerly to grab my phone and press the home button. Nothing happens, so I press the home button again. Waiting impatiently for the screen to light up, so I can dial 911.

Instead, I get the black screen with the red battery icon, and my blood runs cold.

"No, no, no, no." Panic floods my mind as I frantically scan my surroundings. "It can't be dead, it can't be... I had a full battery before I went to sleep." I begin running my hands over the scratchy blanket, desperately searching for a charging cord.

Why is this happening to me?! I did everything right, EVERYTHING.

My eyes start to swell with tears again.

I prayed, I went to church...

I jerk the blanket back, then the sheet.

I volunteered, I got baptized...

I grab the pillow with my other hand and throw it across the room in frustration.

WHY would god forsake me now??

My fingers curl around the edge of the mattress and I pull up, but it barely moves. That only angers me more. I put all my strength into lifting up the mattress and flipping it off the weird floating bed.

At the same moment, my foot slides and I lose my balance. I brace for impact, but it never comes. Instead, a faint beam of glowing lights surrounds me, and I watch as the lights lift me back up to a standing position. More lights put the mattress back, make the bed, and retrieve the pillow I threw across the room.

OH. MY. GOD.

I try to move, but I can't. My body is frozen in place to where I can't move a single muscle or even blink my eyes. I stand there helplessly as the lights move my body and lay me down on the bed with my head perfectly centered on the pillow. Just as quickly as they appeared, the glowing lights fade away and I am paralyzed with fear. My vision starts to blur as my body involuntarily falls back to sleep.

This has to be a dream. That can't happen. That isn't real. This isn't real, it isn't...

40

AVERY

(HOPE)

Sunlight streams through my dorm window, waking me up. I blink hastily, immediately spotting the Thai wrapper on the floor by my trash can. I slowly sit up, my ab muscles straining with stiffness.

Why do I hurt so much?

I had walked around a bit the day before, but nothing out of the ordinary. I didn't even make it to the gym.

I swing my legs over the side of the bed, letting them dangle, and take in my messy room. My desk is covered in old textbooks from previous classes with random papers of study guides and course syllabi stuck in between the textbook pages. The laundry basket is overflowing, and my shoes are scattered across the room chaotically.

Everything looks familiar and yet not. I feel at peace to be in my dorm room, the same sensation I feel when I come back after visiting home.

It feels like I haven't been here in a while…

My eye itches terribly, the same irritating pain when I leave my contacts in for too long. I subconsciously rub the edge of my eye to alleviate the itching as I slid off the bed. My knees buckle when my feet hit the floor, and I frantically grab the edge of the bed frame to prevent myself from falling on the ground.

Shit why are my legs so wobbly?!

After regaining my balance, I walk out of my bedroom and to the bathroom Li Mei and I share. The light is off, and the door is open, which means the bathroom is free for me to use. I flip the light switch and shut the door in one fluid motion. I wash my hands, splash cold water on my face, and then pat myself dry with a hand towel. Then, I use the end of my finger to take out my contacts and put them in the trash. I blink a few times and can feel the irritation in my eyes getting a little better now.

Probably need to wear my glasses for today.

Without my contacts, my vision is blurry, but I can make out enough of the shapes around me to avoid running into the wall. I slowly feel my way back to my bedroom and find my glasses on my desk. With my vision restored, my attention once again focuses on the messy room. My stomach rumbles and I can feel my body temperature rising as a drop of sweat slides down my back. All at once, the messy room feels unbearably claustrophobic.

I bend down to pick up the Thai wrapper and throw it away. Then I start grabbing the papers on my desk, glancing at them to throw into the trash or set aside to keep. From there my body takes over, moving about the room to throw away the trash and organize the items I need. My mind feels numb and thought free, as my hands move from one area to the next to clean. When I make my bed, I find my student lanyard hidden under the sheets. In my thoughtless daze, I slid the lanyard into my pocket, before freezing to pull it back out.

Where is my horse keychain?!

There is an empty ring where the horse keychain should be attached to the lanyard. It looks like it must have broken off. I frantically search under the bed sheets and the bed but can't find the keychain.

How did I lose it??

Two hours later, my dorm room floor is spotless, and my desk is cleared, but the keychain is nowhere to be found.

I must have dropped it on the street somewhere or in the parking deck... which means it is long gone by now.

I feel a dull ache returning to my chest. I lost the last connection I had to Li Mei and there is nothing I can do to get it back.

Ugh, this sucks.

Not wanting to stop my progress, I decide to distract myself with laundry and pick up my basket of dirty clothes. When I step out of the elevator doors on the ground floor, I see Li Mei walk into the dorm building. She's alone, wearing a pair of black biker shorts with a baggy T-shirt and high-top sneakers. She stops dead in her tracks and stares at me. I catch glimpses of the red bloodshot veins in her slanted eyes from a lack of sleep and excessive crying.

I stared back at her hopefully, longing to hold her. My empty stomach is doing summersaults, nervously waiting to see what she does.

Fuck that, I want her.

"I'm sorry," I blurt out at her. "I was an ass, and I shouldn't have spoken to you like that."

Her shoulders slump and her stern face instantly softens.

"I'm sorry too," she says back, stepping closer to me.

I drop my laundry basket beside the elevator and step forward to greet her with a loving embrace.

"You mean everything to me," I whispered in her ear. "And I never want to lose you. Ever."

"Me too. I love you," She whispers back.

"I love you too."

I let go and pull back, picking up my laundry bag.

"I need to start my laundry and then maybe we could watch a

movie? Well, have you eaten yet?" I ask instead.

"No, not yet," She answers.

"Perfect, I haven't either and I'm starving," I say. "Want to come with me?"

"Actually, I need to go up to the dorm to grab my dining card," She starts. "I'll meet you at the laundromat in a few minutes."

"Cool, sounds good."

The elevator dings as the doors open to let students off. Li Mei steps on and I walk down the hall to the laundromat with excitement.

I'm so happy we are good now.

I walked into the laundromat, relieved that no one else was in there. I can hear the hum of one dryer running, but otherwise it looks like all the machines are empty. I approach the first empty washer, throw my clothes and detergent in, then slam the lid shut. After sliding in my quarters and turning it on, I set my empty bag on top so others will know that washer is taken.

I turn to walk out and notice my reflection in the mirror on the wall. There are heavy bags under my eyes from lack of sleep and my hair is a sloppy mess.

My hair looks so vibrant today... Like it does after it is freshly dyed.

I step closer to the mirror to inspect my roots closer.

I dyed my hair at the beginning of the summer... right?

I pat my pockets, trying to find my cell phone to check my calendar and realize they are empty.

Oh well, I guess I left it upstairs.

My gaze shifts to my eyes, how exhausted they look, and the small wrinkles starting to form at the corners.

I need to get a better eye cream.

"Are you ready?" Li Mei calls out from the laundromat door. "I'm so hungry, I never ate last night."

I nod my head instinctively and turn away from the mirror. "Yes, let's grab something to eat. I'm starving."

I leave the mirror and thoughts about my horrible appearance behind. As I approach Li Mei, I hold out my hand to indicate I want to hold hers. She smiles and grabs it, intertwining her fingers with mine.

41

DR. MALICUS

"Status report, verbally."

The computer whizzes to provide the latest update. A male robotic voice fills the emptiness of my lab.

"The fetus from 21ABP06 has died. Cause of death: ruptured lung. There was nothing that could be done, the genes for the lung did not develop as well as they should have during pregnancy..."

Damn it!

"21AN05 is in good standing and has zero complications with the pregnancy. 21AP17 is in good standing and due to go into labor any day now. However, 21ON03 appears to have a complication with the fetus. Would you like to awaken 21ON03 so we can run further tests?"

I grimace at the thought of waking an experiment. It takes away from the resources I have to put the experiment back to sleep until it is time to go into labor.

"Is it necessary to awaken 21ON03?"

"Not necessary but recommended. The fetus has not moved in some time."

That's odd.

"Why would you recommend waking 21ON03 if you can already see the fetus is not moving? Is the fetus not viable?" I ask as I glance through the on-screen reports.

"There is a 99.456834% chance the fetus is not viable. However, there is a 0.54317% that the fetus is sleeping at the same time as 21ON03. The only way to know for sure is to awaken 21ON03."

I lost another one. That is unfortunate.

"The fetus is already nonviable. Remove it from 21ON03. We need to prepare to return 21ON03 to the correct time period."

"Right away, Dr."

I watch as the robotic arms appear in the room, cut open 21ON03 and remove the dead fetus. Then the machines begin the process of repairing her body and removing all traces of the pregnancy. As I turn away, I catch a flash of something sparkly in 21ON03's hair and pause to inspect it.

Oh, it's just that piercing in her ear. I forgot she had that shiny diamond in her cartilage.

I stifle a yawn and glance at the time to see it is almost midnight. I had been working around the clock since returning from the ICO headquarters. As much as I didn't want to stop, I knew I needed to rest and now would be the best time to do it while I'm waiting for results.

I leave my lab and on my way to my bed I see Ziva still awake in the living room. She is sitting on the floor with a puzzle spread out on the coffee table in front of her.

I lurk in the shadows, watching her intently. She is focused on the puzzle, looking at the pieces she has and occasionally jumping with excitement as she finds the right one to add in. A soft smile creeps onto my face.

She seems to be picking that up quickly.

I enter the room so she can see me. "Ziva, dear."

She looks up excitedly at the sound of my voice. "Iacobus, darling."

"I'm surprised you're still up," I remark.

She glances down at the puzzle in disappointment. "I am still struggling to sync my sleep cycle to the correct nighttime hours."

"It will get easier in a few days." She looks up at me as I sit down across the table from her, crisscrossing my legs on the floor. "Have you had any other symptoms? Or issues with your memory loading?"

She considers the question for a moment. "It's coming back in bits and pieces. I know you are my husband, and I love you." She smiles at me. "I know I am one of the most brilliant engineers of our generation..." She suddenly jumps to grab a puzzle piece and place it in the next spot. After that, she giggles before continuing, "And that I love puzzles."

It feels so good to hear her laugh again.

"I have some questions for you," I start cautiously. "About when you were pregnant with our baby girl. Do you think you might be able to answer them?"

"I mean, I wasn't the one actually pregnant with her..." Anger flashes in my eyes and Ziva starts again. "I can try though. What would you like to know?"

I regain my composure before speaking. "Do you remember if she would move around when you were asleep?"

"Hmmm." She thinks for a long time before continuing. "I recall a few nights where she woke me up. But for the most part she only moved when I was awake. It was almost as if she knew it was daylight and time to be awake and active."

"What was it like? Feeling her move inside you?"

"It was... incredible. To know that my body was growing this child, our child. That we had made her together..." "Her voice trails off as she grabs another puzzle piece and twirls it in her fingers. She watches the puzzle piece, and I watch as her mind travels back through the memories I gave her.

"Every kick was a reminder that she was alive and fighting. And when she went too long without moving, I got scared. That maybe I had lost her, that somehow my body wasn't providing everything she needed, that it could be my fault."

Her eyes look up into mine. I stare back into them, intently looking at every speck of green and the occasional hint of brown mixed in. They're foreign and strange to me. Not even close to Ziva's original eye color.

But her personality... Yes, this is much closer to what she used to be. And she can actually speak well. I'm glad I fixed the vocal issue this time.

"I felt so helpless when we lost our little girl. We did everything right, everything we could and still we lost her," I sigh and run my fingers through my hair. "It wasn't supposed to end like that. We weren't supposed to end like that."

Silence envelops us for several moments, broken only by the soft tap of Ziva's fingers fidgeting with the puzzle piece. Eventually, she reaches across the table, carefully placing the piece where it belongs, her smile triumphant.

"We could always try again," she says softly, her gaze fixed on the puzzle.

I feel a lump in my throat and the blood rushing through my body. "I've almost perfected it. The perfect formula for another baby girl. One who will be strong and survive this global extinction crisis. Once I have it, we can try as much as you want to." I smirk at her as I undress her with my eyes.

She giggles and blushes, her soft brown curls bouncing with her movements. "I would like that, very much, Dr."

My heart jumps in my chest.

This is what I have been missing.

There used to be a time when I couldn't even imagine living without Ziva. Then, for a time, I had to, and it was the most painful experience of my life. I sigh with content, happy to finally have my partner back. My best friend, my wife.

"Can I ask you something?"

Her sudden question pulls me from my wandering thoughts. "Of course, dear. What would you like to know?"

She pauses for a moment, looking down at the table and biting her lip. "Not all of my memories have returned. And I know some will take time to resurface... I spend some time trying to remember what I can and doing everything you told me that I liked to do, to help jog the rest of the memories. When I remember our baby girl, while it does make me happy, I also feel... scared."

"I'm sure it's just because of the hysteria of what was happening in the world at the time. Everyone was scared back then," I interrupt reassuringly. "Scared for their babies and what was happening, how it would be fixed and if it could be fixed."

"Well, that's the thing. The feeling isn't associated with a memory exactly or even the baby..." Her face portrays how confused she looks and how she is trying to process into words what she is feeling. "It's more of a fear for... myself? I think? But I'm not really sure why I would be scared for me... It would make sense to be scared for the baby."

"Ziva..." I reach my hand out across the table, beckoning her to take it. She does and looks straight into my eyes. "What happened was a long time ago. Things are better now, more hopeful. You don't have anything to be scared about. I will always take care of you." I smile reassuringly and she nods her head in acknowledgement.

"It's getting late, we both need to go to bed." I pull her hand as I stand up, indicating my demand to her. She complies, standing up to follow me out of the room. Down the hall, we part ways to go into our separate bedrooms in silence.

I change into more comfortable clothes and climb into bed. Our conversation replays in my head, fueling my mind to stay awake.

I need to help create new memories for her, so I don't lose her again...

The easiest memories to create - and the ultimate distraction - would be another pregnancy.

Maybe it is time for 21AP17 to go into labor.

42

GRACE

Bright lights fill the room, and I squint my eyes from their glare. Once again, I am disappointed to see that I am still in my prison.

I thought this was a dream, a horrible nightmare.

I recall the weird lights that controlled my body, the random door that appeared and then disappeared… I haven't seen many sci-fi movies, but I've seen enough to know that somehow this person has better technology and capabilities than I know about. Which makes me wonder what else they are capable of doing, that I don't know about.

I'm scared to move, scared to have my body controlled again, against my own will.

I feel so helpless. There is nothing I can do to escape this.

My stomach growls and I realize since I've been held captive, I haven't eaten anything or even drank water. Suddenly, my mouth feels dry, and I yearn for just a single drop.

How can I even grow a baby if I am not eating food?

The thought disturbs me, that my captor could have such advanced technology that my body was able to grow a baby with such little nourishment.

Come to think of it, I've only been awake a handful of times… how long have I been here??

I look down at my fingers to see my nail polish is completely gone and that someone has cut the nails down.

What the f...

My thoughts are interrupted as the strange lights surround my body again. I try to turn my head, move my arms, or even kick my legs but I can't. My body is completely frozen. My mind, however, is alert. The lights pick me up off the bed, suspending me in mid-air. A robotic arm comes toward me with a needle.

Eyes wide in fear, I try to back away from the needle, but it is useless. The needle is shoved into my arm and the robot pushes the liquid in one swift motion. It hurts so much, stinging and burning my arm, but that pain is quickly overshadowed by the contractions in my lower body.

They are inducing my labor!

The strange lights shift my legs up and push my nightgown out of the way. Sweat beads form along my hairline and blood courses through my body as my adrenaline spikes.

It can't be time to do this yet, I'm not ready, this can't be happening... I'm not ready to be a mother.

The contractions build in intensity, coming more quickly and painful than the last. The strange lights controlling my body make it worse, because I don't have any way to scream, to move to a more comfortable position or to cope with the excruciating pain.

I can't even breathe quicker as my chest is frozen in place. My throat burns desperately because all I want to do is scream. Release this anger and fear and pain that is building up inside of me. Seeking to escape.

No, focus Grace. You just have to survive. You are strong, just focus on surviving.

Every fear I had leading up to this moment is pushed away as my body fights for survival. I don't care that I'm a captive, that I'm going into labor, or even what happens after. All I care about is for the pain to stop.

The room is eerily silent. If someone were to walk by, they would have no idea that I am in labor. It's not at all like the stories I've overheard at baby showers or the few movies I've seen, where the birthing process is portrayed as loud and chaotic.

Another contraction comes and the pain distracts me from my wandering thoughts.

Oh my god, I can't do this! I can't, it's too much! It hurts too much!

My head feels light, and I desperately want to move my legs to a more comfortable position.

I hate these stupid lights! I hate them, I HATE them.

Another contraction comes and I want to scream.

This is it. This is how I die. This is the end for me.

When the next contraction comes, I actually feel the strange lights pushing on my body, somehow helping to push the baby out. A few pushes later and screams fill the silent room.

The lights pull the baby out, holding it up as the robot arms frantically clean it. The umbilical cord attached to its little belly is swaying back and forth. I'm still suspended in the air, frozen, but between the movement of the robotic arms I catch a glimpse of a tiny penis.

A boy. I just gave birth to a baby boy.

The realization of what I just endured is still incomprehensible to my mind. Before I can wrap my head around what happened, the lights start pushing on my body again. I feel something else plop out of my body and one of the robotic arms picks it up. I catch a glimpse of a nasty red blob that is almost larger than the baby itself.

WHAT. IS. THAT?!?!

I don't have long to wonder because the robotic arms stick another needle in my arm. The sudden force stings and burns as the arm pushes a liquid into my body. Then the arms start wiping my body down with a damp cloth and stripping me of the old gown. They dress me in a new gown that is still as ugly and plain as the first one. The lights finally soften their hard grip on my body, and I am able to breathe easier. They sit me down on the bed, propping me up with a pillow. Then the lights move the baby towards me and place him in my arms.

I stare at him with a mixture of emotions. Disgust. Awe. Sadness. Amazement. Anger.

My eyes focus on his little bald head, ten fingers and ten toes, squinty eyes because it's too early for him to open them. He can't be more than 5 or 6 pounds at the most.

I created this… I created him. A child, my child… Mine.

I hate my situation. I hate what I have endured. I hate that I've become a teenage mom against my will. More than that, I hate that I won't be able to protect him. I can't even protect myself or figure out how to escape this place, much less keep him safe from my captor.

Don't get too attached to him. You can't save him and yourself too.

My eyes swell with tears of exhaustion and frustration. As if on cue, he starts to cry too. My breasts perk and I feel a drop of milk come out of my nipples.

Through the tears, I grimly smile. "I guess you're probably hungry by now. Huh, little guy?"

I lift the ugly gown up and pause. It feels weird to just shove my boob into his face. His cries start to get louder, and the sound triggers a small headache. I grimace at the abruptness of the pain and decide to push away my hesitancy. I shove my boob in his face, and he immediately finds my nipple.

As he starts to suck, I can feel his toothless gums pressing into my nipple and creating the necessary pressure to release more of the milk. He pauses to drink it down before pressing down again.

This feels so weird.

I hold him there, letting him drink as much as he wants, until he finally releases my nipple. He stretches his little arms and yawns, before curling back up against me. I feel the warmth from his naked body touching my skin, reassuring me that he is very much alive.

At some point I must have drifted off to sleep. I wake up in a confused daze, still holding my baby. His soft whimpers start to get louder, and my mind wakes up enough to realize he might be hungry again. The breast I didn't use earlier feels sore, so I shift his body around and press his face to my nipple.

Once again, his toothless gums apply pressure to release the milk and pause while he swallows it. He continues repeating the process until I think he is content, and I pull him away. Unsure what to do next, I hold him in my arms and stare at him.

I stroke his head, imagining what color his hair might be. Maybe he will have the darker color my dad has, or will he inherit the blonde hair my grandmother had? I shudder at what traits he might inherit from whoever his father might be.

"You will need a name, little guy. I didn't plan on having you, so what on earth will I even call you?" I pause to think.

I don't really want to name him or even get attached to him. It feels dumb to talk to him, he can't even understand me. But I need a distraction from my current situation, and I don't have any better ideas.

"Hmmm… You don't really look like a Michael or John. Definitely not a Paul. Hmmm… What to name you?"

I spend a few moments thinking through all the boy names I've heard, quickly dismissing the ones I don't like and thinking of others that stood out to me. Something unique that not every boy would be named, but also not something uncommon either. I don't want him to struggle all his life to explain how his name is pronounced.

"I got it! Daniel. I'll name you Daniel. He was always one of my favorite Bible stories, Daniel in the lion's den. How God protected him from the mighty beasts an–"

My words are interrupted by the sudden appearance of the strange lights. They surround my body once again, freezing me in place. My mouth is still open from the words I was about to say. A separate bulge of lights appears around my baby and pulls him out of my arms.

NO! NO NO NOOO!

I watch in horror as he disappears through the secret door that had just reappeared. The door disappears again, and I'm left staring at a blank white wall.

THEY CAN'T TAKE HIM FROM ME!

Hysteria fully takes over my body, fighting desperately to escape and chase after my baby. My darling boy, my Daniel.

The lights pull me off the bed and suspend me mid-air once again. The robotic arms appear, ripping off my gown. One sticks a needle in my arm and collects a sample of my blood in a bag. I would have winced at the pain if I were capable of moving. The other arms attach suction cups to my boobs, and I watch as my breast milk is pumped out of me. The machine squeezes hard, and the process is painful.

Once again, I want to lash out, scream, and cry. But instead, I watch in horror as my captor does whatever they want to my body. Just when I think I can't take the pain any longer, I smell that strange scent again and my eyelids become heavy. The last thing I see as I pass out, is the outline of a man standing in the shadow of the doorway.

43

DR. MALICUS

"Run every test possible on the male baby from 21AP17 immediately. For his current body status and also run a report to predict his future bodily status. Monitor his condition 24/7 and notify me if there are any new developments."

"Right away sir."

I stand outside the nursery room in my lab, watching the baby closely. I don't want to get my hopes up again. I'm also scared that if I walk away, something will happen, and the baby will die.

This has got to be it. This has to be the cure, I'm sure of it this time.

The computer runs various tests on his little newborn body, and I reflect on every step that led up to this moment. The sleepless nights, the research, the dedication. Everything, from the first global conference to trying to fix this genetic issue, to the first time my team gathered in the ICO lab. To Ziva and our baby girl, the depression I felt when I failed and lost them both. To the ICO forcing me on sabbatical and everywhere I traveled back in time to find the perfect hosts for my embryos.

It is all worth it if this tiny baby survives.

While I wait impatiently, I pull up the reports on 21AP17's vitals. Her body temperature is rising, and her heart rate and blood pressure is unnaturally high. I quickly wave my hand over the computer screen, clicking to pull up various options to treat her medical condition.

Can't have her dying from preeclampsia. That would be annoying to fix… not to mention a waste of my supplies.

I indicate on the computer screen what I want the lab to do to treat and prevent her condition from getting worse. I'm reading about 21AP17's family history when a beeping noise grabs my attention: the reports on the baby's condition are ready. I read each and every one, not skipping a single word, chart, or stat. At the end, I stare up at the baby in disbelief.

I did it.

I found the cure, I saved our species, I recreated a human baby. Free of the organ failure that has plagued us for the last few years.

I stumble backwards onto a nearby stool. I reread all the reports again, to make sure I didn't miss anything else.

"I did it, I finally did it," I mumble to myself.

I ran upstairs to find Ziva, huddled over a new puzzle. My sudden outburst startles her, and she looks at me with confusion.

"Ziva, I did it. I DID IT!" My voice fills the empty room, as I throw my arms up excitedly.

Her face immediately transitions to delight and surprise. She jumps up, running across the room to hug me. "I knew you could do it."

She kisses me softly on the lips, then pauses to stare into my eyes. Her large green eyes are searching deep within mine, patiently waiting for my next move.

"Are you ready to be a mom?" I ask her excitedly.

She bites her lip and quickly shakes her head. "Yes, I've been ready."

I pick her up in my arms and start walking down to the lab.

"Then, let's get to work."

44

GRACE

"Grace! Do you want any breakfast?"

Dad's voice rouses me from my deep slumber. I yawn, stretching my arms and legs out. I grab my phone to check the time, only to find that it is dead.

Ugh, I must have forgotten to plug it up last night. At least I don't have to work today.

I get up from the bed quicker than I anticipated and my head spins with dizziness. Pausing for a moment, I wait for the dizzy spell to pass before standing up. My legs feel painfully sore, and I struggle for a moment to walk across the room.

Why am I so sore?!

I think about the last few days and anything I could have possibly done to warrant this level of soreness. My stomach growls, distracting me from my thoughts. Instinctively, I place my hand on my abs and how flat my muscles feel.

I feel so skinny… Maybe I finally lost a few pounds.

Excited by the prospect and curious about my weight, I slip on my house shoes and wander down the hall to the bathroom. I weigh myself and am annoyed to see I've actually gained a pound since I was weighed at the gynecologist's office the week before. My hand reaches for my cross necklace but instead feels my bare neck.

Oh yeah, I took it off last night.

Back in my room, the glint of the cross necklace in the morning light catches my eye, and I pick it up from the nightstand. I ran my thumb over its familiar surface, before putting it around my neck. My fingers adjust the chain, so the cross is in the center of my neck, and it feels comforting to have it on. I leave my room and follow the scent of blueberry pancakes to the kitchen, licking my lips in anticipation.

"That smells delicious!"

Dad turns around, with a spatula in hand. "You should try tasting them." He winks at me before turning back to the oven. "There's some on a plate ready for you."

I grab a couple from the stack, drown them in syrup, and sit down at the table. After a quick, silent prayer, I start shoveling the pancakes into my mouth as quickly as I can. It feels like I haven't eaten in forever, and these pancakes are the best thing I have ever put into my mouth. Dad finishes cooking, grabs a few pancakes for himself, and sits down.

"Wow, you really were hungry!" He exclaims.

I nod my head while I chew, so he knows I am acknowledging him, and am trying to finish eating. He takes a few bites of his pancakes, before getting up to go to the stairs and call for Faith to wake up. By the time he returns, I'm putting my dirty plate in the sink and grabbing a glass of chocolate milk.

I take my glass into the living room, plopping down on the couch to watch TV. The news is still on, probably from when Mom first turned it on before she left for work. I grab the remote to change the channel but pause when I see a photo of the new abortion clinic on the screen.

"Yesterday, Planned Parenthood opened another abortion clinic on 1st Avenue North. Over 100 people showed up to protest the opening, saying that it was a crime against humanity and even God to allow these facilities to be open. Many local citizens are concerned their tax dollars will go towards funding the institution and what it claims as 'medical procedures.' But for many people, this is not just a medical procedure. It is considered a death row for unborn babies. Conservative leaders are urging people to..."

Dear God, this is so awful. I hope they shut down that clinic soon and pray that no babies are killed.

I continue watching the coverage from the protest, as footage is displayed of the crazy, liberal pro-choice group who showed up to disrupt our peaceful protest. I see an array of people from various backgrounds, with wild hair colors, and numerous piercings or tattoos. Sometimes both. All of them angry and screaming out. Many of them carry vulgar posters depicting naked women with 'my body, my choice' or 'abortion is healthcare.'

The footage transitions to the pro-life group, banded together singing hymns. I realize the footage being shown was filmed before the pro-choice group showed up. I even catch a glimpse of myself, enthralled in the crowd.

"You did the right thing kiddo."

I look up to see Dad, standing behind the couch. I feel satisfied and proud that he is happy with what I did.

"Thanks, Dad. I'm trying to be a good Christian."

"If you keep taking a stand like that for Jesus, you will always be a good Christian. The only bad Christian is a silent one."

He pats my shoulder softly before walking away. I turn my attention back to the TV, as it shows a person from the pro-choice group pushing someone in the pro-life group.

Then the news transitions to their next update and I can't help, but notice they only showed bad footage of the pro-choice group. They didn't show the ones in the pro-life group, who initiated the fight or the guy who threw soda cans at the employee's car when they tried to turn into the parking lot. They didn't even show the footage of the police officers arriving.

I suddenly feel cold, a deep pang of doubt in the pit of my stomach. Our behavior as Christians bothers me, but I'm not sure why. It's never bothered me before and I can't understand why it does now.

I take a deep breath and shrug it off. So long as I believe in the Lord and follow His command, everything will be fine. I can't control what other Christians do, but I can control my own actions. I realized I never brushed my hair and decide to go to the bathroom to tame the mess. In the first pass, my brush hits a few knots in my hair, and it takes several minutes for me to untangle them all.

How did my hair get so tangled?! I don't toss and turn in my sleep that much.

When I am finally done brushing my hair out, I check my arm and realize the bandage I put on it the night before is gone.

It's probably buried in my bed sheets somewhere.

I'm pleasantly surprised that the rash on my arm is finally gone, so the ointment I put on the night before must have helped.

My gaze sweeps over my entire appearance. The pale skin, dark circles and finally my eyes, which look extra vibrant. I never noticed the color being so bright before and I admire them for a few minutes in the mirror.

They look kinda pretty for once.

I eventually leave the bathroom and go to my room to search for the bandage under my bed sheets. I can't find it anywhere and decide to sit on my bed for a moment.

I stare at my bedroom, its familiar surroundings and I feel content. Peaceful. Comforted. The same satisfaction I feel when I come home after a long trip or vacation. It feels good, yet odd. I haven't been anywhere all summer besides Church or the Happy Mart.

Why does it feel like I haven't been home in a while?

A cold shiver runs down my spine and I want to push away the eerie thought. I grab my Bible off my dresser and lay on my bed to complete my quiet time for the day. I turn the pages to Exodus 20 and begin to read.

And God spoke all these words, saying: I am the Lord your God…

45

DR. MALICUS
FIVE YEARS LATER

I crack open my eyes as the alarm finishes.

"Good morning Dr. Malicus. Today is Sunday, October 23rd, 4107. The time is currently 7:15 a.m. Would you like for me to continue with your morning report?" Aux's deep voice fills the room.

When Ziva moved back into my bedroom, it became confusing to refer to her artificial voice and her in the same room. I let her pick the new name and voice, much to my annoyance she chose a deep British accent.

"Do we have to get up?" Ziva's groggy voice mumbles from under the pile of blankets she has buried herself in.

I look over at her messy hair that is hiding her sleepy eyes.

"The day will start, with or without you. Time to get going, we promised the kids we would take them to the waterfall today. Remember?"

"Ughhhhh," She groans, pretending she's annoyed, but I know she isn't.

She's grateful we have children and that we get to spend this time with them. I raise an eyebrow at her, and she giggles.

"Fine! Let's get going then!" She exclaims, pushing back the blankets and partially sitting up in bed.

"Aux, continue with the morning report please," I command.

"Excellent sir. Chancellor Cordelia Ni Fhiachra has officially with-drawn from the election. In an official statement, the Chancellor said the decision was difficult to embrace..."

I throw off the covers and get out of bed as the bedroom door flies open. Two children come running into the room and the scientist in me can't help but study their bodies. Prim is the boy with brown hair, rosy cheeks and dull blue eyes that occasionally sparkle against his pale white skin. He just recently turned five years old and loves to be outside. Trailing behind is our daughter, little Elara. She is the spitting image of Ziva with her curly brown hair and lightly tanned skin. It is a stark contrast from her brother's features. I watch her body movements closely, how she runs to keep up with him and reaches out her chubby hands for the side of the bed. They both climb up and start jumping on the bed, playfully attacking Ziva, who burrows deeper under the blankets.

"...the ICO has yet to discover a cure for the ongoing extinction cri-sis. It has now been 7 years since a baby has been born and lived successfully on its own. Even the medical engineers who have con-structed assisted living devices say there have been complications connecting the devices to..."

I sneak into the bathroom to wash my face, change clothes, and listen more intently to my morning report. From the bedroom, I can hear Elara's shrieks and Prim's giggles as Ziva tries harder to avoid them. I chuckle as I grab my watch and put it on my wrist.

"...Dr. Kayitesi speaks out, stating they have exhausted every possi-ble means they can without crossing ethical boundaries. In light of the desperate situation, she has proposed and is actively urging the ICO to adopt a special amendment to authorize time travel to find a cure. In her statement, she said, 'the world is waiting patiently for a solution that doesn't seem to be coming. We have done everything we can, and now it is down to the wire - it is not a matter of finding a cure now. It is a matter of whether we want our species to die out or not. And I for one, don't want that to happen. We have to adjust our methods, even if it crosses some ethical boundaries or we will become extinct.' Critics of Dr. Kayitesi are distraught over her grave message, insisting that there are still other ways to repopulate the human species. Dr. Xaun, who has been a collaborative partner with Dr. Kayitesi is now shying away and claiming that there are still other methods to be explored. The two scientists will be facing off in the coming months for the ICO Chancellor position…"

Ha. If only they knew I had the solution already.

I had almost called them so many times. To say that I did it, to brag, and rub it in their face. To be welcomed back to the ICO with open arms and the recognition that I rightfully deserved.

But all their fucking politics.

I didn't want to get caught up in that world anymore. It made me happy to know I had the cure and that I could repopulate the human species myself. That I could control how the human species will be remade to my standard of perfection.

I only had a few more months left to wait before I started my repopulation project. I had already run all the tests to map out the perfect timeline to let the old human species die out and to repopulate it with my new one.

Screams and giggles erupt in the room next to me, and I walk into Ziva saying, "okay enough, I'm up, I'm up, I'm uppppppppppp!"

Prim and Elara back up slowly, both red-faced and out of breath.

"Come on kids, let's get dressed and ready to go to the waterfall! Mom needs time to get ready."

Ziva mouths a silent thank you to me as I corral the children out of the room. They gleefully run to the other end of the house, where we set up both their bedrooms. I follow Elara into hers, knowing that she might need more help getting ready since she is a little younger.

"Daddy, what to wear?"

I smile at her slightly broken English. Her fourth birthday is coming up in a few weeks and I love seeing how much she resembles Ziva. She inherited all of her best features, except her eyes. She has my gray eyes, which fills me with pride to know she truly is my child.

"Hmmmm let's see we are going to be doing a lot of walking, yes?" I prompt her.

"Uhh huhh."

"We want to make sure you are comfortable, so maybe we just go with something simple like this…" I guide her curious mind in the direction I want her to go.

I pull out a flowery top and matching shorts. She reaches her hands out to grab the pieces and I hand them over.

While she struggles to put the shirt on, I find her shoes. When I turn around, she has the shirt on backwards and both legs in the same leg hole.

"Oops, did you get stuck?"

She looks up at me with the most innocent face and says "Welp." It was her cute way of saying "oh well" and Ziva joked that it was the toddler version of "oh shit."

I chuckle and help put the clothes on her correctly, then slide on one of her shoes. The tip tap of Prim's shoes echoes down the hall as he runs to the kitchen, most likely half-dressed.

At least he has shoes on this time.

"Wait Prim, wait, Elara!" She cries out after him, before running off with only one shoe on her foot.

"Elara, wait…" My voice trails off as she runs out of the room.

Her second shoe is still in my hand, and I stand with a huff before following her down the hall. I find them both in the kitchen, sitting in their chairs, and Ziva handing them plates of food. I grab Elara's barefoot and put the shoe on, double-checking that both shoes are secured tightly.

Ziva has two plates ready, one for each of us and we eat quickly knowing the kids will be done soon. They never sit long to eat their food, especially if they know we have something fun planned. Like going to the waterfall today.

I feel my throat tighten and on cue, Ziva slides a glass of water over to me at the same time she takes a sip of her orange juice.

Damn, she is so perfect.

I chug the water, setting the glass down, and checking on the kids out of the corner of my eye. Ziva follows my gaze and we both stare in disbelief as Prim climbs out of his chair and jumps down onto the floor. Elara is whining, struggling with the straps that hold her in and trying to figure out how Prim escaped.

Ziva and I exchanged a laugh.

"Divide and conquer?" I ask her.

"Dibs on Elara." She laughs back, rushing forward toward the easiest child to retrieve.

"I need to get better at calling dibs." I laugh and take off to find Prim. I quickly found him in the living room, grabbing Ziva's latest puzzle.

I lurch forward, picking him up from behind and saving her puzzle from destruction.

"Haha! I got you."

He shrieks out in surprise and playful frustration.

"Dad! I was just going to move one piece."

"Boy, you know I know you better than that," I smirk, looking into his strange blue eyes.

He isn't our true son, but we made him one of us. Besides, he will never know the difference.

I sling Prim over my shoulder and march back to the kitchen. Along the way, Aux calls out to me from overhead.

"Sir, there has been a development in an old test you asked me to run."

I sigh. Ziva would kill me if she knew I was trying to work today.

"Aux, I'll take a look at it when I get back. Thank you for updating me."

"Very well sir."

In the kitchen, I find Ziva has Elara ready and a backpack in hand with various snacks and drinks for our day outing. I sit Prim down and say "Alrighty, are you kids ready to go to the waterfall?"

They both squeal with excitement, jumping up and down. "Yesssss!"

"Alright, let's get this show on the road then!" I lead the way out of the house and hear the pitter patter of their feet behind me, knowing that Ziva is watching them closely.

As soon as I opened the door, they both took off running. They know the way and the waterfall is barely a quarter of a mile from our house. Ziva and I watch them both lovingly, running along the worn path. Occasionally, Prim will pick up some bug he found to show Elara, who will say "ew gross" and swat his hand away.

It doesn't take long before we hear the rushing of the river and see the waterfall. Next to the water is a beautiful meadow, with tall brown grass.

Prim and Elara run through the grass, the tops of their heads just barely visible. We aren't worried about losing them though. They don't know it, but they have genetic trackers within their bodies, so in the event something terrible happens we will be able to find our children.

Ziva turns her back to me and I reach in the pack to pull out the blanket. We set up our picnic, admiring the peaceful scenery and listening to the giggles of our children. She pulls out some crackers and cheese, as well as a hidden bottle of wine.

"We did it, baby. We finally have the dream life we always wanted." She smiles at me, with a slight gleam in her eyes.

"Yes, we did. We have two beautiful children and a wonderful home for them to live in. The perfect life, away from the distractions of the city, the politics of the world…" I take a deep breath in and look at the nature around me. "I wouldn't trade anything for this."

I smile at her and lean back on the blanket.

"I wonder if…" Her flirty voice trails off. I turn towards her and watch her face change from playful to concerned. My body tingles and I follow her gaze. That's when we both hear it.

Elara is shrieking. Not her normal playful shriek. This is a noise we have never heard her make. One full of panic and fear. We both jump up and run to where we think the noise is coming from.

Elara finds us along the way, crying and mumbling words we can't understand. Ziva instinctively picks her up, shielding her from the unknown danger we aren't prepared to encounter.

"Where is Prim?!" Ziva asks frantically.

I don't answer her rhetorical question. My eyes are already scanning the meadow, and I see a clump of grass swaying in the direction Elara came from. I take off, sprinting as hard as I can. I find Prim lying on the ground convulsing. He is gasping for air and struggling to breathe. I try to pick him up, but his little body is thrashing around too much. I sit on the ground next to him, trying to comfort him in my arms, but I feel helpless.

What is going on?!

I frantically rack my brain for answers to help him. He has always passed his physical evaluations, I run regular tests on his body to make sure he doesn't have any complications...

Oh no.

Aux tried to get me to look at a report before I left the house.

And the stupid robot wouldn't have known how serious the report could be. FUCK.

I stand up and bend down to pick up Prim, to run him back to the house, but it is too late. His little body stops moving. I put my ear to his chest, listening for a heartbeat. It is silent. His strange blue eyes are staring back at me. His cold, dead blue eyes.

My body is shaking, and I somehow bring myself to turn around to Ziva. I don't utter a single word, I don't have to. She hugs Elara tighter and closes her eyes. The tears are streaming down her cheek, and she finally opens her eyes to release more tears.

"Iacobus, what do we do?! What do we do about Elara!? I can't lose her, I can't, I can't..." Her voice trails off as the tears fall harder. Elara sees the fear in her eyes and starts crying too.

I stare at both of them blankly, completely void of emotion.

It's happening again. Why is it happening again??

My legs shake and I crumble to my knees. All that work, everything I did for the last 7 years... I thought I had a cure. I thought I did it. I thought we would finally have a happy ending...

I throw my hands behind my head, the quick movement creating a flash of light from the watch on my wrist. I freeze, then bring my arm back down to stare at the watch. Memories of our 10th wedding anniversary come flooding back. It was when Ziva gave me the watch and promised we would always be together, no matter what.

I take a deep breath and get back up. I look at Ziva and Elara with determination. My family, my girls, my world.

I have to protect them. I have to, at all costs.

No matter what it takes. Only the strong survive.

Ziva's Letter
FIVE YEARS EARLIER

Cordelia,

I'm so sorry. I can't do it. I knew what was at stake and I knew what protocol would dictate, but I can't move forward with the investigation.

You've known me for years, you know I never wanted children in that way. I wanted to wait for the cure to be found, and I was conflicted throughout the entire pregnancy. Who knows, maybe if I had found out sooner, I might have aborted her.

For that moment I held her, I was glad I didn't abort her. Looking at her little hand wrapped around my finger, I instantly fell in love. It hurt so badly to lose Elara, I couldn't sleep for weeks. And he knew that. He knew how I felt about the pregnancy, what he did to me. I was shocked when he asked if we should "try again" - as if I had any say in it the first time. That is when I realized he wouldn't stop.

I told him my team was so close to having the technology ready to sync with the organ reactor and that I have strong reason to believe this could be the permanent solution we need to save the human species.

We had spent months sifting through every project file we had ever worked on - together, apart, for the ICO, before the ICO, and even for ourselves. I even showed him my classified project files.

There was no other answer. The organ reactor was our best chance, and I insisted that I just needed a few more months to test it before we could present it to the world.

He wouldn't hear of it and insisted I had lost my mind for even suggesting such a thing. I realized then he stopped taking his medicine and begged him to get back on it.

For a while I was able to sneak it in his morning drink, but eventually he caught on to that and it started another fight. That was when I finally gave up and came to you. I can't help him if he can't help himself.

My heart aches Cordelia. My best friend, my husband, is gone. Even after everything I've been through, I still love him. But the man I love is dead.

I don't know at what point I lost him, and he became the person I see today. I watch him as he works in his lab and for a moment, I can almost forgive everything he has done.

Then that small part of me remembers what he did to me, and it physically hurts. And honestly, at the end of the day, I can't bring myself to betray him, even though he betrayed me.

My dear friend, after all these years, I'm grateful you put up with me. I have loved you like a sister and will miss you dearly. Please find it in your heart to forgive me one day.

Only the strong survive, but first they must recognize that strength lies not in trampling on the weak, but in lifting them up.

Fortis,

Ziva

ACKNOWLEDGEMENTS

To my sisters, thank you so much. You both helped me tremendously and I could not have completed this book without you. Thank you for putting aside your own beliefs, accepting the story I wanted to tell, and supporting me throughout this process.

To Callie, my ever-faithful furry companion, thank you for keeping my toes warm and reminding me that sometimes I need to take a break from writing to throw the tennis ball for you.

ABOUT THE AUTHOR

Courtney Clem, a native of Moody, AL, finds inspiration in both the serene landscapes of her hometown and the bustling energy of Birmingham, where she currently resides. A graduate of the Alabama School of Math and Science, Class of 2013, and the University of Alabama at Birmingham, Class of 2017, Courtney's passion for storytelling is matched only by her love for nature and adventure.

When she's not crafting tales, Courtney enjoys exploring the great outdoors, often accompanied by her loyal golden retriever, Callie. She finds solace in hiking trails and unwinding with a good glass of wine, moments that fuel her creativity and enrich her narratives.

www.ingramcontent.com/pod-product-compliance
Lightning Source LLC
Chambersburg PA
CBHW030242120726
47903CB00005B/1587